MAC'S WAY

REG QUIST

Mac's Way
Reg Quist

CKN Christian Publishing
An Imprint of Wolfpack Publishing
6032 Wheat Penny Avenue
Las Vegas, NV 89122

ISBN: 978-1-64119-049-7

1

THE BURDEN OF POVERTY BECOMES A PART OF SOME MEN, overshadowing all else and impacting everything they do.

The weakest of these men, discouraged by failure and loss and seeing the road ahead as too rough or too steep, may eventually give up, accepting whatever fate deals them.

For other men, the struggle with poverty is like bearing the weight of a buffalo-hide coat; heavy, threatening to drag them down but not stopping them completely. In their darker hours, these men may despair of finding an answer but they move forward nonetheless.

Walker Samuel McTavish was the latter type.

Walker spent the early morning of his last day at home sitting bareback on an old slope-shouldered mare, the only riding animal on the small Missouri farm. With his long legs nearly reaching the ground, Walker headed to the village called Jenkinsville hoping for a day of paid work. His eighteen years had brought him to his full height of slightly over six feet while his broad shoulders and toughened hands were testimony to the work demanded of a young man on a small family farm.

Leading the old mare out of the corral for the three-mile trip to town, Walker looked without pleasure at the animal. He picked up and then threw down the worn-out saddle, then examined the horse again. "Queenie, you're about the sorriest excuse for a riding animal I ever did see. If it weren't that shot and powder were so expensive, I might just take a notion to shoot you. Of course, then I'd have the whole family on my back and I'd have to dig a hole to put you in with no one helping with the digging. I'd turn you loose and chase you off but you're so lazy I expect you'd come right back and stand here with your face in that haystack, and me having to cut and stack the hay, too."

The horse made no noticeable response.

A young girl's voice broke into this monologue of self-pity, "Are you talking to that horse again, Walker? I swear you need to get away more often and visit with folks. Of course, if that horse were to answer you, now that would really be something to tell around."

The embarrassed young man waved Nancy off and turned again to the horse. He had been relishing the opportunity to grumble a bit and he resented his sister's interruption.

The saddle was no longer fit for use and to walk would be too close to admitting his poverty. Finally, he slipped a bridle on the old mare and climbed aboard bareback.

Living in poverty was one thing but making a public show of it was another thing entirely although there were really no secrets in this well-settled but cash-poor farming community.

Walker knew nothing at all about conditions in the rest of the nation but 1855 had been a difficult year in his area of Missouri and, so far, 1856 didn't show much promise either. Although the small family farm sitting snugly in the fertile Mississippi Valley always produced enough food to live on - stored in glass Mason jars and in bins down the root cellar - there were no extra funds and the day-work Walker had come to rely on to purchase a few items beyond the basics was a some-times thing at best.

Finally, Walker pointed the old mare toward town, his youthful pride an awful burden to carry. His future looked as dreary as a winter day where the dark clouds blocked the sun and bare tree limbs dripped with the remainder of a cold rain.

Having about given up on the prospects for the family's small farm, Walker - determined to find a way to improve his future - thought of little else. Those thoughts were consuming a sizable portion of his waking hours as well as intruding on his sleeping time.

The old mare and her rider were traveling on a familiar road through the only country either had ever known or seen. Walker looked around him. What came to his eye was a sunny spring morning with the ripples of the creek he followed dancing like stars in the sunshine and the roadside bush alive with birds and insects. He saw spring crops shooting through the ground, carrying with them the promise of full larders come fall. He saw his neighbor's small dairy herd grazing along the split-oak-rail fence line with several cows craning through the fence to reach the grass on the outside. He knew the land was good and that the future held opportunity for those in the position to accept it. But, as in past travels on this road, the sight was tempered by the knowledge that none of what he saw belonged to him. Nor would it likely ever belong to him, at least until his parents passed on. Best if he did something for himself he decided.

A small step toward his goal was getting to town to find a day's work. A day's work that would provide a small income that could be put toward the family needs or perhaps be salted away against whatever the future brought his way.

The dusty road between the farm and Jenkinsville told of a dry, hot spring although Missouri always seemed to get an abundance of rain in spite of the occasional dry spell. The red dust that rose from the horse's hooves covered horse and rider both, settling beneath Walker's collar and causing an itching irritation.

Riding slowly along, his thoughts were on the prosperous future that he hoped would somehow be his and the girl that would share it with him. The trouble was that he had no idea how any of this fantasy was to come true.

He settled his wide-brimmed straw hat at a jaunty angle, fitting with his fantasy of prosperity. Black wavy hair hung below his hat and down past his collar; at least it would have if his shirt had a collar. Running his hand up the back of his neck to wipe away the dust, he admitted that he needed a haircut. But he was unwilling to spend the ten cents the barber was asking so his curls now covered his shirt top and a good portion of his forehead. He straightened the hat as he neared town while shifting his weight, looking for a more comfortable position on the back of the horse. "Queenie, you're ruining my nether region. We get to town, I just might see if some fool will give me a dollar for you. I'd take the dollar and call it a profitable day."

Walker knew that his thoughts about wishing for a better riding animal were carrying him dangerously close to sinful pride. He had heard about the dangers of pride often enough on Sunday mornings to be wary of that trap.

His father, Hiram, although holding no formal training, delivered the Sunday morning lessons for their small congregation. The traveling preacher had died at a mature age the year before and there was no one else available so his father had stepped in to do the job. Sunday after Sunday he stood before his friends and neighbors, holding his well-worn Bible before him as he talked quietly of the love of God. He seldom looked at his Bible, quoting lengthy passages by heart. Walker knew his father was a strong, humble man who had proved to be a perfect fit for the spiritual needs of the tight-knit farming community. Pride and self-reliance were among his favorite topics.

Jenkinsville lay boiling in the morning sun with a wagon team trying to pull some sparse grass from beneath the small porch in front of the general store and a scattering of chickens trying their luck around the hitching posts. Not many folks were around this early but Clive Jenkins had on his white apron and was out sweeping the porch in front of his store.

"Good morning, Walker. You're up early this morning. How are the folks? Well, I hope."

"Family's all well, thanks, Mr. Jenkins. I'll tell them you asked."

Walker had figured that perhaps Mr. Jenkins was one of the wealthy folks in this cash-strapped community. He had said as much to his father just a few days before.

"Well, son, I can see how you might think that. But Clive Jenkins depends on us and our neighbors paying our accounts. That doesn't happen on any regular basis. I expect Clive is hurting just like the rest of us."

Walker had thought for a moment longer about Clive Jenkins and then asked about the banker. "So how can the banker always seem to have money when mostly he spends his time writing numbers in a book? I never hear of him doing any real work."

His father aimed a small smile at his son. "To a banker that is real work, I guess. Can't say as I ever really figured it out myself. Probably we'd best just leave it alone."

Walker made his slow way toward the Sampson Sawmill. As he rounded the last building and entered the wagon trail leading to the waterfall and the water-wheel-driven mill beside it, he was bothered by the silence. When it was working, the mill produced a piercing, shrieking sound of circular saws tearing into the flesh of hardwood logs, cutting the boards that were sold to deliver what little prosperity the village enjoyed. But this day there was no movement of the water wheel that drove the saws and there was no sound of sawing.

Cletus Sampson, the mill owner, greeted the young man in the mill yard before he even had a chance to dismount from the old mare. "Morning, Walker. If you were hoping for some work, I have to disappoint you. That order you helped me with last week was the last I had. Business seems to have dried up. No work for now. Sorry about that."

Walker thanked the man and turned for home. He considered walking to spare the horse as well as himself but finally decided to finish the ride, plodding along barely faster than a man could walk.

The temperature seemed to climb with each painful minute and each painful mile. And now it was also becoming muggy as only the Mississippi Valley can be muggy. Walker knew that the worst heat of the day was still to come, and the worst of the summer. As the home place came in sight, he took a critical look at the rundown shanty he had been raised in. Lazy smoke from the last of the breakfast fire drifted into the sky from a leaning-over stovepipe. Flour-sack curtains fluttered through open windows. A windblown lilac bush that had been planted too close to the house left scratch marks on siding that hadn't seen paint in many a year. The single wooden step that had led to the veranda had rotted away, breaking under the weight of Walker's foot. He had dragged a large flat rock up from the creek bank to take its place. That and a dozen other memories caused him to say out loud, "It ain't much, Pa; not for all the years of work."

Two blood-red hounds watched his approach from the shaded comfort they had dug beneath the low veranda. He knew the dogs would rise to his call but he also knew they would rather not. Nothing wanted to move in this heat and humidity. But the clank of a hammer on an anvil told him that his father was up and working down in the repair shop. There was always enough work to go around and then some. Farm work didn't wait for the weather.

Riding closer, Walker could see his mother sitting on the porch. Pipe time, he thought, smiling to himself. I wonder where the kids are. He knew his two younger sisters and two younger brothers would be taking advantage of their respite from daily chores. What they had come to call pipe time was one of the few opportunities the farm allowed for escaping work.

Rebecca Della McTavish, known to her friends as Della and to her family as Ma, was sitting in the shade of the veranda, fanning herself with a piece of oak shingle as she gently rocked away a part of the morning. Not that she had time to waste in rocking chairs but she allowed herself one vice: that was to spend a few minutes puffing on a pipe of homegrown tobacco after each meal was served and the dishes cleaned up. She saw the pipe as her reward. She received few others.

His gaze found the tired-looking barn with the outdoor milking stall attached. Two stub-horned red cows stood lethargically, suffering the heat of the morning and giving suck to their calves with whatever milk was left after the family needs had been met. The rail fence running from the corner of the barn to form a small corral and then a garden enclosure was strong and straight and new. It looked out of place in a yard that was dominated by worn-out buildings and sagging fences. Walker had built the new fence himself from materials that had cost an excess of muscle and sweat but which had not encroached on their meager cash reserves.

What little reserves the family had, his mother kept hidden away in a rusted coffee can behind a sack of flour in the pantry.

"Hard times, Queenie. Hard times. Seems that's all I've ever known."

His father worked the small farm and sought out day labor whenever the opportunity arose, sometimes at the mill with Walker and sometimes taking his team of strong black mules to help a neighbor.

His mother had learned to hatch together enough food and clothing to keep the family from starving or going naked. The root cellar was well stocked as was the smokehouse. Ma oversaw the killing, cutting up and smoking of the hogs and the canning of the chickens. The huge garden was a family task. But the effort was starting to tell on her. She was old before her time. Nor was there any end in sight with the four younger children still needing considerable growing before they could claim their independence.

Walker had heard talk about the beautiful young blond girl that had been the desire of every boy in the area. But the blond beauty had been attracted only to Hiram McTavish and in the twenty years since their marriage she had not changed her mind or questioned her decision.

He thought some days that he could see his mother's youthful beauty in his two sisters. Nancy was already catching the eye of some of the boys at school and Walker figured there would be visitors walking the dirt roads in her direction sooner than her parents would be ready for.

He had thought a lot about independence and about the future. His thoughts of independence took his mind far from the home valley, into lands that he had heard about but had never seen and knew nothing about. He knew the schoolteacher had come from a town more than fifty miles east across the big river, an unimaginable distance to Walker, and he was tempted to ask her questions. But his pride held him back, not wishing to sound ignorant. Still, he couldn't help believing that opportunity lay outside the valley.

By noon of that day, Walker had thought his situation through and confirmed the decision that he had made weeks before. This time he was determined to act. He talked about it quietly to his mother on the veranda and less quietly to his father down in the repair shop.

"Pa, there just ain't no work around here that can be depended on and this farm barely feeds the family. It's never going to repay the work you put into it without me adding more years of my effort. I see no place for me on this farm or in this valley. I'm eighteen soon, Pa. Seems to me I have to start making my own way in the world."

His father's eyes bore into him with a fierce intensity until Walker finally dropped his own eyes to look at the dirt floor of the shop. He had intended to say more but thought better of it. The two men stood there in silence.

Walker's father whipped off his sweat-stained hat and slapped his leg with it, raising a small puff of dust. He paced back and forth in the shop a couple of times and banged on the anvil twice with the hammer.

He was impossibly thin and tall enough that he resembled a carpenter's rule when he sat down or stood up, unfolding in the process. The thinness disguised a strength that few men could match. Constant work at the mill or in the home smithy or behind the team of mules as they pulled a plow or harrow had left oak-hard arms and shoulders as its reward.

Walker asked, "Pa, how am I ever going to get a farm of my own or make my own way staying here when you and Ma barely get by after all the years?"

Hiram looked at the floor but offered no response.

Walker waited a moment and then continued, "I want land and an opportunity of my own, Pa. This is good land but there ain't anywhere near enough of it. You're hemmed in on all sides by other small patches of land farmed by other hard-working men and ain't none of you making a living."

He paused, looking at the older man. When his father said nothing, he completed his thought. "I've heard tell there's land for the taking, off to the West. I want to go have me a look."

Hiram looked startled. "West? That's a mighty big and wild land. No telling what's out there. There's a good chance we'd never see you again."

"I doubt as how it's all that bad, Pa."

The two men settled down and quieted their voices. They leaned back, squatting against the wall of the machine shop, elbows on knees, one man looking like the older version of the other.

Getting over the initial shock at the idea of his son leaving, Hiram looked at him. "I knew this time was on the close horizon. Your ma and I, we've talked about it. But looking it right in the eye is a sight more difficult than talking about it."

After a further pause, he continued, "Takes money, son. Even with the land being free, it takes money to farm. How you figure to get that kind of money?"

"I don't know, I surely don't. But I ain't going to get it staying here."

His father pulled his old hat off his head again and scratched the few hairs that were left. He stood, unfolding his long lanky body, leaned back against the wall of the shop and looked out the open door toward the west.

"You're right about this old farm. It ain't ever amounted to nothing much and it ain't ever going to amount to nothing much. But it's fed us and provided a bit of security. You'd have to go some to starve out a farmer but cash money is another thing altogether. Still, there's been a lot of folks talking about the West, son. Maybe you got it to do. You go, and God bless you. Your ma and I, we'll pray that you find just exactly what you're looking for."

Walker gripped his father's hand, knowing what that admission and that short speech had cost him.

The next morning, he put aside what little he could call his own, bunching it together in a flour sack and setting it on the front veranda. The whole family was there to see him off.

He looked at his mother, tall and pitifully gaunt, her original beauty barely a memory on a face that bore too many worries. A worn-out, flower-patterned dress hung limply from broad shoulders. Her bare feet were shoved down into men's shoes that were so oversized for her feet that she had to scuff her steps just to keep them on. Her hands were gnarled and reddened by the continual work; the scrubbing of clothes, the cooking, the cleaning.

"That's not for my wife," Walker said to himself and then felt guilty for the thought as if he was somehow being disloyal to his mother.

He kissed her and shook hands with his father.

Hiram had a twitch on his cheek that had never been there before and his voice was husky. "Where you figure to light, son?" He waited for an answer that didn't come.

"You write, boy, you write to your ma. We'll want to know where you are and how you're doing. Sure going to miss you. I hate to see you set out like this, son, with no more than I've been able to give you. It isn't going to be easy for you to find your way. You save your money and watch out for the sharpers. I've got a lot of faith in you, boy. I have faith in the Lord, too. Don't you pay no mind to circumstances. You work hard and keep your eye on the Lord. He'll have His eye on you."

Except for Sunday mornings gathered in the little church with their friends, that was the longest speech Walker had ever heard his father make.

2

WALKER SET OUT WALKING ON THAT HOT, CLOUDLESS, EARLY
spring day, determined in spite of his nervousness. He was tall
and strong, not quite eighteen years old. He had no experience
of the world beyond the farm and the village. His younger
brothers and sisters walked with him for most of a mile, talking
and asking questions that he had no answers for. He pressed on
but at the crossroads where the farm road joined with the road
to town, the four children stopped, watching until their big
brother passed around a clump of bush and out of sight. Only
then did fifteen-year-old Nancy raise one hand and say quietly,
"Bye, Walker."

The boys, Bobby and Jeremiah, agreed with "Bye."

Ten-year-old Jessie, the youngest in the family, was silent.

After standing and staring at the empty road for a while, they
turned toward home. Nancy was crying but doing her best to
hide the fact.

Eleven-year-old Jeremiah stopped and began pitching stones
at a fence post.

"Come on, Jeremiah," called thirteen-year-old Bobby.

"Leave him be," said Nancy. "He'll be along."

Walker's total earthly wealth was represented by the clothes
on his back, the shaving kit and spare clothing in the flour sack,

and the very few dollars saved from work at the mill. He had set those dollars aside with the family funds but his mother had counted them out to him before he left. He took them reluctantly, knowing the family needed them but also knowing it could be some time before he found work and, eventually, his land and the longed-for wealth.

Leaving the home valley behind, he headed west. Alternating between walking and hitching rides on farm wagons, he wended his way to Independence, Missouri. There he met up with a group of teamsters who were rigging out for the long drive to Santa Fe.

"Who do I see about work?" he asked a group of men hunched over a simmering coffeepot.

A coffee drinker pointed his thumb over his shoulder. "You can try talking to that gent over there. He don't speak no more than what is absolutely necessary but he's the boss. Course, none of us listen too well either so I guess it comes out even in the end."

Several of the men chuckled as they looked Walker over.

Walker wasn't sure what his next move should be but he stepped over to the boss and spoke right up, "I need a job and I can drive mules." Then he waited.

A slow minute went by and then a rumbling voice said, "Got drivers. Need swampers. But you have to be dumb to do a swamper's job. You dumb enough to load freight and harness mules and put up with this bunch of lazy drivers?"

"I'm not dumb but I could act dumb if that gets me the job."

"We leave at sunrise. Be here or be left behind."

"Thanks," said Walker. Turning to the group of men, he asked, "Can swampers drink that coffee?"

The driver who spoke before answered, "This coffee ain't for newborns, son. It'll either kill you or make a man of you. Help yourself."

He spent the first year away from home loading and unloading freight, caring for mules, and doing general swamper and roustabout work on the Santa Fe Trail. The next year, he was given his own team and wagon to drive. He saw the move as an improvement but the small extra pay still didn't make his vision of land come any closer. His search for wealth and land wasn't going as planned.

He discovered that freighting was an occupation that offered will-testing hard work but little promise for the future.

Toward the end of his second year on the trail, as the wagon train was nearing Santa Fe with the end of the long hot trip in sight, they pulled into camp. One more camp, a twenty-mile run into town the next day, and the crew could call it a job well done. Not that the trip's completion would change much for the men. They would simply take a few days in Santa Fe to rest, purchase some new clothing, visit a barber and a bathhouse and make their plans for the return trip. They would be back on the road in less than one week. Always fearful of winter's cold and howling blizzards, the freighters tried to keep the wagons rolling during the hot dry summers.

A few of the men had wives and families in Santa Fe. A few would blow their pay out on rotgut whiskey. Two of the drivers had left their pay on the green felt of the gaming tables after the last trip. Walker wasn't sure if they were any the wiser for the experience.

He left his pay with the company for safekeeping, a hedge against his dream of owning land and a barrier to any temptation to follow the activities of the other drivers.

3

WALKER HAD HITCHED AND UNHITCHED HIS MULES HUNDREDS OF times. He knew the temperament of each animal; which would bite and which were known to kick. But that knowledge couldn't account for the clumsiness of the kid the company had hired as a helper. Zeke, his name was. Most days Walker thought he would be better off without the help.

Walker never really knew what Zeke had done to startle the mules but just as he stepped in front of the doubletree and bent to unhook the trace chains, the six-mule hitch took a disjointed and startled step back and then bounded forward. Walker was knocked off his feet with his legs beneath the wagon and his head and body at the mercy of the prancing feet of the rear mules. As he fell, he first heard and then felt his leg break. He knew he had probably screamed at the pain but he didn't remember doing it. One mule stepped on his arm and another mule slid a hoof down his back in a glancing blow, tearing his shirt and a distressing amount of skin beneath. The soft sand of the campground saved his arm from a break. Four other drivers ran to his rescue and soon had the mules under control.

As the wagon was high enough to clear a prone man, the drivers carefully eased the team and wagon forward until Walker lay in the clear.

Noble Reid, the foreman on the crew, bent over Walker. "You awake, Walker?"

Walker eased his good arm over to lift the injured arm into a more comfortable position. "I'm awake but it ain't no pleasure. I'd just as soon not be as bad as I hurt."

"I don't even have to lift your pant leg to tell you got a real bad break there, son. I've set a few bones in my time but I don't think we had better try this one. The boys are making a space for you on the wagon and we're going to make an all-night run into Santa Fe to find you a doctor. The mules won't like it but they have it to do. You're going to have to tough it out." The foreman tried to hide his concern from the injured man but wasn't totally successful.

Four men carefully slid Walker onto a wagon tailgate that they had removed and lifted him into the back of a wagon on top of the load. Walker knew they were trying to be careful but the break had left the lower part of his leg at such an angle that it didn't fit onto the tailgate. A driver tried to support the angled leg but still Walker screamed in pain and passed out when they lifted him.

After a five-hour rushed trip to Santa Fe, the mules staggered to a welcome stop in front of the doctor's house. Noble Reid banged on the front door until the sleepy doctor arrived, carrying a low-burning lamp. "I heard, I heard," the doctor hollered through the door. "Me and the whole town as much noise as you're making." The door opened as the doctor grumbled, "It's the middle of the night. What do you want that won't wait till morning?"

"Got a broken leg that won't wait, that's what. The boys are bringing the lad in now. Where can we put him?"

"Bring him in here," answered the now awake doctor. "How long ago did it happen and what have you done since? Did you try to set it?"

Noble said, "Happened about five hours ago just as we were going into camp. We were afraid to touch it as bad as it looks. Nearly killed the teams getting in here as fast as we could."

Walker broke into a cold sweat and ground his teeth in agony as the men moved him. He didn't cry out until they slid him off the tailgate onto the surgery bed. Like the wagon tailgate, the bed wasn't wide enough to support the broken leg.

The driver holding the leg stood there looking helpless. The chemical smell of the doctor's small surgery room in addition to the sight of the dreadful angle of the broken leg was more than the driver could handle. He didn't say a word as he let go of the leg and crumpled to the floor in a faint. Noble dove to catch the leg but again Walker screamed and passed out.

The doctor hollered at the drivers who had escaped to the outer room. "Come get this man out of here and all of you go back to your mules. I expect they need you worse than I do."

The doctor turned to Noble. "You going to fall down, too, or can you hang in there? You can see that I'm going to need help but it ain't going to be pretty. I can't have you quitting on me halfway through this job."

"You go ahead, Doc. I'll hang and rattle. I may close my eyes so's not to see what you're doing but I'll be here."

"All right, you take off that filthy shirt and go wash your hands."

The surgery to repair the damage and set the leg took three hours and the doctor and Noble were both exhausted at the end of it.

Noble thanked the doctor. "That's good work, Doc. I've seen it done a time or two. I hate to mention any more trouble, Doc, after this long night. But it could be you should take a look at his back. I do believe a hoof cost him a mite of skin."

"Roll him up on his side so I can see. Gently, he ain't no side of beef."

The doctor cut away Walker's shirt, soaked the cloth from the dried blood, and gasped. "Don't take much more hide than that to make a fair-size jacket." As he cleaned and bandaged the scraped area, he said, "I swear, as hard as you men are on your bodies, I don't know why the Lord don't just give up on the lot of you. This man will go through all of this and won't learn a thing. He'll be back doing just the same as he was and doing it three weeks before I want him to."

The doctor was wrong. Walker was back at work six weeks before he wanted him to.

After three days recovering in the small clinic, the doctor arranged for him to be moved to a boarding house where he often sent recovering patients. Run by a Mexican widow named Maria, the boarding house offered meals, a private bedroom and enough personal care to ensure a small bit of comfort to a patient. Meals were brought to the room when the patient was unable to join the larger group in the dining room. The one-dollar a day cost was more than Walker earned driving the team.

After one week of bed rest and thinking about the foolish expenditure of his hard-earned wages, Walker decided that he might just as well get up and try his hand at driving again or at least find a place to live that wouldn't prove to be such a serious drain on his hoarded cash reserves. With this in mind, he sat up in bed and swung his good leg onto the floor. He then grasped his broken leg and swung it over the edge of the bed. As the leg swung past the supporting edge of the mattress, a fiery pain shot lightning bolts into the back of his eyes and threatened to burst his head in two. He knew a cry of pain was escaping his lips but was unable to stop it. Nearing unconsciousness from the pain, he lost his balance and fell to the floor.

A startled cry and running footsteps told Walker that his painful cry had been heard and that someone was coming. The door burst open and Sal, the neighbor girl that helped around the boarding house, stepped into the room. She took one look at the crumpled form of Walker lying on the floor and screamed almost as loudly as Walker had in his fall. "Maria! Maria!" she hollered down the stairs. "Come quick!"

The last time Maria had moved quickly had been thirty years and forty pounds before. Still she was there in no time at all, scolding Walker and telling Sal how to help him back into bed.

When the patient was back in bed and his pain was more or less under control, Maria asked, "So, what were you planning on doing? Were you hoping to go to a dance or did you think to go out back and split me some firewood?"

"I thought it was time I got back to work. Looks like that will have to wait another few days."

Maria, hands on her ample hips, said, "That's the kind of thing my Miguel would have done. Neither one of you are any smarter than the mules you work with. You stay in bed. Sal, you stay with him for a while and see that he doesn't do anything dumber than what he has already done."

Conscious of propriety and youthful indiscretions, Maria usually cared for the bed patients herself. Walker had seen very little of Sal although she had brought a meal a few days earlier. This was the first chance he had to talk with her and now he had no idea what to say to this very attractive girl. Her presence tied his tongue completely in knots.

Walker guessed Sal's age at about close to his own. She stood perhaps five-foot eight, tall for a girl but slim and strong with a fine figure. Her straight blond hair hung halfway down her back. Walker's mother would have said she carried herself well. She looked Mac in the eye in a way that caught his attention and made him swallow twice before saying, "Thank you for helping me."

Her smiled "You're welcome" caused a pressure in Walker's head that he couldn't understand.

Walker stayed a full month. He figured that was more than enough time to heal a simple break. One of the returned drivers had put together a crutch for him.

He climbed out of bed and reached for his clothes. The usual long johns were set aside as being impossible to get on. With his pocketknife, he cut the legs off the long johns from just above the knees. It wasn't easy but he finally pulled them on. With the help of the crutch and considerable patience, he managed to worm his broken leg into one leg of his canvas pants. The second leg was much easier.

He pulled a shirt on, stretching the healing skin on his back and causing considerable pain, but was pleased when he saw no sign of blood. The biggest test was his boots but he was finally ready to go; he had broken into a sweat getting there but he was feeling better just being dressed.

With his kit bag in one hand and the crutch under the other arm, Walker made his way to the top of the long flight of stairs. There he paused, not sure of his next move. He stood there, his leg throbbing at the unfamiliar movement. Finally, trusting the strength of the wooden railings, he gripped one in each strong hand, gripping the crutch in his fingers as they extended below the railing. Straightening his arms, he was able to lift himself off the top step by an inch or two. Very carefully he lowered himself to the next step and stood on his good leg. He did the same for the next two stairs and then reached back for his kit which he had left lying on the top landing. Hanging on with one hand, he tumbled the kit down the stairs to be picked up again when he arrived at the bottom.

His shaving kit made a clunking noise as the bag of clothing rolled down the stairs. The clunking noise brought Maria and Sal running from the kitchen. Sal screamed while Maria simply looked up the stairs, shaking her head and mumbling about stubborn, foolish men and suggesting that they would all be better off living in a brush jacal; that they didn't deserve the care and comfort of a good woman. Walker heard the comments through his intense concentration but he chose to ignore them.

He reached the bottom with some feelings of accomplishment and no small amount of exhaustion, hoping to never again be faced with a set of stairs before his leg healed. He reluctantly counted out some coins to Maria, said his thanks to both women, hobbled out of the boarding house, and moved off toward the freight office with grim determination to see about his job. As he walked, he considered the happenings of the past few weeks and what his meeting of Sal might mean.

During his month at the boarding house, Walker and Sal had struck up a friendship, often visiting when Sal's work duties allowed. Walker was still sparing with words but he was comfortable talking about farming and the land. Sal seemed to understand Walker's desire to own land although she talked more about cattle ranching than farming.

"New Mexico is good country, Walker. You could do worse than to look around here for a place to settle."

He got that pressure in his head again, the way he had when he first met Sal. Quickly, a vague image of a ranch or farm with Sal welcoming him home after a day's work, flashed through his mind. He took her simple words as an invitation. He was sure Sal could see how he felt about her. He didn't see the need for words and gave no thought at all to the possibility that she was only passing the time with a boarder. He'd started to put a face and a name to one part of his long-held dream.

By the time he was at the freight office, he'd broken out into a sweat and was exhausted. He hobbled up the two steps into the cramped and sweltering office and sat down on the closest chair.

Buster Murphy, a large, loose man once strong and work-hardened but now running to fat, was the freight manager. He looked up from his desk and with a startled expression asked, "What are you doing here? Aren't you supposed to be in bed?"

"I've been in bed. Ain't no need for it anymore. I need to go to work. I can't do all the camp work on a trip east but I can drive. I'll drive for half-pay if you'll give me a good swamper to care for the mules."

The freight manager leaned back in his swivel chair and grinned. "How be I give you Zeke? He'd like to go back on the road. He hasn't been out since your last trip and I'm sure he's available."

Walker didn't see the joke. "If Zeke is the best you have, I might just as well go back to bed."

The manager laughed and finally Walker joined him although he was still not sure if the offer of Zeke was a joke or not.

"Seriously, Walker, are you up to taking a trip? It ain't no picnic even on two good legs." The manager sounded genuinely concerned.

"I'll be all right driving. By the time we return, I should be back on both legs and as good as new."

Buster thought for a few moments and finally said, "All right, there's a train leaving in three days. You find your own swamper. We pay swampers fifteen dollars a month. I'll promise you the half-pay you mentioned and if the trip goes well, I'll up that to your full pay."

Walker hobbled to his feet and shook the manager's hand. He would have to start asking around right away if he was going to find a competent helper.

Maria solved that problem for him by introducing him to Yuan Aribay, a Mexican boy that Walker judged to be a year or two younger than himself. The boy had been raised on a ranch and was familiar with horses and mules. Walker liked the looks of him and after getting the approval of the freight manager, the deal was finalized. The only drawback Walker could see was that Yuan didn't speak English. Walker thought that perhaps by the end of the trip he would learn a bit of Mex while he was teaching Yuan some English.

From Santa Fe to Independence, Missouri was a long slow trip. If drought, storms and Indian attacks could be avoided, the return trip required about four months. The daily pace was leisurely at best, giving the drivers ample time to think and watch for Indians as they sat on the high spring seats of the wagons. Walker cut off his leg cast before he reached Independence partly because he guessed the break, even as bad as it was, must be healed but mostly because the itching was about to drive him crazy.

As the slow, tedious trip progressed, Walker thought only about land and Sal. By the time he returned to Santa Fe, he'd pushed the land to the back of his mind and was dreaming almost entirely about Sal. He filled his imagination with all kinds of pleasant thoughts; all of them wrapped around her. He was sure they'd come to an understanding even if no words in that direction had been spoken clearly. Upon his arrival back in Santa Fe, the wagons were unloaded and the mules cared for. The men were then free of work for the next week.

Walker immediately visited the barber and bathhouse and then made his way over to the boarding house. Maria greeted him at the door with inquiries about his leg and about the long trip.

"Leg's mostly as good as new, Maria, and the trip went all right. I was hoping to see Sal. Is she working today?"

Maria gave Walker a hard study for a moment and then looked at the porch floor, obviously uncomfortable with the question. Finally, she spoke, "Why, Walker, of course you wouldn't know. You've been away so long. Sal doesn't live here anymore. She married a rancher from south a ways. She moved out to the ranch over two months ago."

Walker just stared, not wanting to believe what he had heard. He couldn't find any words so after a few moments he turned and started to walk away. A pressure had returned to his head but not the same pressure that he'd experienced before when talking with Sal.

Maria rushed down into the yard and caught up with him, taking a light hold on his shirt sleeve. "I'm sorry, Walker. I didn't know how you felt but I can see it now on your face. But didn't Sal tell you? She's been friends with Willie Burton for at least the past two years. They planned their wedding almost one year ago." After a pause, Maria continued, "No, I can see that she didn't tell you and that you misunderstood her friendliness. That wasn't fair of her. I'm very sorry."

At a slight tug from Walker, she let go of the sleeve and as he walked away he heard her say, "That girl ought to be horse-whipped."

Walker went straight to the freight office. Buster Murphy was sitting behind his desk. Without preamble, Walker asked, "How soon can I get a trip east? One way. I won't be coming back this time."

"You just got in a few hours ago; you want to leave again already?"

"Right this minute if you have a train set to go."

"Well, I don't," answered Buster. "But there's one leaving in a few days. We have enough drivers but you can go as a swamper and fill-in driver if you want. But I don't like the sounds of one-way. I hate to lose a good hand. You've got the makings of a team leader, Walker. The fact is that I would have given you a fore-man's job before now except that I was afraid some of the older drivers would resent it because of your age. Sure you won't reconsider?"

"No good reason to stay here," was the answer.

"Want to tell me what happened to lead you to make that decision?"

"The decision was made for me," was all Walker would say. "But I would appreciate a letter from you so I can collect the wages you're saving for me when I get to the other end. Or you can give them to me now."

"I'll have the letter ready for you before you leave. I hope you're making the right decision, Walker. This west grows on a man. You get back east and you just might wish you were back out here."

Walker gave a slight nod and said, "I had no idea how big or how grand the west was before I came here. You're right, though. It really does grow on a man. I'm guessing that I'll be back some day. But for now, home is sounding kind of inviting. I've not seen the folks for over two years. And as much as I've appreciated the work from you, I have dreams of land that I won't pay for in two lifetimes with this job. So it's time to move on. But I sure do owe you and the company my thanks. I'll be ready to go when the train is ready."

THE TRAIN WAS MADE up and standing in the street when Walker hobbled up to it a few days later. He shook hands with the drivers standing close by. He was glad to see Yuan Aribay standing there.

"Are you taking this trip, Yuan? I thought you might want to stay home for a while."

Yuan grinned up at Walker. "I go with you, *amigo*. Much dinero for doing easier work than I do at home. See? I buy new boots." He pulled up his pant leg to show off his shiny store-bought boots, the first he had ever owned.

The train made its slow way east, arriving eventually at Fort Dodge. Walker thought the world might be better off without places like the ugly little military post. He thought of it as he would have thought about a boil that was in need of lancing. Still, the team stopped there on each trip to purchase a few extra supplies and to sit up to the table in a woman-run eating house.

The drover crew was just finishing up their dinners of fried potatoes and buffalo steak when the door opened to let in a man of indeterminate age dressed all in buckskin, wearing a hat that looked like it had lost a battle to a buffalo stampede. He was sun-bleached and dirty, his buckskins shiny from wear. Most frontier men had let their beards grow but this man was clean-shaven. His five-foot-eight frame didn't hold enough meat on it to hardly hold him down through a prairie wind but he carried a long gun with considerable authority and his eyes bore into each person in the room, one by one.

"Howdy, boys. I see by the lay of your wagons out there that you might be heading east."

He leaned his long rifle against the edge of the table, swung his legs over the bench and sat down. He pulled a plate off the small stack in the center of the table and reached for the steak.

"Don't mind if I do, boys. Kind of you to invite me. A man surely does get weary of his own cooking. Mind you, I'll put my own fixings up against that Greta woman anytime. Yessir, old Jimbo can cook up a mess of buffalo tongue or a cougar stew that would make you give thanks and howl at the moon. But still it's nice to sit up to a woman-cooked meal when the offer is made.

"Oh, Greta was fair enough on the eyes and for the first while that was enough for me. But after a month or so even that started to wear thin and I found myself longing for a better class of vittles. Liked to have starved to death that first while with Greta. Finally had to let her go. Oh, she didn't like it one bit when I brought her back to town and turned her loose. She didn't appreciate all I had done for her either. Tried to shoot me there at the end, she did. That was one fearsome woman but I didn't see it right there at first. Do you want to pass me that coffeepot?"

Josiah, one of the younger drivers, spoke up with a grin, "Do you talk the entire time you're awake, old man, or is this just our lucky day?"

Jimbo laughed and slapped the table with his left hand. "Why now, I like that, sonny. I like a man who speaks right up. Fact is, when a man knows as much as I do, it is just his natural responsibility to share his knowledge with folks. So I guess you could say that this is your lucky day.

"The other fact is, I plan to go east to Independence. Now you take the Indians hereabouts and west to the Rockies. I know them and they know me. I've lived with them and fought them. I've hunted buf with them and trapped fur with them.

"I even married one some time back. Notional girl she was. Unpredictable. Stayed with me for over a year and then ran off with some buck from another village taking our young son with her. There's no figuring a thing like that so I left the village looking for greener pastures.

"But we're still friends, those folks and me, and I see some of them from time to time. I ain't ever seen that girl again though. I send a gift down to Chief Runs His Horses when opportunity allows. He never has enough shot or powder so I drop a little over his way when I can. Just enough to shoot a buf or two, never enough to raise any ruction.

"But now these tribes to the east of here, that's another matter altogether. They don't know me and they just might decide my hair would make a fine decoration on the end of a war lance. Hard to judge folks you don't know. I figure a man would be foolish to travel alone. If'n you're heading east and I surmise you are since your wagons are heading that way and you haven't said anything to the contrary, I thought I would just ride along. I could add another gun if there's trouble and keep your fire supplied with meat. Yessir, this old Hawkins and I have brought a lot of meat to a lot of fires. Expect we can still do it all right. Now, if you was to…"

Josiah grinned again. "If we were to agree to let you ride along with us, would you stop talking?"

Jimbo looked around the table at the crew and then over at the young man. "Hard to find a youngster any more with a good upbringing. Show no respect, most of them. Still, I said that I liked you, young feller, and I do. Could be you can still learn. Who do I see about riding along?"

Josiah answered, "The foreman's out at the wagons. Mike, his name is. We're going out there now so you might as well come along."

The freight crew walked out to the gathered wagons with Jimbo walking along beside leading an Appaloosa stallion the likes of which none of the crew had ever seen before; sixteen-hands high, carrying his head proudly as only a stallion will do, prancing on delicate feet at the end of his lead rope and with a shiny coat with more spots and speckles than you could count.

"Seen you looking at my ride. And might you well look, too. Ain't another ride like Idaho anywhere around these parts. This here's what's called an Appaloosa. Not many around on account of the only folks that's got them is the Nez Perce tribe up in Idaho. Tried for an entire summer to deal the chief out of this here horse but he wouldn't hear of it. Brought him buf robes and shot and powder, gave him a Green River knife I truly admired, but he still wouldn't part with this here horse. Not that that stopped him from accepting the gifts. Finally had to take the borrow of old Idaho here. I had about seen all of that country I needed to see anyway and with winter coming on I thought it was time to head south a ways. Sure do get some winter up in those hills. Why I've seen snow near to the moon and lasting so long a feller might think that spring would never come."

Josiah asked, "You stole the horse?"

"You're a judging young feller I can see. No, I just took the borrow of it. I intend to borrow it back to the chief if'n I ever get back up that way. In the meantime, I take good care of old Idaho and he takes good care of me. A natural fit you might say. So which one of those fellows is Mike?"

Josiah led Jimbo up to where Mike was talking with a swamper. It was Mike's habit to check every wagon and every animal and talk with every one of the crew before starting out on the trip. He had just completed his inspection.

"Mike," called Josiah, "this here squaw man and horse thief

wants to ride along with us. Wants to talk with you." He looked at Jimbo with his grin still in place.

Mike took a long look at Jimbo. "How do you know he's a squaw man and a horse thief?"

"Told us so in considerable detail. This here is the talkingest man I ever did meet. If he rides along with us, he'll have the mules kicking over their traces and running off just to get some peace and quiet before the week is over."

Jimbo spoke to Mike, "This here young feller is a little sparing of the whole entire truth but the pure fact is that I'm planning on going to Independence and I surely don't want to ride the prairie alone."

"Well," said Mike, "we don't have any squaws to worry about. You going to run off with one of our mules?"

"Don't figure to," answered Jimbo. "You let me ride along, you'll find me doing my share of the work and we'll both be the better for the arrangement."

"I'll let you ride along. But understand this: we had a train attacked last year. Three men died. It was the work of Indians all right but they were led by a couple of white renegades. If I even get a reason to be suspicious of you, I'll shoot you dead and leave you beside the road and never give you another thought. If we meet up with Indians, you had better be shooting at them not with them. Are we clear on that?"

"Clear and agreed. I'll give you no reason to regret traveling together."

The train was led out of Fort Dodge by Mike riding a big bay gelding. He was the only one of the crew that was riding; the rest of the men were working the wagons. Jimbo ranged a mile or more ahead and nearly as far to the north. After a few miles, he swung over to the south. When he was satisfied with the emptiness of the Kansas prairie although you could never be sure what with all the rolling hills, he pulled in closer to the train and rode from wagon to wagon, visiting with the drivers and the swampers. True to his word, he brought in two antelope for the evening meal.

AFTER ABOUT ONE week on the trail, Jimbo pulled up beside Walker's wagon. Walker was swamping for a driver named Bo Hill. Bo never explained how he came about having such a name and Walker didn't ask.

Bo called out to Jimbo, "Hey, Jimbo, I'd sure admire to have a ride on that Appaloosa. How about you trade me places for a while?"

"Well, young feller, rightly this is a lot of horse. But you don't need a lot of rein to tell him what you want. You do it with love and understanding. Of course, I talk horse and that helps but not many as can do that. Shoshone medicine man taught me. Swore me to secrecy he did so I'm bound to keep the secret. But I'll trade you for a while. You stay right close where I can see you."

Walker took the reins and Jimbo climbed up beside him.

"I don't believe I've ever met a man to say less than you do, young man. They were telling around the fire how you're a first-rate driver but that you're quitting when you get back east. Must be a reason for that. Most folks, when they come west, get themselves hooked on the openness and the sheer size of the country. This is a man's country with room and more for a strong woman to walk beside him."

Jimbo had been looking at Walker as he talked. As soon as he mentioned women, the look on Walker's face changed and Jimbo started to understand something that none of the crew had bothered thinking about. For the first time since he had joined the train, Jimbo was silent.

Finally, "Want to tell me about it? It ain't just exactly an uncommon experience. Might be some talk would help."

Walker took a slow study of Jimbo. "You talk and make out like you're a simple man but you ain't no such thing. You've got eyes to see which is more than most folks have. As for me, what's done is done; there's no going back. I expect I'll live through it all right. I just thought I might live through it a bit easier if I had a change of scenery. And then I haven't seen the folks in two years and it's time."

That conversation led to many hours on the wagon seat where Jimbo talked endlessly about the west, telling Walker about the rivers, the tribes, the existing settlements, the land itself. Walker was a good listener, asking just the right questions to bring out the information that might be useful in the future. He and Jimbo became fast friends.

After Walker had explained about his desire to farm or ranch, Jimbo advised, "Ranch, that's the thing, and no better place for it than out on the plains and hills around the Purgatoire out in Colorado. The buf will soon be gone and some of the tribes are already moving to the reservations. Soon be millions of acres there for the taking. Why I know of a valley that would make you weep when you first see it, it's that beautiful. It was that valley the Lord was referring to when He called His work good after the creation. It's on the fringe of a Spanish land grant but those grants don't have clear borders. Runs His Horses tribe claims it. If you were to let them hunt a buf or two from time to time and you didn't run roughshod amongst their women, I'm guessing he'd sell it to you. You get back out west, you look me up. I'll show it to you and help you make a deal."

CLOSE ENOUGH TO Independence that the crew was starting to feel pretty safe from raiders or Indians, Mike, riding lead, came over a rise and frightened off several coyotes that had been tearing at the horribly mutilated remains of a family scattered around a burnt-out wagon. He called a halt to the train and rode back to bring up some men and shovels. Leaving the mules cropping the rich grass, most of the men made their way forward. Jimbo was among the first with Walker beside him.

Jimbo took one look and shook his head. "Fools, out here by themselves. They didn't make it a week on the trail. Too late in the year to be setting out anyway. Fools. Feel sorry for them but they were still fools."

Yuan Aribay pushed his way forward, took a quick look, then ran a few feet before bending over and throwing up. Walker stepped over to him. "You going to be all right, Yuan?"

Yuan couldn't speak. He just waved Walker off and sank to his knees, retching. Walker left him alone.

There was nothing left of the wagon or the family's possessions. "Indians would haul it all off before they set the fire," Jimbo said.

A wide, single grave was dug and the family placed in it, one by one, wrapped in spare blankets from the freight wagons. Father, mother and three children would share the same piece of prairie forever.

When the grave was covered, Mike asked, "Does someone want to say some words over them?"

When it became obvious that no one else was going to volunteer, Walker pulled off his well-worn hat and stepped forward.

In a strong, clear voice, he started in from memory, "The Lord is my Shepherd, I shall not want." He continued on to, "Even though I walk through the valley of the shadow of death, I will fear no evil for Thou art with me; Thy rod and Thy staff, they comfort me." He ended there and then bowed his head and prayed in the same strong voice; praying for the souls of this family that none of them knew and asking the Lord to be merciful to them, to comfort those who would wonder what became of them. He closed the prayer asking for safety for the crew for the remainder of the trip.

The men replaced their hats and silently made their way back to their wagons. Mike watched Walker move away, a new respect in his eyes.

Jimbo rode up to Walker's wagon. Bo had decided to walk for a while so Walker was alone. "You're just full of surprises, aren't you? Well, I say, good for you. Might interest you to know that I studied for the ministry many a year ago, long before I came west. I'd appreciate you not telling that around. I ain't never told many folks. Pearls before swine and all that, you know. Anyway, you set me to thinking thoughts that I haven't thought for a long time. Might be I'll dredge up some memories and see where they lead me."

4

WALKER LIMPED INTO THE FARM YARD, HIS LEG NOT COMPLETELY healed, and hollered a greeting at his mother. Startled, she looked up from sweeping the porch, dropped her broom and came running. By that time, the hounds were baying their mournful song and the rest of the family - except Walker's father - was running toward him, too.

"Go get your father!" Walker's mother yelled at no one in particular. "Tell him Walker's home."

The tumultuous greeting was followed by more questions than Walker had any chance of answering and the best supper he had eaten since leaving home.

Sitting on the porch in the cool of the evening, Walker's father looked his much-matured son over again. "Well, son, you've seen the west or a part of it at least. What are your plans now?"

"I've got some money put aside but it ain't anywhere near enough to start a ranch or a farm. Most of the west that I saw might be farmland someday but right now it's more suitable for cattle ranching. Dry. The land is dry. Good grassland but dry for farming. I expect someone will figure a way to get water to it but that won't be in time to help me. And then there's the matter of

Indians who have been there for generations and the millions of buffalo that range the entire area."

"Maybe you're a few years too early for the west," offered Walker's mother.

"For parts of it I am but there are some settlements and some ranches along the Big Sandy and the Purgatoire River in Colorado, and a few have even pushed further into the mountains. And New Mexico has been partly settled for generations. Still, it's a long way to the markets in the east and, no matter what else is happening, it still costs a lot of money to establish a ranch. I'm going to have to work and save my money for a while yet."

Hiram nodded in understanding. "The mill in town is looking for a foreman. I was talking with Cletus just the other day. He has more orders than he can fill. Maybe you should have a talk with him."

Walker went the next day to see the mill boss. He was welcomed back with a hearty handshake and the offer of a job. He took the job, determined to continue saving his money. He buried the gold coins brought home from the freighting job, placing them in a sealed metal can under the rock front step of the farmhouse.

He bought a horse so he could ride to his job while living with the family. Queenie had been retired; she roamed at will in the farmyard and around the garden fence.

He built a lean-to on the back of the house for his bedroom, hauling home scrap lumber from the mill to complete the job.

The family spent the long summer evenings drinking coffee and discussing the future and its possibilities. Walker especially enjoyed Sundays. The mill shut down on that day so the town was quiet. His father was still leading the little church in town and Walker came to enjoy his father's teachings from the Scriptures. He especially enjoyed the music as the small group of believers raised their voices in the familiar songs. Walker had always enjoyed singing.

But he was restless. And even though he was continually frugal, his carefully hoarded funds were growing at a discouragingly slow rate. So after a year of working at the mill, he again said farewell to the family and headed east this time having heard about abundant work and high pay on the Mississippi riverboats.

On the waterfront in St. Louis, Walker approached a stern paddle wheeler. He had noticed the "help wanted" sign at the bottom of the boarding plank. He hollered up to a uniformed man leaning over the railing of the pilot house, "What kind of help are you looking for?"

"The kind that knows something and can work hard," was the answer.

"Well," hollered up Walker, "I'm your man for half of that. I know I can work hard but I don't know the first thing about a boat. Expect I can learn though."

"Come aboard."

By the time Walker had made his unsteady way up the shifting boarding plank, the ship's officer had come downstairs and was waiting for him. "What kind of work have you been doing?"

"I was raised on a farm and recently spent a year as foreman in a saw mill. Before that I spent two years driving a freight wagon on the Santa Fe Trail. None of that work is designed to allow a man to run to fat. What kind of work are you offering?"

"Except for officers, boiler men and cabin staff, everyone starts out loading freight; everything from cotton bales to barrels of sugar and cut lumber. Lately we've been moving more military supplies than I'm happy with but we have to accept whatever might show a profit at the end of the run. That sound like something you might pick up on?"

Walker took a moment to look over the boat, as much as he could see anyway. "And if a man starts there, what might he work his way up to if he was to learn the ropes?"

"A good man can move into firing the steam boiler if he shows ability and with some training, he could work on the engines and the repair of the boat. You have to understand, there really aren't that many workers on a boat as small as this. But if you fit in, the life is pretty good even if the work is hard from time to time. Between stops where we load and unload, there's little to do and we have a good crew. No troublemakers. I won't tolerate them,"

"What's the pay?"

"We pay forty a month and you live and eat on board."

"When do I start?"

"My name is Rylie, first or last, it's all the same to me. And you've already started."

WALKER TOOK the job and because the boat was already loaded, he had little to do. The next morning after the passengers were boarded, the boat pulled away from the St. Louis wharf in a splash of churning, white water. Walker feared he might fall over or go for an unwelcome swim each time the boat took a turn or crossed over a wave. But by noon the first day he was getting a feel for the movements of the boat and was able to walk the deck without reaching from wall to wall or post to post.

Never one to stand around, Walker soon found that the fireman welcomed some extra help tossing the cord-length hardwood logs into the roaring maw of the boiler. He soon understood that the fierce fire was virtually insatiable and he started wondering if there might be opportunity for a wood supplier. But he found the life on board the boat growing on him so he decided to give it a longer try.

The steam engineer saw Walker looking at the maze of pipes, valves and gauges surrounding the boiler and steam engine. Never one to make friends, the engineer ignored the rookie laborer.

Walker stepped over to the engine and let his eye follow the various pipes that connected the engine to the boiler. Finally, he came close enough to the engineer to be heard over the roar of the fire and the working of the engine. "What do those gauges tell you? I never seen the like."

"They tell me that you should stick to loading cotton bales, farmer."

"I expect I can do a lot more than load cotton bales. I expect I can figure out this contraption for myself, too. It just might be a bit easier if you were to tell me. But I don't mean to trouble you. Maybe I'll take over your job after a while, too."

After the third trip on the river, Rylie called Walker over. "The big boats keep stealing our crew. I need a foreman. Think you're up to the job?"

"I can do it."

"You'll be on your own. There's no one to cry to. Remember I said I won't tolerate troublemakers. If you can't control them, I'll have to get someone else who can. You have to remember that these are mostly men from the saloons and the gambling pits. There ain't no college graduates among them."

"I can do it," Walker said again.

His way of controlling the men at the sawmill had been to first talk to the troublemaker, or try to, hoping that reason would prevail. It usually did. Most of the men at the mill were either townsmen or local farmers so the task was not difficult. But Walker had learned early that the boat crew was an entirely different situation. He knew there were men among the crew who would gladly give him trouble and who were not really too interested in living peaceful lives.

The first man to challenge him was a big Dutchman named Hans. He was older and bigger than Walker and had several years experience on riverboats and in logging camps. He considered himself bull of the woods.

He challenged Walker right after lunch on his second day of being foreman. "So how come you get my job, kid? Did your mama come crying to the captain?"

"I got offered this job and I took it, Hans. There's no need for trouble. We've all got a good boat to work on and a good thing going here. No need to upset it."

"Those are fancy words, young feller. But they don't mean noth'n to me. I think you're a mama's boy off the farm for the first time. I think maybe it's time you learned how it is to work among men." Then he hit him.

Walker didn't see it coming. The blow landed squarely on his chin and mouth, well-placed and well-timed. He flew backwards, backpedaling across the boiler-room floor and was brought up hard against the doorpost leading to the outside deck.

Walker knew he should have been expecting it but somehow he hoped the man would be reasonable.

He'd been in a couple of fights with the wagon crew along the trail but although he had won those handily, when he got right down to it, he realized he really knew nothing at all about fighting except to bore in and see what happened.

Walker wiped blood from broken lips with a dirty rag he pulled from his hip pocket. "You're wrong again, mister. I left the farm some years ago and if that's the best punch you've got, you're in a world of trouble. Step up and let's see what you've got."

The two men squared off, looking for openings and opportunity. Hans hit Walker twice more before he was really set. Walker found himself sitting on the deck. Hans was aiming a boot for his head when he rolled to one side and got to his feet.

The crew had gathered around and were yelling encouragement to their favorite.

Hans rushed and the two men fell into a bear hug. As big and strong as Hans was, he was no match for Walker's strength. Clearly surprised, Hans broke off and took a short step backwards. He would have been wiser to take a bigger step.

Walker moved in close and aimed a thundering left to the man's jaw. Blood and teeth fell from broken lips. His eyes glazed and the big Dutchman crumpled to the floor and didn't move.

Walker turned to the watching crew. "Is that it or do we go again?"

No one took him up on his offer, looking instead at the big man lying on the deck.

Walker turned to leave and saw Rylie watching from just inside the doorway. Rylie gave him a short nod and walked away.

That wasn't the end, of course. There seemed to never be an end to trouble but at least now he understood more clearly what was expected of him.

He continued to hang around the boiler and engine studying the piping and gauges, watching the movements of the engineers. Within a few months, he felt he had the hang of it. After six months on board, Rylie promoted Walker to the engineering crew. In resentment, the chief engineer walked off, saying he wasn't going to work with untrained farmers. The second-in-command moved up one space and Walker was firmly on the boiler crew, taking a shift on his own within a few weeks.

Walker stayed with the boat for a full two years. He sent most of his earnings home for his father to add to the tin can under the rock step. At the end of that time, the war between the North and South was almost a year old. The boat had been moved further south to be used exclusively for military travel, both materiel and troops.

Walker went to talk with his boss. "I have to leave you, Rylie. I want to thank you for the work and the trust you've placed in me. But I feel it's my duty to sign up. The South has a continual call out for men and I can't think of one good reason not to go when so many others are going. So I'll be saying good-bye at the end of this run."

Rylie looked his surprise. "You don't have to go, you know. An exemption for a job like you have is automatic. This is critical work we're doing and no one is going to think less of you for staying with it. You don't necessarily have to be in uniform to be serving."

"I know you're right. But I've made my decision."

The two years on the riverboat were followed by three years of war that Walker lived through wearing a gray uniform, slogging through the heat, the rain and the mud alongside thousands of other foot soldiers. The war was long and bitter and eventually his side lost. He didn't take the loss personally like so many did.

He ended the war with a lot of grim memories, a nearly new carbine, two good pistols and a sack of ammunition, all picked up off the abandoned battlefields. He also had a black saddle horse with a small US brand on the left shoulder that he'd found standing over an officer who wouldn't need him again.

Walker Samuel McTavish, who by now was known as Mac thanks to the long military tradition of assigning nicknames to buddies, headed south and west into Texas; west because going west had been his original plan. He then angled south because it sounded warm and winter held no appeal after the long cold nights on the battlefield. Both directions held the promise of distance that might dull the memories of war.

He had maybe sixty dollars saved from Confederate pay script that he had carefully exchanged for US dollars as the opportunity had presented itself. Army pay was a seldom thing but the soldier was always careful with his money. His frugal nature had caused him to save his money when so many others were spending freely on drink and gambling. But it was his cunning that had given him the thought to change his pay into Federal currency before the opportunity passed him by. He managed to hold onto the money by hiding it in his socks when the war came to an end.

He could only hope that his previous savings, stuffed into the tin can buried under the rock step on the farm, had survived the war. He was determined not to touch that money until the time came to buy his much dreamed about land.

With the war's end, the fighting men just drifted away; some to go home, some to where they thought there might be opportunity, and some to where they would not have to witness the death and destruction that had surrounded their old homes.

A good many men whose lives were broken beyond repair headed out into a world that was broken almost as badly as they were. Some headed for the riverboats, a few to logging camps, and some got lost in the big cities. But a lot of them found their way west to the grasslands and the buffalo herds where they would be unknown and might get a fresh start. Many changed their names. Some tried to find honest work but some couldn't or wouldn't hold down a steady job. Some of these men became outlaws. It would be a good many years before they were all brought under control.

Mac was paroled at Wittsburg, Arkansas after a short stay as a prisoner of war following the surrender. He'd fought for nearly three years, doing things and seeing things that he never dreamed were possible and that he would never forget. He ended his service attached to a cavalry outfit led by Brig. Gen. M. Jeff Thompson. They were among the last to surrender.

He considered riding home to Missouri from Arkansas but in the end chose Texas, feeling that the last thing his family needed would be another mouth to feed and that opportunity would lie in another direction.

5

WHEN MAC SMELLED CAMPFIRE SMOKE AND THE FAINT ODOR OF cooked beef, he was as weary and hungry as he had ever been. He had used up the last of his supplies two days earlier except for a small bag of coffee beans and a bit of rough ground corn flour. He had just a few inches of water left in his canteen. The scorching spring sun seemed to draw the last of the strength from him and his horse both. He found himself wondering if it ever rained in south Texas.

Following the smoke and in need of food, he reluctantly turned his dusty, tired horse toward a small gathering of cattle being held by a handful of derelict-looking men hunched in the sorry shade of some scrubby trees. A quick glance at the tattered clothing and worn-down boots on the riders told him that these men were gnawing on the leftovers of life just as he was. Still, his throbbing two-day-old hunger drove him forward in the hope that there might be some scrapings left in the bean pot. As he drew near, he saw a group of eight or ten men lounging in haphazard fashion with saddles, bedrolls and gear scattered over a wide area. Mac didn't like the looks of it. The shambles of a camp went against his very nature. Yet need to feed himself forced him to overlook the disarray around the gathering.

"Hello the camp," he said just loud enough to be heard,

knowing that he had been watched into camp. With the land as flat as it was, there was no chance of arriving unseen.

Several heads turned his way.

"Any chance for a cup of coffee?"

"Light and set," was the reply, a common response on the frontier.

Mac stepped down, fished his battered tin cup from a saddlebag and made his way to the fire. A filthy camp cook offered him a plate of half-raw beans with a big slab of leather-dry beef. The meal required two cups of acidic coffee just to choke it down. But poor as it was, the food was offered freely. He finished it all and could have eaten more. He ignored the dust and the flies.

It would take many a meal this good or better to fill out the remnants of the gray uniform he wore.

The gathered men, busy scratching map-like sketches in the dust and talking quietly, had paid him no heed at all. Mac dropped his empty plate into the cook's water-filled crash bucket, thanked the cook, and turned to leave.

A grating voice like you might expect from a half-hanged man stopped him, "You hunt'n work, soldier, or just a free meal?"

Mac turned toward the voice of gravel and didn't like what he saw. The man was as dirty as the cook and was armed like he was going back to war. His long scraggly hair and his uncombed beard added to his unkempt appearance although Mac knew he wasn't being totally fair in his judgments. As little water as there was in this dry country, it was nearly impossible to keep clean; he was in serious need of a bath himself.

"I'll be need'n work, all right. Ain't got no set plans yet though. You offering?"

"Name's Jones." The voice grated on Mac's ears. "A few of the boys and I are planning on moving some cattle north to the market. We could use another hand or two. I watched you ride in. You ride like you could go the distance."

Mac took offense at the entire camp setup in spite of the free meal. He lifted his hat and ran his fingers through his black wavy hair. He thought again how he needed a haircut but that looked like it would have to wait.

"Jones, is it? Right common name. Met a lot of Jones' in the Army. Kin of yours perhaps. One or two good men among them, I expect."

Jones tightened his fists at the insult but Mac continued, "Now I'm wondering here, Mr. Jones. I don't see no more than about a dozen cattle. You're holding a bunch somewhere close by, no doubt."

Jones smiled with his lips and glared ice with his eyes. "A name is of little importance on the frontier but mine happens to really be Jones. You could blame my grandpa I guess; he shortened it from something that didn't spell proper in English. But it ain't a name that will move cattle. It's hard work and sweat. Either you're up to it or you ain't. And as far as the cattle are concerned, the country is full of them with the owners gone and forgotten. We'll have cattle enough to drive."

Mac took a moment to tighten his saddle cinch, thinking about those cattle. Finally, he said, "Mr. Jones, could we leave that offer open for a day or two? I need to go sit by a stream somewhere and get the stench of war out of my nostrils. Should I decide to take up your offer, I'll ride up here ready to go to work. Much obliged for the meal."

Mac knew he wasn't being honest. He wouldn't be back. These were not his type of men. But he was thankful for the meal and he felt there had been enough controversy for one fifteen-minute stay. He swung his leg over the saddle and lifted his horse into a trot away from the camp.

Around noon the next day Mac rode up to a picket shelter that passed itself off as a roadhouse offering rooms, meals and drinks, and some basic camp supplies for sale. The grim exterior disguised the fact that the food was actually pretty good, served up by a woman who looked stout enough to wrestle steers, testimony to her own cooking. Her beanpole of a husband was kept busy tending the little bar although he had no customers when Mac entered. And they did, indeed, have a room or two at the back that could be rented if a traveler wished to spend a few coins to escape the elements. Mac bought a twenty-five cent meal, seasoned so as to bring tears to his eyes. He didn't bother with the drink or the room. He purchased a small sack of beans and a piece of cured and salted side meat along with a bit more flour and some cooking salt.

After eating, Mac took his coffee cup and stepped outside into the shade of an overhang. Six or seven men lounged there, some on tilted-back chairs and a couple squatting on the ground, all of them absently swatting at the clouds of flies that swarmed them. Mac leaned against a post, observing the group and listening to their talk while he drank his coffee. No one spoke to him although a couple of hard-bitten men nodded a slight greeting. The group, a ragtag bunch at best, included two who were wearing remnants of blue uniforms and who appeared to be at least a step or two above the others. The conversation stopped with Mac's arrival as the men sized him up. Still no one spoke to him. But there seemed to be an air of acceptance.

One of the men in a tilted-back chair, taking advantage of the break in the talk, looked over at the two men wearing blue. "No offense, friend, but that blue shirt could get you into a mite of trouble down here. Mostly we see those shirts on carpetbaggers or crooked sheriffs with a lot more like them on their way to take over Texas if the word I heard was right. And I looked at more than just a few shirts like that over the sights of a rifle although I must say that I've done things I enjoyed more than that."

The man spoken to answered with a grin, "No offense taken, friend. I'd like nothing better than to ride up to the best emporium in the country and deck myself out in style. But broke as I am, if I threw away this shirt, I would have to cut arm holes in a flour sack and pull it over my head, always assuming that I could find a flour sack." He seemed in no way intimidated by the question or embarrassed by his answer.

Mac, looking at the broad chest and shoulders of the speaker, allowed to himself that it would take a sizable flour sack to make a shirt for the man.

The conversation drifted back to its previous topic. These men didn't interest Mac much but their talk did. The talk was of cattle, the second such talk in two days.

Mac had always been a listener with little to say himself. It had been drummed into him by his patient father that a man learns absolutely nothing while he is talking. So Mac had learned to listen.

Mac noticed that the two Northerners had little to say either. The rest were a rowdy bunch but they talked a line of talk that interested him for they talked of selling cattle and making money. He didn't have any cattle to sell but he liked the idea of making money so he listened, the vision of land of his own strong in his mind. And the vague image of the girl that would share it with him although he admitted to himself that his experience in Santa Fe had considerably increased his inborn caution when it came to his relationship with women. He also knew that to turn that vision into reality would require money.

The self-appointed leader of the ragged group who called himself Shorty although he stood over six feet in his boots, spoke out, pointing at the ground, "There must be a million cattle within a week's ride of right here. Now it's true those cattle used to belong to someone. At least their mammies or their grand-mammies did before they took to running wild. But it's also true that most of them carry no brand and have had no contact with human people for all their entire lives. What owners used to be here mostly went off to wear the Gray and will never be coming home again. What few people stayed after the start of the Northern aggression were run off either by the Comanche or hunger. You might have noticed that there just aren't a lot of people around here. Empty ranch shacks and run-down corrals are about all that's left of the old ranches."

Mac thought about the gravel-voiced rider from the day before. He had talked the same kind of talk.

"What are you suggesting, Shorty?" asked a beak-nosed teenager who was doing his best to whittle away the awning post.

"What I'm suggesting is that those cattle are free for the

taking although I'll allow as how the taking might be no easy matter."

"What would we do with them? There ain't no market around here and even if there was, Texas is broke. I'll bet there ain't a hundred dollars gold within fifty miles of this roadhouse. And if there was someone who wanted cattle, he could just go out and catch his own.

"The market is in the big eastern cities. The war left a big need for meat that ain't no one set out to fill yet. These here Texas longhorns are a bit tough and a mite stringy but most people would still call them beef. They could go a long ways toward filling those eastern stomachs."

"Speaking of a long ways," said another rider, "it's an almighty far ways to any of those eastern cities."

Mac had trouble holding in the excitement of an idea being born but he thought he had done a pretty good job of it when he turned and left.

He rode a few miles to a copse of willows growing beside a small stream where he tied his horse and made a simple camp. Careful to assure that he was alone, he stripped off and had a bath in the stream although the water was barely six inches deep. He dried himself in the sun, ready to dive for cover if someone came close enough to see his nakedness. If someone happened by, he knew what they would see: a big man topping six feet and near two hundred pounds. At least he had neared two hundred before the war. He was a gaunt one-seventy standing there naked in the sun and he wondered how many plates of rough beans it would take to fill out his ribs again. But even filled out, he knew he would still appear slim to the casual glance. He was tall and slender like his father. The slimness was a disguise. He had the oversized shoulders and hands of his father, and a natural strength that was the envy of lesser men. The disguise was complicated by an inborn gentleness taken from his mother combined with a fierce determination which was a further gift from his father.

He didn't figure many folks would consider him handsome. Reasonably good-looking perhaps but not handsome although there had been a girl back home who had said the words. Mac figured those words had lacked conviction. But he knew he was solid and strong with more natural muscle than most men. He did his share of work and looked a man in the eye when he spoke. He stood by his word and finished what he started. Mac figured that would just have to be enough.

He washed his clothing without soap and spread the wet articles on the willows to dry. Looking at his worn-out pants and shirt, he thought about how it had been back on the small family farm the day he had left looking for opportunity all those years ago. He had been a long, lanky farm boy with the shoulders and hands of a man and the dreams of a boy. The thin material of his homemade shirt as well as his pride had been stretched to the limit. His worn and patched bib overalls and equally worn and patched work boots showed him for what he was: a dirt poor young man grasping for a better life than he had known but having no real assurance that he would ever find it.

Looking at the clothing spread out on the bush to dry, Mac thought, "Why, I'm no better off than I was when I left home all those years ago. I set out to change that but I've still got it to do."

His carefully-hoarded gold coins hidden in the tin can on the farm never entered his thoughts. That gold was for the purchase of land and cattle and he wouldn't use it for anything else. The few coins tucked down safely in the bottom of his saddlebag were held as a hedge against hunger. A new shirt would have to wait.

By evening, both Mac and his clothing were dry so he got dressed and started to settle in for the night. After combing the long grass and the brush carefully to lessen the chances of a night visit from an unwelcome snake, he laid out his bedroll.

Just before full dark, a quiet voice came to him through the brush, "Hello, the camp. Two men here. May we come in?"

Mac had pulled back from his fire so he knew they couldn't easily see him. He had seen enough men die during the war when they had foolishly allowed themselves to be backlit by their fires. He wasn't about to make that mistake.

Mac pointed his carbine in the direction of the voice and said just as quietly, "Come in friendly or you'll not see the morning."

The two from the roadhouse - the two wearing the remnants of Blue - stepped into view, each holding the reins of a horse.

"You hid yourself well, friend," said the taller of the two. "We looked for you closer to the settlement and so did a couple of those others. I doubt as how they were up to any good. We finally saddled up and made as if to leave. I don't think we were followed."

Mac thought that if one rough-built roadhouse passed as a settlement out here, then ten houses and a livery barn would be a city. "Well, you found me. My question is why."

"Fair question," said the tall man. "My name is Jerrod Thompson. My friend here is Luke Black. The war left us foot-loose. After the hostilities, we rode home and found that the war had been fought over our farms and homes. There's little left but some wooden grave markers and a land that will need a lot of time to heal. We figured we didn't have that kind of time or the heart to help in the healing. We set out riding and ended up here, trying to find a future. We're nearly broke and robbing banks doesn't appeal to us so when we heard those men talking cattle, we listened. You keep a straight face, friend, but you listened, too. We both saw it in you. We also saw in you a man we might like to ride with. We sure prefer not to ride with the likes of those others."

"Tie your horses and set a while," invited Mac.

The two men were near opposites. Jerrod was tall and slim. Mac knew that when a girl called him handsome she would really mean it. He made an imposing figure, showing brownish-blond wavy hair with a strong tinge of silver falling from under a worn-out hat and with his backbone ramrod straight. He looked every bit the cavalry officer he had been if you could forgive the mixture of well-worn clothing.

Luke was shorter and built like a bull. His chest and arms were massive. A broken nose and the scars on one cheek spoke of past misunderstandings. Mac wondered if the scars were the result of the war or of some private venture. He tried to picture the man in a flour-sack shirt but couldn't quite complete the image.

Both men were clean shaven. Mac had let his beard grow for a while after the war but hadn't liked it. He had shaved in the cold water and without soap that afternoon.

Sitting down with his back to a small live oak, Luke pulled off his sweat-stained hat to wipe his forehead with a dirty sleeve. Mac was startled to see that he was completely bald.

Luke noticed the look and grinned. "Lost my hair to the war. We fought three solid days in the prettiest valley I ever saw. Hand-to-hand at the end and sheer terror the whole time. A lot of blood and a lot of hurt but no real winner. I woke up the next morning with my hair lying beside me on the blanket. All in all, that wasn't a good week."

Mac looked the ex-cavalry sergeant over for a moment or two. "Had me a week or two like that myself."

All three were silent for a while after that, sizing each other up. Mac finally nodded his head toward the men, "Well, you're the ones with the idea. Better spit it out. I'll listen to anything that makes sense."

Thompson took the lead. "Cattle. Same as those others were talking about. We came south looking for opportunity not having any real idea how broke Texas is. I could write a book about what we don't know about Texas. We had just about made up our minds to turn north again before we became flat broke when we arrived at that shack this morning. After hearing the talk, we got to thinking that perhaps opportunity was all around us and we just hadn't seen it. We got to wondering if you had seen the same and if we might be smart to try working together."

Mac looked from one man to the other and finally asked, "How much do you know about wild cattle?"

Jerrod looked at Mac and chuckled. "Why, you hit the nail right on the head. We don't know the first thing about wild cattle. We can both milk a yard cow and have been around field cattle all our lives but that's not going to be much help with these wild critters we've seen around here."

Luke spoke up, grinning, "We figure we're as smart as most

and we can learn. Anyway, it's a long ride north to our homes. If we're going to make that ride, we might just as well be pushing a few cattle along ahead of us. Seem a shame to ride all that way with nothing to show for it."

After a short pause while he studied his two visitors, Mac stood and picked up the coffeepot. "You see if you can stir up that fire. I'll dip some water."

So the three campers who a few weeks before had been on opposite sides of a war that had dragged them in, mostly against their will and their better judgment, drank up most of the coffee they held between them talking the night away, swatting flies and mosquitoes and listening to the coyotes singing in the distance. By midnight, with a few dry clouds making their slow way over a half moon and with the coyotes finally deciding they had serenaded enough, a partnership was born. A cattle partnership. One with no cattle, one horse each and with a little over two hundred dollars between the three of them. But a lot of grand ventures have been started with less and no one could slight their will to work or the strength of their hopes.

Mac found himself wondering if, after all the years of wandering and trouble, this could develop into the opportunity he had set out looking for.

6

WHEN MAC FINALLY LAY DOWN TO SLEEP, HE FOUND HIMSELF thinking about the winding path that had brought him to this place. He thought about his godly, hard-working parents who had never known anything but striving and hard times. He thought about the poverty of his youth; a poverty that seemed to follow him like an unwelcome shadow.

His main goal in life was to rid himself of this plague of poverty. He had two other goals that depended on the first one. That was to find a home for himself and to find a girl who would share that home with him.

Thinking about home and his own dreams, Mac thought to himself, "I set off to make my fortune, Pa, but I've still got it to do. I wish you were here with me. You understand cow critters better than I ever will. It would be good to be doing this together."

Although Mac's mind was swirling with possibilities, he finally went into a shallow sleep, thinking about home and listening to Luke snore.

Now, sitting by the morning fire with his two new partners, discussing how to get started in the cattle gathering business and drinking up the last of Mac's coffee in the morning sunlight, he spoke up, "There's got to be a few things understood if we're to travel together."

"What did you have in mind?" asked Jerrod.

"First, the war is over. No good can come of talking about it."

"Mac, folks like you and us had no say in the starting or the stopping of that sad foolishness. The soft-handed men sitting in tax-paid offices made all those decisions but they aren't the ones who paid the price. I'm happy it's over and I'm content to never talk about it."

Luke simply nodded, indicating his agreement.

"Then," continued Mac, "we three are equal and there is no boss. I've taken enough orders the past while to do me for the rest of my life. If we agree on something, we do it. If we don't agree, we take another path."

Both men nodded in agreement.

"Finally, it ain't a partnership as you might rightly think of a partnership. We work and ride together, split the costs and split the rewards, always assuming that there will be rewards. But this ain't no permanent thing. If we manage to gather us some wealth, I'll have plans of my own. The fact is, I already have the plans and I expect you both do, too. When I leave out toward those plans, I don't want any hard feelings. But I promise not to leave you before the work is done."

Jerrod and Luke looked at each other and then both nodded at Mac. They were silent a while as if waiting for his next condition.

"That's it from me," Mac said.

"It about says it for me, too." Jerrod glanced at Luke.

"I got nothing to add."

Mac got up and headed for his horse. "Then let's get to work."

Luke watched Mac walk away, then looked over at Jerrod and grinned.

The three men saddled up and rode back to the roadhouse to ask for directions, hoping to get some kind of a feel for the country.

The skinny bartender flattened out a piece of brown wrapping paper onto the top of the bar, licked the end of a dull pencil and said, "I'll draw you a map. This here line is the border with Mexico. That's maybe a short three- or four-day ride south of here. You didn't ask for advice but were you to, I'd say to stay away from there. No good can come from wandering down that far. There's a good many Mexs around here and most of them are right fine folks. But there's some of the other kind, too, and mostly they gather around the river. Of course, you're apt to find an unwelcome anywhere south of the Nueces. Mexico never was very happy with the result of that little set-to between Santa Anna and Houston and the holdouts still claim the strip of land between the Nueces and the Rio Grande.

"So this here line is the Nueces," he said, drawing a line across the paper. "The Gulf water is right about here, off to the east a few days ride. Never been there myself so that's a bit of a guess. And you go more than maybe fifty miles to the west and you better learn to speak Comanche."

THE THREE MEN had just enough food between them to prepare one meal each day, supplemented by some coffee and other necessaries purchased at the roadhouse. They talked about killing a beef but, knowing that between the heat and the flies most of it would go to waste, decided to locate a campsite first.

The partners spent a few days scouting the land, marking out sizable groups of cattle and getting to know each other.

Mac found himself starting to push the war into the back of his mind. The work being done and yet to be done was having a calming effect on his memory. And although the rations they were preparing would never cause concern about overweight, Mac was feeling better than he had since he left the riverboat and put on a uniform. He might even have put on a pound or two. He wondered if sleeping without fear and the sounds of cannon were making a difference, too.

Neither Jerrod nor Luke had suffered from hunger quite as much as Mac but still, they were looking better also. Perhaps just more rested.

Mac looked at Jerrod's tall, slim frame and his handsome face and thought, "Ma would call him a fine figure of a man. She might even be sizing him up as a possible son-in-law but, of course, she would never speak of that."

His study turned to Luke. "I'd say he was a man who enjoyed a good scrap," Mac thought. "And I wouldn't like to try him on. Looks strong enough to straighten out horseshoes and grin the entire time he was doing it. Ain't handsome, though; not by a long shot. He's going to have to win a wife some other way. Looks ain't going to do it."

After looking over a badly-neglected ranch site, they decided to make it their home base. The weeds and brush growing in the corral and barnyard spoke of a long vacancy but the barn still stood and the house looked livable.

"It's not pretty," Jerrod said, tying his horse to a desert shrub. "But she looks solid. The roof appears to be intact and we'll enjoy that on a rainy day. That's assuming it ever rains in Texas."

Mac walked over and lifted the dried-out cover on the wooden well casing. The hinges creaked and some dried wood flaked off. He took a slow study of the well and then turned to his partners. "Holding water. The pulley is rusty but usable. But the rope is rotten and we don't have another. I expect we have to use the creek for water."

Luke sat down on one of the cots and Jerrod looked over the table and chairs. The few pieces of crude home-built furniture left in the shack were judged to be usable.

"These must have been rich folks," Luke said with a grin, "At a time when most folks were cooking over an open fire in the fireplace, these folks had themselves a for real cook stove. Why, just looking at it makes me want to stop and light a fire just to see if it does work."

Mac looked at Luke. "I expect we have time for coffee."

The three partners spent one day patching up the corral so they could pen their horses. They found two shovels which were used to clean out enough of the barn to where they had three stalls available for their three horses. "Be good to lock them up of a night," opined Mac. "Might still be the odd Indian around looking for a riding animal. Or a white man with a poor under-standing of property ownership, for that matter."

A further search of the barn yielded a curry comb, a lot of old harness, several halters and bridles and a wooden bin half full of oats that somehow the mice had missed. They also found a branding iron showing a Bar-H.

By this time, they knew they needed supplies.

"Where do you suppose there's a town?" asked Jerrod.

Mac threw out the dregs of his morning coffee and looked at his two partners. "This whole operation of ours is based on guesswork. Now, if I was to guess, I would say that the border with Mexico is not too far south. According to the sketch map that bartender gave us, that's the Nueces we rode along yester-day. And we've come less than fifteen miles north from there. Seems doubtful there would be a town down that way if what the bartender told us is true. My guess would be north but it's purely a guess."

"Good as any," Luke agreed.

Jerrod said, "You boys ride along and see what you can find. I want to stay here and straighten this place up a bit more. Might take a gander down through that bush to the west; we haven't been there yet.

Mac and Luke agreed and left out, riding north by a bit west.

Riding along Luke, said, "You told us you were raised on a Missouri farm, Mac. Do you still have folks there or is everyone scattered like our families are?"

"The last letter I received from home said that they had all come through the war all right. One battle was fought through the farmyard but the family found shelter in the root cellar so they were safe enough although a mite scared. Probably no more scared than I was many a time. The folks are there along with two sisters and two brothers, all younger than me and not near old enough to join the forces."

"Did you think about going back?

"I did, but I figured they didn't need another mouth to feed and whatever opportunity the home valley offered wasn't going to help me to get my ranch. Of course, I wasn't quite sure what I was looking for when I came to Texas either."

After a few more minutes of riding, Mac asked, "What about you and Jerrod. You going back after this little venture is finished?"

"I won't. I like this western country and the life it can offer when the war becomes a memory and things settle down. You can already see that I'm a bit rough around the edges. Town life would never be enough for me and although I've put in my time looking at the south end of a mule, I never did feel that my hands fit a plow handle too well.

"Jerrod will probably go back. He fits well into town life. Mixes well and gets along with folks. The ladies like him. Don't let those good manners fool you though. There's nothing soft about Jerrod. If there was anything soft before the war, there for sure isn't after. I've seen him ride into the face of cannons leading his men when most of us wanted to go the other way. I've also seen him give orders to men when the odds were that no one would survive the carrying out of the orders. Near broke his heart to do it but that didn't stop him. And because he took more risk that anyone else, we couldn't hardly do anything else but follow. No, sir, don't you misjudge Jerrod. He'll be there when the need is upon us."

About twenty miles north of the ranch house, they found a small settlement that boasted a combination saloon and eating house, a livery barn, a general store and a lawyer's office, all side by side in a ragged line on the one-street settlement.

The two men pulled up to the hitch rail in front of the general store and stepped down.

As they were tying up, Luke looked over at the lawyer's office and grinned. "Don't that beat all. Lawyers just seem to want to be the first on the scene so they'll be handy when trouble starts. And often enough they start the troubles themselves."

Mac just shook his head as if somehow it was no surprise that there would be a lawyer in this sun-baked and dust-soaked settlement.

They purchased a supply of beans, coffee, sugar, flour, side meat and a few other necessaries. They also purchased a new rope for the well plus a cattle rope for each of them although none of them had any idea about how to work cattle with a rope. They looked at the oilskin slickers but decided, for as often as it rained in Texas, they would save their meager funds for necessities.

They spotted a no-longer-young horse standing with drooped head in the corral at the livery barn that they figured they could use as a packhorse.

The hostler was sitting in the shade of the saloon porch. When he noticed the two visitors looking over his stock, he sauntered down to the corral showing no hurry. "Sell you that there mare for seventy-five dollars, son, although I shouldn't as good as that horse is and as few horses as there are left in the country."

"As good as that horse is," answered Mac, "you should really pay me to shoot her for you. Tell you what, though. You throw in a pack saddle and I'll take her off your hands to save you feeding her and we both benefit."

Luke grinned at Mac and hunched his shoulders. "Never heard any bargaining start out quite like that before," he said quietly.

"Son," said the livery man, "if'n we had a sheriff, I'd holler him up. Tell him I'd caught him a horse thief. But since I can see how much you want that there horse, and to keep you from getting arrested for horse stealing, tell you what I'll do. You dig around and find me fifty dollars and I'll dig around and find a pack saddle."

"Well, I like the part where you find a pack saddle but I don't much think I can find fifty dollars that I want to spend on that worn-out horse. But just so that you can tell the boys down at the coffee shop that you suckered a greenhorn into buying a worn-out mare, I'll dig around and have five dollars ready for you when you come back with the pack saddle."

"I just couldn't do that, son. I have expenses to pay and how can I pay them if'n I let people steal from me, and me watching it happen?"

"I'm losing patience with you, old man," Mac said with as stern a voice as he knew how to use. "You bring out that pack saddle and a bill of sale and I'll double the five dollars. Take that or we saddle up and ride away."

They did saddle up and ride off; and the old mare, following on a lead line, was saddled and loaded with the food and camp gear that they had just purchased.

7

THE TWO EX-SOLDIERS, NOW GREENHORN CATTLEMEN, HEADED back to the ranch yard. They stowed the supplies in the shack and put the packhorse in the corral with a pail of oats from the bin.

Mac took another look at the mare. "I doubt if that nag even knows what oats are."

The next day, the three partners rode to a small copse of bush about one mile from the shack where they had seen a good grouping of cattle.

"What do we do first?" asked Jerrod. "I doubt if these critters will make themselves into a herd just by our asking. They look as wild as deer to me."

"Let's just start in and see what happens," suggested Luke, never one to bother with an excess of details. "I'll go around the far side of this bush and in through the middle if you two will hold the sides."

Without waiting for an answer, Luke rode away to circle the bush and Jerrod said to Mac, "Luke has never been noted for patience. Right or wrong, I expect he'll make something happen."

The experiment drove eight cows and two calves out of the

brush. As soon as the cows spotted Mac and Jerrod, they turned aside and headed right back into the bush, their tails aloft and their calves running to keep up.

Luke came out of the brush with his shirt torn and with both his horse and himself bleeding in several places from thorn scratches. He walked back in and found his hat. "Well, I don't know as I expected to get it just right on the first try."

The next two weeks were a mixture of work, sweat, dust, bruises, cuts and very small successes. The two weeks of work allowed them to boast fewer than one hundred head of mixed cattle, loose-herded on a few acres of grass beside a slow-running creek just a short ways from the old ranch shack.

Sitting exhausted beside the noon cook-fire, Mac said, "If anyone came and told me that we didn't know what we were doing, I would probably feel duty bound to give him a whopping, or try to, but he would be right nonetheless. These cattle can breed faster than we can catch them. We got to try to be smarter."

"What are you suggesting?" asked Jerrod.

"Well now, you boys know as much as me but two things bother me. One is that the more we chase these critters, the lower they shake their horns and the higher they hold their tails. They just aren't enjoying the chase even a little bit. And once they get excited, I'm not sure even a week-long hunger would get them out of that brush even if'n we was to lay out green cut hay for them. Plus, the chasing is killing our horses.

"Once they've come out of the brush on their own with their minds set on grazing or slaking their thirst, I'd like to try just easing them along to join the ones we already have. Let them come out of the brush in their own good time. If we were to just slowly move up beside small groups and encourage them along a bit, might could be they would join the others up by the shack and forget about this here brush. They're almighty skittish though. We would have to take it slow.

"The other thing is, it seems that we're trying to be too thorough. Yesterday I lost six cows while I was trying to get the seventh one out of the bush. I would've been better off to take the six and leave the one. Seems to me, anyway. As it is, I have nothing but scratches and experience to show for all that work."

"You're saying we should skim off what we can get and try to work them into a herd?" asked Luke. "I like that. Our horses are nearly dead and our grub is seriously shortened. Yes, I like that idea a lot."

Jerrod's way of agreeing was to go saddle his horse.

Within a week, they had three-hundred and fifty head gathered and reasonably content by the creek. Another two weeks saw the herd rise to eight hundred. They kept the bulls that had followed the cows but cut out the cows with small calves at foot. Any with brands were turned back.

After discussing the problems of driving that many cattle with just one horse each, the men decided to be satisfied with the group they'd gathered. They spent the long days riding slowly around the herd, hoping to keep them from darting back into the brush and giving them time to settle down to their new surroundings.

Jerrod rode over to where Luke was wiping sweat from his bald head with his kerchief and asked, "What's your count, Luke?"

"I make it eight-hundred and three, mature cows and bulls together with a few yearling heifers. What do you make it?"

Jerrod said, "I gave up trying to count them. If you say there are eight-hundred and three cows, then I say there are eight-hundred and three although just how you can be so sure when they never stop milling around is beyond me."

Mac rode up about that time and was asked for his number. "Eight-hundred and three," was his answer.

Luke grinned and Jerrod just rode away after hunching his shoulders and giving the two men a quizzical look.

"Your turn to make supper," Luke hollered after the departing Cavalry officer. Then he turned to Mac and said with a grin that Mac was to see many times and over many circumstances, "He's pouting because he can't count past twenty and every time a cow critter moves, he has to start over again.

Numbers are surely not his strong point. He'd burn the beans on purpose and not talk for a week if he knew you and I had agreed on the number before he asked."

They took their meals beside the herd, afraid to leave them without at least one rider available to watch for trouble. After a predictable supper of beef and beans plus biscuits that Jerrod really did burn, Mac took another cup of coffee and looked at his two partners.

"I say one day more of rest for the horses and then we move north. What do y'all think?"

Luke ventured one of his rare opinions. "I don't think these horses are going to make it very far without they get more than a single day of rest. That big black of yours might be the exception, Mac. Now I know we agreed we wouldn't talk about the war and rightly I'm not. But I wonder about that horse. Not that the Union couldn't spare a horse or two. But I never knew them to pass them out as a consolation prize to Southern soldiers on their way home." He let the statement hang right there.

Mac pulled a few lengths of grass from where he was sitting and let them sift through his fingers. He set his coffee cup on the ground, took off his hat to wipe his forehead and took a long look at Luke and then at Jerrod. When he spoke, he spoke so quietly the other men could barely hear him, "Old Able Prieses and I were on our way out, walking as most of the boys were doing. The war was over a few weeks but feelings hold fast and die hard. We had given up our weapons, of course, but there was no shortage of them lying around where they were easy to hand. So Able and I were both armed although the weapons we had were far from new and had been hard used.

"Somewhere in southern Arkansas, we walked out of a hard-wood thicket and into an acre of clearing. We surely didn't mean no harm and we were purely tired of killing and being killed. On the other side of that clearing was an officer in Blue who was paying more attention to cooking his lunch than he was to the noise in the woods. He was alone and I guess our weapons and the gray uniforms startled him. Seems he was miles from anywhere that made sense but there he was nonetheless. Able was a bit ahead of me and when that officer heard our steps in the long grass, he turned with a weapon in his hands. Able and I both hollered to stop him but he was turning almighty fast and he fired as he turned. Able returned the fire mostly from habit and self-protection but he fired accurately. He shot that officer clean through the lung.

"I didn't think Able was hit so I ran to the officer. He stared right through me with glazing-over eyes. Then he lifted his arm to the sky and said, "Ain't it a pretty day." Well, it was a pretty day. The trees were in full leaf and there seemed to be birds everywhere. A few fluffy white clouds accented the deep blue of the sky and there was not a sound anywhere excepting the birds. It was far too nice a day to be dying for nothing. But dying he surely was."

Mac couldn't help noticing that Jerrod was studying him intently but he let it pass.

Mac continued, "I went back to see Able and found that he was shot in the hip. A nasty wound that broke bone and spilled blood freely. He would've lived if we'd had any medical help but all I could do was try to stop the flow of blood. It wasn't enough. It took him the most of an hour but finally he died there. The pretty day had turned into a pleasant evening and old Able died right there. He lay there in the long grass with the hardwood trees casting a shadow and with the evening birds singing their songs. He gripped my hand something fierce right at the end but he never said a word. Able and I had dodged bullets and bayonets together for over two years and here he lay, dead on the grass, weeks after the war had ended.

"There was nothing I could do for either of them so I left them right where they lay. I took an address from Able's pocket and later I wrote a short note to whoever was at that address. I have no idea if it was a mother or a wife or a stranger. But it was all I could do. I took that officer's horse and traded my worn-out weapons for the better ones that officer had and here I am."

"Did you find a name for the owner of that horse," asked Jerrod.

"No. I figured they would both be found soon enough so I let it be. Anyway, I wanted to get away from there. Even though I hadn't fired a shot, I figured I'd be blamed if someone came along. Seemed best to be somewhere else."

"Good horse," was all Luke said but a melancholy of memories settled over the camp for the rest of the evening.

8

JERROD WAS THE FIRST TO LEAVE THE SHACK THE NEXT MORNING. Opening the door, he was surprised to see an exhausted horse standing droop-headed in front of the shack. The horse was solid black except for one white front stocking. It would be an easy horse to recognize.

Sitting bareback on the horse was a scarecrow of a young man, really little more than a boy, who looked as worn out as his horse. His six-foot frame was gaunted down to no more than one-hundred-forty pounds. His long blond hair hung straight and tangled over his dirty collar. His filthy wool trousers were tucked into shabby boots. But he was well armed with a belted side arm, a carbine tied over his shoulders with scraps of twine, and a wide-bladed knife hanging from the light rope that was holding up his pants.

The tired horse stood with head hung, his front legs splayed wide for support. By the looks of the exhausted young man, Jerrod was afraid that if he tried to slide off the horse he might just fall and not get up again.

"Morning," spoke Jerrod seeing no threat from the rider. "If I am any judge, both you and your horse could use some break- fast. Why don't you slide off and come inside? We are just about to fry up some side meat. You make yourself at home and I'll take your horse and feed him."

"I am at home. I don't need your invite." Even through the weariness a touch of anger and a touch of pride showed itself. "This is my land and that's my house."

Jerrod leaned back inside the door and said, "Better come out here, Luke. We have company."

Luke came out carrying a carbine. He walked up beside Jerrod and looked at the young man and the horse. "Who's this?"

Mac was still riding night herd on the cattle.

"This young man says this is his land and his shack. He hasn't offered his name yet or any proof that this is his land but we knew it belonged to someone before we got here. So why don't we invite him in for breakfast while we sort this out? Maybe you could holler up Mac and bring him in? I think the cattle will be all right for a few minutes."

Jerrod looked at the weary rider. "We're friendly, young man, and we hold no threat. Why don't you just ease yourself down and come in? If I do say so myself, you and your horse both look like you've come some distance on poor rations."

While the young visitor was hesitating, Luke and Mac rode up.

The young rider finally lifted his right leg over the horse's neck and slid to the ground. He couldn't stop himself from going to his knees. He crouched there a moment or two and then found strength to rise to his feet. "Reckon I am a bit tuckered. Breakfast sounds good as long as I'm not being asked to eat my own beef. There should still be a few head of Bar-H around these parts somewhere."

Luke grinned at him. "You're running in luck then. We have side meat this morning, just about the last of what we bought a while ago but enough."

Jerrod took the reins of the young man's horse and said again, "I'll care for the horse. You go in and sit down."

He led the exhausted horse toward the barn until its head perked up and it stepped forward, tugging at the reins in its eagerness to get inside. As soon as the horse was led through the barn door, it headed directly to the first stall and tugged until Jerrod finally let him go. "Well now, I would say you've been here before. Welcome home."

There was a bit of hay left in the manger and Jerrod scooped a small pail of the precious oats into the bin built into the manger for that purpose. He tied the black to the manger, gave the horse a friendly slap on the hip and walked to the house.

When he walked in the door he smiled at the sight of the young visitor sitting hunched over a cup of coffee held reverently in both hands.

"First coffee I've had in months. Missed coffee just about as much as I missed the meals."

Jerrod balanced on a three-legged, crudely-built chair across from the visitor and asked, "Do you have a name? Mine's Jerrod and this here is Mac and the cook this morning is Luke."

"Name's Tyler Hobson. Most folks call me Ty."

"Well," Mac said, "if this really is your house and land, you deserve an explanation. We've been here about five weeks. Strangers to this part of the world. We were scouting cattle when we come upon this ranch site. It looked like the roof wasn't about to let in the spring rains and there were cattle close by so we moved in. We've done no harm so, if this is really your place, you've lost nothing."

"It's mine all right." The thought of breakfast seemed to set the young man's mind at ease with the three strangers. "We was a family until the war started. I had an older brother rode off to join up and we never heard from him again. My pa died lying under a no-good horse that fell and drove the saddle horn into his ribs. My sister rode off in a wagon with the neighbor boy who was determined to not wear a uniform. No telling what happened to them. Ma just pined away and I buried her back in that clearing beside the creek. I was too young for the war when my brother rode off but then, when I was alone, I decided I had it to do. I rode north and east and got to the closest battlefield just in time to hear about the surrender. I never did put on a uniform or fire a shot but they still put me in a stockade. Called me a prisoner of war, they did. Made me mad enough to want to go to war on my own."

Ty looked over at Luke and Jerrod. "They were all wearing shirts just like y'all are wearing."

"Well you're here now, Ty," Mac said with one of his rare smiles. "So I guess someone should say 'Welcome home.' Don't appear that you're coming home to much but, even at that, I guess it's as much as we've seen anywhere else in Texas. And don't let those blue shirts worry you. These boys are all right. At least they have been so far."

Luke dished up the side meat and biscuits which they spread with molasses and the men ate in silence. Mac didn't touch his plate of food, watching Ty. When Ty's plate was empty, Mac picked it up and slid his full one in front of the young man. Ty looked his shame and his gratitude.

Mac said, "Go ahead, son. We have plenty and can cook up as much as we want," which wasn't exactly the entire truth.

Finishing another cup of coffee, Mac stood up. "I need to get back to the herd. Ty, why don't you stretch out on that bunk and catch up a bit?"

"How are the cattle for restless?" asked Jerrod.

"They're fine for now, grazing nicely. You hear any commotion, you come a running. Otherwise, I think the horses will benefit from the rest. Maybe one of you could ride out that way around noon. I'm all right until then."

Luke spelled Mac off at noon and he rode in and unsaddled his horse. He gave it a quick rubdown and a small pail of oats. He walked into the house to the smell of coffee and the sight of Ty and Jerrod in conversation. The boy looked more rested but perhaps not fully awake yet.

"We've been talking cattle, Mac," said Jerrod. "Ty says there's no shortage of the brutes in the thickets just south of here. Myself, I've seen enough of thickets but Ty says the local boys manage to work the cattle out without too much trouble. Most of those boys are Mexican. *Vaqueros*, Ty calls them. Says they're born to the thickets. The possibilities do give a man something to think about."

"We'll talk more about that when we're all together. Luke has to hear this, too. But, Ty, I would like to know how you got home and where you managed to get that horse and the weapons. I was in a prison camp, too, so I know what you went through up to that point. Do you mind telling the rest?"

Jerrod spoke up, "I would say he's telling the truth as far as the horse is concerned anyway. There's no doubt that horse is at home in the barn. Stepped eagerly into the first stall like he was born there."

"He was born there. Born there, gelded there and spent all his life there until I foolishly rode him east."

Jerrod chuckled. "Well, I don't suppose he remembers being born and I hope he doesn't remember being gelded. But he for sure remembers that stall."

Ty looked at Jerrod and Mac over the rim of his coffee cup. "I'll have to trust you boys to not repeat this but I stole that horse and the weapons. Now it's not quite as bad as that sounded. I rode east on that very same horse with a good side arm and a fairly new carbine. Pa raised that horse from its birthing and if you look you will see the Bar-H brand on his left hip. When they threw me in prison, they took away everything I had, even my Confederate money which wasn't no more good by that time."

"How long did they hold you?" asked Mac.

"Just two weeks but it sure seemed longer as rough as they treated us and as little as they fed us. They turned us all out with nothing at all and told us to go home with threats of what would happen if we ever took up arms again. Well, I figured my weapons were gone for good but I surely wanted my horse back.

"The soldiers had a pretty good-sized remuda held outside the prison camp so I figured my horse would probably be there. I hung around careful not to be seen, watching for a chance. Finally, I spotted a soldier riding out on my very own black. He wasn't on any special duty it seemed because he just rode into town for a drink.

"I didn't dare to just up and take that horse in broad daylight so I waited around and when the soldier came out of the saloon, it was dark. He rode slowly down the street in no hurry to get back to the camp. I expect he had more than just the one drink. I walked along in the dark until we passed the last building. Then I called softly to him. He rode over as innocent as could be and I just lifted his foot out of the stirrup and dumped him on the ground. I was on him before he could even call out and one kick in the jaw kept him from even thinking about hollering for help. Might have heard something break, too. Can't be real sure.

"Well, I took back my horse and the borrow of his weapons and lit out for home. A close call some days later cost me the saddle. It wasn't my own saddle but it was good enough. A few soldiers surprised me sleeping in the shelter of a ranch shed. I didn't have time to saddle up. But old Blackie there, he outran them and here we are."

Jerrod looked seriously at Ty. "That horse is real easy to spot and identify. It's true you're a long ways from that prison camp but, just the same, I would rid myself of that horse just as soon as possible if I was you. You wouldn't want to go through all of that and then have someone spot the black."

Ty studied Jerrod for a moment or two. "I hadn't thought of that. But you're right. I'll ride down and see my Mexican friends and make a trade. They can pass it along south and in a week or so they'll ride it across the river and trade it again down into Mexico. No one will ever see it in Texas again. I'll go tomorrow."

Ty slept the afternoon away and after a brief supper and a quick check on the horse went right back to his cot.

"That there was a tired-out man," Luke said with a grin.

The following morning, Jerrod spoke to Luke and Ty who were finishing up breakfast. "We have some things to discuss. Let's meet Mac at the herd and talk there just in case our live-stock decide they preferred living in the brush and head for home."

"A couple more bites and I'm with you," answered Ty.

When the four were together at the bed grounds, Jerrod asked, "How are we going to do this? Neither the horses nor the cattle are trail-ready yet but they're close. I suggest another two or three days of rest for the horses. I'm hoping we can hold the herd that long."

"That sounds good to me," answered Mac. "What do you think, Ty? Will the herd settle better when they're being driven?"

"It'll take a few days for them to figure it all out but I expect the walking will pretty much take their minds off going home."

Mac looked at the others. "Then, if you all agree, that's what we'll do."

Ty spoke again, "Boys, it will just take a couple of days to ride south and trade this horse off. If I leave now, I can be back in time to help you get them off the bed grounds."

"Go ahead," answered Mac. "We'll be all right."

As if to prove the men wrong, the cattle milled and were uneasy all the next two days.

"I'm not sure we can hold them," hollered Luke, "and I don't like the looks of the sky. I've never seen a South Texas storm but that could be about to change. Might be better all around if we were to hit the trail. We're wearing out the horses anyway and we're not any further north than we were yesterday."

Mac was about to speak his agreement when Jerrod spoke up, "I'll go gather our stuff and load the packhorse. We won't get so far off that Ty will have trouble finding us."

The words were no sooner out of his mouth when the skies opened and a cold, drenching downpour soaked the men and animals causing the cattle to hump their backs and turn their tails into the wind. There was thunder and lightning but it was centered miles to the west and didn't much bother the animals.

"We'd better let this pass, Luke; I can't hardly see across the herd for rain. I think driving them is out of the question." Mac seemed to be trying to curl up under his hat as he spoke.

That statement didn't really need an answer so Luke just bobbed his head in agreement and rode to push a cow back into the herd.

The storm swirled and circled in a clockwise direction bringing the lightening closer by the minute. There was no sun left to see and the darkness, on top of the pounding rain, seemed to distress men and animals both. By the time the first close lightning struck, the men, cattle and horses were drenched. Their backs were sore from the pounding rain and the black, churning sky showed no promise of relief.

When it came, the lightning storm was brief but noisy. The cattle seemed to take the thunder more or less in stride having heard it many times during their wild, free lives. But when a lightning bolt struck the ground fairly near the herd and lightning flashes started dancing like fairy lights across the tips of the cattle's wide horns, the brutes started to run. The men were dangerously close to losing them all. Mac and Luke were trying desperately to hold the two leading corners of the frightened herd and were in dread of losing the battle when Ty charged up on a strange horse and took charge of the effort.

Yelling and slapping cattle with his coiled lariat, he started the cattle turning and milling back into themselves. Mac and Luke watched from a short ways off and when they recognized what he was doing, they joined in. Jerrod was frantically driving strays back toward the larger group.

The horses were lathering but the rain was washing it away as fast as it formed. The men charged the cattle, moving them tighter into the mill. The horses danced and slipped on wet grass as brutally sharp horns grazed their sides. Mac took a horn in his boot; the leather ripped and the horn punctured the skin above his ankle. He felt nothing and rode on, thinking the blood forming in his boot was rainwater.

The cattle ran over a half mile of Texas grass before the men got them into a tight mill and they settled down.

Mac rode over to Ty. "I don't know where you came from or where you got that horse but I never seen anyone more welcome. You can see what greenhorns we are. I never would have thought of turning them that way." He still had to shout over the noise of the pounding rain.

"Got the horse on a trade down south. When the storm started, I came right along figuring you might need help. Glad it worked out."

Mac smiled at Luke. "We talked about moving them to new grass. I guess you could say that's done."

Luke shook his head at his partner. "I really wonder about you sometimes."

Soaked to the skin, Jerrod hollered at Mac, "Makes me consider all the storms we could encounter driving these brutes north. I owned a slicker once, long ago. I don't remember what became of it."

"I had a sheepskin coat once but never a slicker."

The men started taking turns returning to the shack for food and warmth. There were no dry clothes to change into but a few minutes backed up to the cast-iron range helped. And the rain continued.

Discouragement started to set in on the second day of rain. The horses were stumbling in weariness and the men had taken to walking and leading their mounts to allow them a bit of rest.

The first sign of temper showed itself on the third day of the storm.

Luke hadn't spoken for several hours and the men seemed to sense that it was time to let him be.

Mac was afraid that one wrong word and Luke would go to chasing rattlesnakes with his bare teeth.

Luke was walking beside his horse when a young cow turned as if to wander off, challenging Luke's authority. With a roar of stored-up rage, Luke leaped at the critter, grabbed her by the horns and twisted. The cow took a couple of jumping steps but Luke held on, his heels tearing up wet Texas grass. His biceps bulged and cords of muscle stood out on his neck as he gritted his teeth and twisted. The cows head came around and Luke kept twisting. The cow slowly turned onto her side and then her back. Luke let go of the horns and grabbed the animal's head, still twisting.

"That will probable do it, Sergeant," said Jerrod. "I think she gets your point."

Luke let go and gave the cow a kick in the ribs. He gave Jerrod and Mac a slow look and mounted his horse, riding away without a word.

"That's new," Mac said after a moment.

"Luke does have a way about him that usually gets his point across."

The cow lay for a minute before struggling to her feet and rejoining the herd.

The storm rained itself out on the third day and after drying by the stove and having a warm breakfast, Luke was more or less back to his old self. No one mentioned the incident with the cow.

By the morning of the fourth day, the sun was drying out the land and the riders. But Jerrod and Luke were starting to have some doubts about the task they had undertaken.

9

Ty had traded the Bar-H black for an unbranded sorrel. His Mexican friend threw in an old saddle that wasn't much but was maybe a bit better than riding bareback.

He had cleaned up the old Bar-H branding iron and suggested that perhaps the men could help him brand the new horse before they left. "Ain't no easy thing branding a full-grown horse."

He looked somewhat rested but otherwise not much better than he had when he first arrived. It would take many more meals and more nights of sleep to recover from his long, useless ride to the battlefield. And nothing at all would help his ragged clothing.

Looking at him, Mac figured the years before he rode east hadn't been easy either but he didn't ask Ty about them. He saw nothing wrong with leaving a man a bit of personal dignity.

Mac called a meeting of all four of the men. "We can't leave the cattle for long enough so let's just have our meeting in the saddle, ready to go to work if need be."

He looked at the gathered men. "Ty, we have a proposition for you. Jerrod can best explain it."

"I'll listen to anything that might show a future."

Jerrod gathered his thoughts for a few moments before

speaking as if searching for just the right words. "Ty, you've already figured out that there is a long chance this drive won't end well. Still, we're determined to try. We know we need more men and more horses but we're foolish enough to set out north without them. We just don't have any way to pay wages or buy horses even if either horses or men were available. So we have it to do, just the three of us.

"If we're successful, we'll want to do it again but with a larger herd next time. We know we lucked out with this bunch. As gentle as we treated them, I'm not even sure they understand that they've been moved. Your good grass and that steady-flowing creek have given us a contented herd for the most part. We also know that free cattle are just too good to pass up. More men will be chasing them which will thin out the herds and make them harder to catch. These came pretty easy for us."

Luke interjected, "Depends on your definition of easy."

Jerrod ignored the remark and looked back at Ty.

"What we're proposing is that you throw in with us. You have the ranch here and miles of grass. You have friends about and no shortage of cattle running free. You know the country and you know cattle. My guess would be that a few of those *vaqueros* would want to earn a wage helping you gather a herd. You put a herd together, brand it Bar-H, and with any good luck at all we should be back by early fall."

Jerrod looked at the other men and saw no sign that they had anything to add.

"We'll work with you to hold the cattle on your grass, under your brand, until spring. Then we'll buy them from you at the going price and push them north. If this drive turns out half all right, we should have enough money to hire some riders. We'd like to try for two trips next summer but that will require a lot of luck as well as an early spring start and will leave no time for a gather. But if you do the gather and have a second herd together when we return, we just might get it done."

"Your plan might work. But what if you have trouble and don't get back?" asked Ty.

"Then you'd have a herd to sell to anyone with enough gold.

Or you and your friends could drive it yourselves," Mac answered.

Ty seemed to consider that for a few moments before saying, "There's another problem. I can't even feed myself except for beef and I don't suppose my friends or I either one want to live on just beef. I'm thinking I have to find a job that pays enough to buy beans and coffee if nothing else."

"We thought about that," answered Jerrod. "If you like the sound of what we're saying, we'll spot you to forty dollars in supplies. I wish it could be more but we're almost broke, too. But if you're careful, that much might keep you in enough beans and flour to round out the beef and hold you till we get back. If we don't get back, you have the forty dollars for wages and rent on the cabin."

Ty looked at each man for a moment and then stuck his hand out to Jerrod. "Deal, and I wish you luck on the drive. I'd like to see your herd branded but I can see how just the three of you couldn't get that done. Still, I intend to brand my gather."

THREE MORE DAYS of rest found them ready to start the drive. After discussing how they would do it, they broke camp and headed the herd north. With just three men there wasn't much to decide. Jerrod and Luke made up to try to direct the herd and also catch any bunch quitters on the front half of the drive. Mac took up the rear and most of the task of keeping the herd together. Ty rode along intending to purchase supplies at the settlement before heading back to the ranch but he also helped Mac with the drag.

By late afternoon, they had only made eight miles and Mac figured they could go no further. "Good creek over here," he hollered to Jerrod. "Maybe that's enough for the first day."

The men and horses were all worn to a frazzle and the herd was restless not knowing what was happening to them. But the cattle hadn't run or turned toward home. He took that as a victory. And they had all learned some things. The men had started to get just the barest feel for the task, the horses were starting to understand their job of chasing cows, and the cattle were moving more or less in a pack.

Two mature bulls had moved to the front and had challenged each other for the leadership. But with the constant forward motion they eventually separated and took up positions on either side of the leading edge of the herd. Cows and younger bulls fell in behind and seemed to sense their place in the order of things.

"I never saw such as that," Mac said with some amazement. "Who would ever think that these brutes would act like that?"

"There's no telling what they're thinking," added Ty. "But maybe it will be a help in the drive."

Mac was still studying the two bulls. "Old bulls aren't noted for their speed of walking. That could present a problem next summer if we intend to take two herds north."

The four men cooked a meal and took turns sleeping and riding around the herd. By morning, Jerrod and Luke were having doubts again.

"How far is it to this railway?" asked Jerrod over his breakfast coffee knowing that none of them knew the answer.

"Don't matter how far it is," Mac answered. "We started out and we got it to do. At ten dollars a head, we have more than eight thousand dollars in that herd. And my hope is that we can do a lot better than ten dollars. Now you compare that to the less than a hundred dollars we have between us. And then you tell me what our options are."

They sat in silence for a few moments and then Luke said, "Let's saddle up."

It took three days to cover the twenty miles to the settlement and both horses and men were at the end of their endurance.

Mac looked over at his partners. "Seems like we've come a long ways. Luke, how about you take a little hike up that hill over yonder. I bet if you look off to the north you'll see coal smoke from an engine or maybe even hear a train whistle." He said it with a tired smile.

Luke managed a lopsided grin. "Like I said before, I really do sometimes wonder about you."

As the herd rested a mile from the settlement, Luke and Ty rode in for supplies. A group of riders came out from town to look over the herd but they didn't ride in or speak to the herders.

Jerrod pointed off in their direction. "You see that bunch over there? I wonder what they're up to."

Mac took a slow look. "Can't be real sure at this distance but one of those men looks an awful lot like a Mr. Jones that I scrounged some burned beans from the day before I met you fellows. He was getting set to make a gather. Invited me to join his group but I couldn't see anything good coming from it. I wonder what he's doing here."

There seemed to be no threat so they ignored the riders.

They rested two more days and then pulled out. Ty sat his sorrel and waved one final time as they moved out of sight.

By the end of the first week, they had made maybe fifty miles and the horses could go no further. They bedded the herd by a small lake and staked the horses out to rest, leaving loose saddles in place in case the horses were needed in a hurry. They circled the herd on foot just to let the dumb brutes know that they were not alone, hoping none would try to run for home. But the herd was pretty much settled into the routine and showed no notion of leaving the lake and the abundant grass.

Ty had told them that the old-time ranchers used to sing to the herd. Not that the brutes had much of an ear for music but to reassure them that they weren't alone.

Mac figured both he and Jerrod might be accepted into the church choir but Luke's voice was another matter.

Jerrod finally said good-naturedly, "Three years I rode with you, Luke, and I never once heard you sing. Gives a man something else to be thankful for."

But sing they did, just loud enough to tell the resting cattle that the riders or in this case, walkers, were still there. Mac wasn't sure if it was doing any good or not but it didn't seem to be doing any harm so they carried on with the singing.

"Might be we should be keeping notes, men," Luke said when they stopped for supper. "I don't expect as how anyone else has ever driven cattle afoot before, at least not as far as we intend to go. You could write yourself a book, Jerrod, telling all about your experiences. Might make more money selling the book to eastern greenhorns than you will driving these beasts. "

Jerrod brushed off the suggestion with a wave of his hand. "I kind of think we'll remember the most of this and I have no mind to write more than a letter home some day."

They had planned to rest for two or three days and then set out north again. They weren't sure that even that much rest would be enough for the horses. In truth, Mac realized they needed at least four horses each. Even more would be better.

Just before full light on the third morning, a group of raiders rose up out of a small coulee running hard at the herd, yelling and firing their pistols.

Luke, on foot patrol at the herd, dove into a small willow clump. From there he took a couple of pistol shots at the raiders but they were soon out of range and his shots fell far short.

Mac and Jerrod were still in their bedrolls when the first shot brought them wide awake. Barefoot and wearing only their long handles, they grabbed for their carbines.

The cattle had just risen from their bed grounds after a night's rest. At the first sound of gunshots, the cattle raised their heads in panic and were soon in full flight away from the noise. They circled the lake and headed north with the raiders giving chase.

Two riders charged the camp, sweeping up the three pick-eted saddle horses plus the packhorse. They were clear of the camp within seconds but not before a rifle shot from Jerrod knocked one of them out of his saddle. The downed rider's horse kept running, keeping up with the rest.

Within one minute, there was nothing to show for all the work that had been done gathering the small herd except dust, sore muscles and one dead raider.

Luke came running and puffing into camp. "Let's get after them. They can't get far as slow as those cattle move."

Mac shook his head. "They were moving pretty fast the last I saw of them."

Luke looked at the trail of the departing herd. "Makes my blood boil. Losing that herd after all our work just doesn't suit me at all."

"It doesn't suit any of us, Luke," said Jerrod. "We'll figure something out but it will have to be something other than scrambling after a running herd."

The three walked over to the downed man and Jerrod turned him over with the toe of his boot.

Mac looked closely in the dull light of early morning. "That's that kid that was whittling away the porch roof post at the picket roadhouse, the one where that Shorty feller was doing all the talking."

"I do believe you're right," Luke agreed.

"I figured that bunch was up to no good but I never once suspected this. What will we do now?" Jerrod asked.

Mac looked grim. "We'll go get our cattle back, of course, just like Luke suggested. But I'm not up to trying to run them down. Let's get started. We can develop a plan as we go along."

Without further discussion, they set out north carrying their gathered camp gear. Jerrod finally said, "I can think of just one good thing about this."

"I must be going stone blind," answered Luke. "I don't see even the one good thing."

"Well, consider those boys are driving our cattle north which is where we wanted to go in the first place so the distance isn't a loss. When we catch them, we'll be that much closer to the railway."

"My sore feet are telling me that there thinking is a stretch of good common sense," responded Luke. "For myself, I'd just as soon be riding no matter which direction we were headed."

"Then consider this," spoke Mac. "If we hadn't left those horses saddled, you would have still been walking but then you'd also be carrying your saddle.

The other two grudgingly agreed.

Mac continued, "These thieves aren't as smart as they think

they are. They probably ran the cattle for a while thinking they'd be leaving us behind and they did. But those cattle can't run far. Except for the first few miles, we're covering more ground than that herd will be so, given time, we'll for sure catch them."

"I have no doubt," he continued, "that a walking man can catch a cattle herd. With the cattle making twelve to fifteen miles a day at best, the walking man can gain five to ten miles each day with steady walking."

Luke nodded. "You might be right in what you say, Mac. But you two tall galoots are built more for walking than I am. Short as I am, walking just holds no appeal at all."

Closing in on sundown on the third day, Mac pointed out a campfire and a herd of cattle about two miles ahead.

"All right," asked Luke, "what's our move?"

No one spoke for a while and then Jerrod said, "We were cavalry, Luke, and since cavalrymen without horses aren't much good for anything, we'd better let our infantryman come up with a plan."

Mac thought about it for a minute. "It's less than two miles to that camp. These boys ain't smart but they just might be smart enough to have a guard posted this side of the camp. I say we drop our bedrolls and gear here so our hands are free, and that we separate some and walk up quietly. If we can get within a short way of the camp, we'll settle down for the night and then see how they feel about a visit just before sunrise."

Luke answered, "Sunrise sounds good to me. That will give my sore feet a bit of a rest."

Mac looked at Luke and chuckled lightly. "I don't know as I ever met a man who fussed over his feet so much."

"I'm built for riding or sitting."

Mac continued with his plan, "If we spot a guard, we pass around him if possible, getting between him and the camp. If he spooks, we will have to drop him. Quietly. Guns only as a last resort. I would just as soon these cattle didn't run any further else we will be walking all the way to Kansas or Missouri or wherever that railway proves to be."

They stacked their bedrolls and other gear in a pile behind a small bush and sat for a short rest.

The night was cool but pleasant. There was a bit of a moon showing but the slowly drifting clouds kept it hidden most of the time.

Mac stayed alert for noise from the camp but the steady hum of night insects was the only sound to be heard.

Luke sat cross-legged facing Mac and Jerrod. He stretched out his tired back muscles, then massaged his feet right through his boots. "My feet are so sore they feel like they'll never be normal again. It'd give me pleasure to take off these boots and rest a while but I doubt I could get them back on again as swollen as my feet are.

"Boys, we're going to have some stories to tell our grandchildren. All we have to do is live through this night and a few hundred more like it." For once Luke wasn't grinning.

After a few minutes, Jerrod spoke, "Has it occurred to either of you that we don't even know where we're going? We know there's a railway somewhere north of here but we don't know where and none of us have ever been there. Then when we get there, who do we sell the beef critters to? There's a chance we might have to walk these cattle all the way to the stockyards in Chicago, all the time assuming that we get the cattle back and somehow get past the Indians and other outlaws."

Mac was lying in the grass with his hat over his face. "If it was easy, everyone would be doing it."

"I'll say this for you, Mac," Luke said with a small laugh. "You're not easily discouraged."

After an hour's rest, the three sore-footed men separated a bit and headed toward the outlaw camp. Mac knew that as slow as they were walking it would take a good while to get into the positions they wanted to be. But there'd be no sleep this night anyway so the time was unimportant. He walked as quietly as possible, skirting clumps of sage and the odd patch of prickly pear.

Mac pulled a handful of grass and looked at it carefully. He then scuffed his boot through the grass to loosen some soil. "Good cattle country," he said quietly.

A flared match just off to his right stopped Luke in his tracks.

"Dumb as an ax handle," muttered Luke. "No soldier would ever light up while on guard duty; none on my command anyways."

Seeing it was unlikely that he could sneak past the guard, Luke carefully turned in his direction. After a bit, he dropped to his hands and knees and made his way forward.

Just as he was thinking that his silent mission was successful, the guard turned sharply and called out, "Who's there?" The voice wasn't loud enough to be heard in the camp.

Before the guard could make another call or fire a shot, Luke was on him; a powerful hand clamped tightly over his mouth and the blade of his ten-inch campaign knife imbedded between his ribs. The guard let out a slight gurgling noise and slumped to the ground.

Luke let the man fall and then wiped his knife blade on the man's shirt. Too late to make any difference, he said to himself, "I sure hope this is the right herd. If it isn't, I just killed an innocent man."

Neither Mac nor Jerrod had heard or seen anything of the scuffle.

When they were within about one half-mile of the campfire, the three men drifted back together centering on Mac who had taken the middle position.

"See anything?" asked Jerrod.

"Not me," answered Mac.

There was no response from Luke. The silence dragged on for a few moments and then Mac asked, "You, Luke?" Again, there was silence.

Luke finally spoke up, "Found the guard," he said quietly. "He won't be following us or warning the camp."

In the near total darkness, both Mac and Jerrod looked toward Luke. Neither spoke but Mac was thankful the man was on his side, blue shirt or no blue shirt. That thought led without warning to considering how easily the two of them could have met on the battlefield.

Mac thought about the war for the first time in weeks. He had fought and killed and seen too many of his buddies killed or maimed but he never really accepted the need. He did his duty, and more, but he often wondered at the foolish waste. He had seen men become hardened and callous in their effort to survive and he hadn't liked what he saw. Although a strong man when it was required and always determined in whatever he set out to do, he was - at heart - a peaceful man.

Mac figured Luke was one of the many undocumented casualties of the late war, a casualty that wouldn't show up on any military list. Luke had never said much about his life before the war but he had probably changed considerably. He'd become a complete warrior to whom all threats were taken seriously and to whom a fight usually ended in death. An ending that Luke took as natural and which he didn't question.

Mac had wondered a bit why the raiders had made no attempt to kill them when they drove off the cattle. They had seemed to be satisfied with taking the animals. Mac was prepared to take the animals back without violence if possible.

"I figure at least an hour before first light," Jerrod said to no one in particular.

Again, they waited, crouching in the sage studying the camp. Through the gray of the pre-dawn, they could see a rider circling the herd and just the barest outline of resting cattle.

Mac whispered to the men, "Be light within the hour. We ain't going to get far with this venture if those sleeping men decide to rise and saddle up. I know we talked about waiting for first light but I say we go now as quiet as can be and with no shooting if that turns out to be possible."

Luke, always ready said, "Let's go," and started walking before either of his partners gave an answer.

Mac and Jerrod tucked their carbines under their arms and followed.

"Let's come up behind the wagon. If the cook happens to be

an early riser, we might see him before he sees us," suggested Mac and they all turned in that direction.

"Men," Luke whispered, "this is knife work if we want it to be silent. One gunshot might spook those cattle into a run that will undo all our hard walking."

"I'm not much on killing if we don't have to," answered Mac. "I know we might have to but let's see what happens before we do it."

"If you say so. I'm not exactly sure what you think this bunch will do, Mac. I really doubt if they'll saddle our horses for us and apologize for the inconvenience. We'll see, but I won't hesitate when the need is on us. I want those cattle back and I purely don't take to being robbed and shot at."

"I can't say as I enjoyed that either, Luke; we'll do what's necessary."

They moved off in the direction of the open-topped wagon.

The thieves had a small horse remuda grazing alongside the sleeping cattle and Mac looked at it longingly, knowing what those extra horses would mean to them. They might capture the horses later but the men were their first concern.

Mac reached a hand to each of his partners and whispered, "Look behind the wagon. Ain't that our own horses?"

"I do believe you're right, my friend," Jerrod agreed. "For some reason, they're keeping them saddled and tied to the wagon. Perhaps they're afraid those nags will cut loose from the bunch and head home."

"Whatever the reason, it's fine with me. Let's get up to the wagon."

As they approached the wagon, they were able to see that the camp was well placed beside a stream that wound its crooked way through a goodly copse of trees.

Mac counted the bedrolls in the firelight's flicker and whispered to the other two, "There's only two of them and I don't see a cook. And I only see one riding with the herd."

Jerrod looked where Mac was pointing. "I do believe you are correct again. Luke, why don't you give Mac and me a few moments to catch our horses and then crawl up on those two sleeping thieves? Maybe you can thunk them on the head with your rifle butt and keep them quiet while Mac and I bring that other feller in. Then we can decide on our next move."

Jerrod and Mac walked cautiously toward their horses but still the beasts shuffled their feet and one let out a low whinny.

"I wouldn't make much of a horse thief," Mac said quietly to himself. "Can't even sneak up on my own horse."

As he reached out for the tied reins, he turned to look toward where the two sleeping thieves were bedded down. The noise from the horse had awakened one man. He sat up and laid out his arm and shook his partner. They were both sitting up when Mac saw Luke walk up behind them. Luke swung his rifle butt with a force that could have split an oak fence rail, once to the right and again to the left, and the two thieves were laid out cold.

Mac cringed at the sound of the two skulls cracking like eggs. He whispered to Jerrod, "Well, that should hold them, maybe for eternity."

Mac and Jerrod were soon mounted and headed around the herd, one going each way. They hadn't discussed that tactic; it just seemed natural that they should trap the outlaw rider between them. Mac thought about their teamwork and was pleased with the partners who had chosen him.

As they approached the rider, they heard him call out, "Slim, is that you? You're up early."

Mac recognized the raspy voice and said just loud enough to be heard, "Why, no, Mister Jones. This isn't Slim. Slim decided to go back to sleep, quite a long sleep if my guess is correct. Now you just sit quietly while I ride over there and we'll discuss your future."

Jones turned his horse in a panicked attempt to ride away and turned right into Jerrod's mount. There was just enough light to see. Mac watched as Jerrod leveled his pistol at Jones. Jones slumped in his saddle and raised his hands.

Jerrod relieved Jones of his weapons, took his horse's reins in his hand and started back toward the camp.

Mac had ridden up alongside; Jones rode beside Mac, showing no fight.

Arriving at the camp, Mac was surprised to see that Luke had hoisted the unconscious raiders from their bedding and onto their horse's bare backs. He had them sitting beneath a spread out live oak limb, their saddle ropes looped around their necks, over the limb and tied off around the trunk of the tree.

"You should have stuck to your original plan and made your own gather," Mac said to Jones. The prisoner just gave him a vicious look.

Jones looked at his two partners, sitting their horses and roped to the tree limb, and knew that they were just one step from being hung. "Where's Willy," he asked. "We sent him a ways south to watch for you boys."

"He won't be joining us," answered Jerrod.

"What's your name?" demanded Luke. "And if you lie, I'll shoot you."

"Why, this is Mr. Jones," answered Mac. "He invited me to go into the cattle business with him. Good thing I didn't. We would have sure come to a disagreement about just how the business should be run."

"Name's Jones," confirmed the rider, "and that's the truth. You going to hang me, too?" He asked the question with evident fear in his voice.

"Don't figure to," Luke answered, "lessen you think being hung now will save you a site of misery in the future. I just don't see no bright future for you at all. What do you want? You want to be hung now to end your misery or you want to go free so you can tell everyone you see that the McTavish herd should be left alone? You got just no time at all to make a decision."

"Fellas," growled Jones, "I want to live. I want to live a whole bunch and I didn't really understand that until just right now. You let me go and I promise you will never be bothered by me again."

Mac looked at Jones and saw the kind of fear he had seen many times on the battlefield. He figured Jones would go to groveling at any moment; he had a growing wetness spoiling the front of his canvas pants but he didn't seem to notice. Mac turned away in disgust.

"You can go," Luke said after getting nods from his two partners. "But we're keeping the spare horses and the guns." With that he picked up the reins of the two horses under the tree and walked them forward. The two tied men slid off the horses backs and flopped to the end of the ropes. It was all over in a few seconds.

Jones fainted and fell out of his saddle.

10

ON THE FARM IN MISSOURI

BOBBY, one of Mac's young brothers, rode a harness mule into Jenkinsville for a few supplies his mother needed and to ask about the mail. The post office consisted of a wicket at the far end of the serving counter in the general store. Clive Jenkins, the store owner and postmaster, was helping to load a wagon in front of his store when the young rider slid off the mule.

"Morning, Bobby," greeted the grocer. "What brings you to town today?"

"Ma has need for a few things. Been a long time since we heard from Walker, too. Any chance of a letter?"

"This must be your lucky day. A letter arrived for you just yesterday. Come in. I'll get it for you and the things your ma needs."

Bobby helped the grocer load the purchased items into a flour sack. With no saddle on the mule, he had to carry the sack in one hand. He carefully folded the letter inside his shirt for safekeeping and hurried home as fast as the reluctant mule would take him.

His sister Jessie saw him coming and hollered for her

mother, "Ma, you better come. Either Bobby has news or he just feels like kicking that mule. I never seen the like."

Ma McTavish stepped onto the small veranda wiping her hands on her apron. Dried bread dough crumbled from her fingers and fell to the floor. A blood-red hound rose from the end of the veranda and came to examine the crumbs before curling up again in the shade to rest. He had been resting all morning but it appeared that he wasn't quite finished yet.

Jessie, always ready to cause a problem for her brothers, said, "I do believe Bobby is going to cave in that poor mule's ribs kicking him the way he is. That mule will be useless for field-work for a week." She glanced at her mother to see if her comments had taken effect.

Ma McTavish responded, "As much as you know about mules and fieldwork, young lady, you might want to just leave it alone. Your brother never hurt an animal in his life. He's walked many a mile behind that mule working this land. I expect now he just wants to get here with some news. The mule won't suffer any."

Bobby leaped from the still-trotting mule, reached inside his shirt and ran, the groceries flopping in the cloth sack and calling out all at the same time. Tangling one foot in front of the other, he tripped himself and landed in a dusty ball at his mother's feet. The mule trotted off toward the barn.

"Land sakes, young man, what in the world has you so worked up in this heat?"

Bobby had knocked most of the breath from his lungs.

His mother bent and picked up the grocery bag. "I don't expect you're hurt any so when you get your breath back, perhaps you could tell me what all the rush is about."

Still lying on his back in the dirt, he reached for the letter and passed it up to his mother. He tried to say, "From Walker," but it came out as a gasp.

"Go get your father, Jessie, and see if your other brother is around. Tell them we have news."

Ma McTavish sat down in her rocker on the veranda, the rocker no one else had ever even thought about sitting in, and used a fingernail to open the letter. Again, she tried to work the bread dough from between her fingers before touching the letter from her eldest son.

Hiram McTavish and his youngest son Jeremiah were coming up from the barn. Jeremiah was running. His father didn't run but his long legs covered the distance almost as quickly.

Hiram pulled up his favorite cowhide chair and sat down. The three young ones found space on the steps or on the veranda floor.

"Have you read it yet?" asked Hiram.

"Not yet."

"Well," he drawled, "reckon this would be as good a time as any."

Ma McTavish drew the single page from the envelope and read:

DEAR FOLKS

I'm in far south Texas. I've teamed up with a couple of ex-Yanks and we have rounded up some stray cattle. I never knew there were so many cattle in the whole world as there are running loose down here. We have 800 of the beasts more or less under our control and are planning on heading them north to find a market. We don't know exactly where we're going or where there might be a railway but we're heading toward Kansas in the hopes that they are laying tracks there. I know that these longhorn cattle aren't welcome in Missouri. If we are successful, we plan on gathering another herd and doing it all again. We'll make money if we find a market and if we don't, we won't be much worse off than we are now. We figure on about two months for the drive.

I'm fine and working hard. My plan is still to find some land and these cattle might be the key to it.

I MISS YOU ALL.

Love

Walker

WHEN THE READING FINISHED, Hiram reached over and took the letter from his wife's hands and read it again to himself. He was silent for a few moments and then passed the letter back. Saying nothing, he got up and walked back toward the barn. He'd been cleaning stalls but now the task seemed like it could wait. Ma McTavish was used to her husband's lack of words but as she watched him walk away, she wondered what was on his mind.

On the south side of the barn in a corner made by a lean-to addition, Hiram had long ago built a rough wooden bench. He sometimes sat there enjoying a pipe of strong tobacco while he soaked up the sunshine and rested from his labors. It was his place to be alone and normally the family knew to leave him to his quiet time. Ma found him there.

The bench was tight for two but she sat down anyway. "You have thoughts," she stated after a minute or two of sitting.

"Yep."

Again, a delay. "Want to share them?"

Hiram tapped the leavings out of the pipe bowl onto the palm of his work-toughened hand. He rubbed the warm tobacco between his palms until he was sure the danger of fire was gone.

"When Walker was talking to me about leaving, he said something like this is good land but there ain't anywhere near enough of it. Then he said this old farm ain't ever paid back for the work put into and it never will."

"And you've been thinking about that ever since?"

"Once in a while my mind goes there."

"Why didn't you say something so we could talk about it?"

Hiram looked off into the distance for a while and then shrugged his shoulders. "I guess I was embarrassed to. It's almost exactly what you said twenty years ago and I didn't want to open that discussion again. I must have heard a thousand times growing up that a rolling stone gathers no moss. I don't think anything on this earth could have made my father consider selling this farm or making a change, for better or for worse. I brought that thinking into our marriage and when you questioned it, I remember that I didn't make myself proud with my response. But you were right and Walker was right. That's not an easy idea to get into this old head although it's been there for quite some time with me pushing it down so's not to be a bother."

She wrapped both her arms around Hiram's right arm and leaned her head on his shoulder. Time went by. Finally, she spoke, "So where are your thoughts taking you now?"

"Well, it scares me half to death but my thoughts for quite a while have been that we should do something for ourselves. Not exactly sure what. It's an awful big world out there and it's always felt so safe here, even living hand-to-mouth and season to season like we've done. But the war woke me up a bit as to how quickly our comfort could be taken from us. Made me wonder, it did. What do you think about that big world out there? Does it scare you as much as it scares me?"

"It might a little," she responded. "But we survived having a war fought through our barnyard. Cowering in our root cellar while those young men died in our yard and knowing that Walker could have been one of them was as much fear as I ever want to know. And it makes everything else that might frighten me seem small. Those three young soldiers lying in those cold graves up the hill will haunt me all the days of my life even though I know the graves are now empty. It was at least some small comfort to know those boys were carried back to a more formal burial. Maybe to their family homes, I don't know. But even that made me think of Walker and how I didn't want him coming home that way.

"Anyway, I am not real sure if fear and excitement are the same thing or which it is that I might be feeling right now."

Hiram said quietly, "I've thought a lot about the west since Walker left. I'm sure it's the land of opportunity for young folks but I'm no longer young. I'm not altogether sure if I'm up to that kind of a challenge. Don't know if I could start again or not."

"People a lot older than us are going west. And I have every confidence that you can face any challenge we might run into. I never seen anything whup you yet."

"We've always whupped things together, Ma. Might could be we could do it again."

"I'll bet we could. And we have almost adult young ones to go along and help. All of the children have talked with me about the west at one time or another. I just listened without saying much. I prayed that if the right time came you would know it."

Hiram said, "Big change. It would be an almighty big change." Then they sat in silence for several minutes.

Finally Hiram spoke, "You say the kids have talked about going west? Why didn't you say something? Or why didn't the kids?"

"You're much loved and much respected by each of us and we take our lead from you. Anyway, this hasn't been a bad life at all and I figured that if the time was right for a move, the Lord would put it in your heart and you would know."

Hiram gave his wife's hand a squeeze. "You send someone to town for Jonathon and Nancy. Tell them to come out for supper and a family gab. We don't see enough of them since they got married anyway. Be good to have them for a visit. We'll lay out as much as we know and get their reaction. Leaving Jonathon and Nancy behind would maybe be the hardest part. I'll hike over to see Collie. He wants a bigger farm and has talked about selling but he could do real well if he joined the two pieces together. He just might be interested."

They parted then to put the plan into place.

Later, when everyone was seated for supper, Nancy asked, "So what is this all about? What's the big news? Is it about Walker?" They had read the letter when they first arrived.

Hiram answered, "Enjoy your supper. We'll talk on the veranda with our coffee."

Nancy didn't seem to like the answer but she held her peace.

When they were all seated on the veranda with coffee which Nancy poured, she said, "All right, we're here and I'm not waiting one minute longer. Let's hear it. If it's bad news, we're as ready as we will ever be."

"Not bad news. Unless someone chooses to take it that way. Your mother and I, we're thinking of selling the farm and going west."

This brought on an excited babble of voices. Hiram had more to say but with everyone talking at once there was no point. He packed his pipe as he waited for the talk to slow down.

Again Nancy took the lead, "What brought this on and what exactly do you plan on doing? And did you think to just walk away and leave me and Jonathon stuck in this little town? Our only reason for being here is because of family. What other possible reason would there be for staying here?"

"Well," answered her father, "we don't have exact plans. Just west. Maybe lay a claim to some free land. Might even find enough land to get your sister and brothers a start in a few years."

Jonathon spoke for the first time, "We'll be ready to go when you are. We've been talking about just that same thing but we were worried about how you would feel if we up and left. Now that worry is gone we'll be ready to go."

Ma said, "It would be so good to have the whole family even if we can't settle exactly together. Perhaps we can at least be close."

Hiram turned to the younger children. "You three are old enough to voice your thoughts."

Bobby was bursting with enthusiasm. "If we could ranch instead of farm, I wouldn't have to follow that mule around and around a field. I favor that."

The other two young people voiced their excitement and asked how quickly they could go.

"Will we go find Walker?" asked Jessie.

"We can sure try," answered her mother. "But there's a lot of space out there so we can't be sure."

Hiram said, "I went over to see Collie this afternoon. He agreed to buy the farm and the stock except for the team of mules and that lazy old mare. We'll keep some chickens and one milk cow, too. We agreed on a price. The problem is that he only has about half the price now and he refuses to go to the bank for a loan. Can't say that I blame him as much as either of us trusts bankers. Anyway, we made a deal based on his promise to make a payment every fall until the farm is paid for. I trust Collie but we'll put a paper in place just in case something happens to either of us."

Just less than a month later, the entire family was but a few miles short of crossing into Kansas. Two large wagons with canvas tops, teams of mules, saddle horses, the old mare wandering loose and coming along at her own pace, one milk cow, a crate of laying hens and one rooster who threatened to go to battle with anyone who came close to his cage made up the entourage. That and the two red hounds running along behind.

The women had chosen the food supplies carefully, aware of their needs but also mindful of the weight each wagon would bear.

Hiram had carefully selected the farm tools.

"I'm not cooking over an open fire," Ma McTavish told him. "We can leave the big kitchen stove behind but that small sheet iron stove goes with us."

A small barrel of water was strapped to each side of each wagon.

The traveling group, young and old alike, had trouble holding down their excitement as the Kansas border came in sight, marked by a crudely lettered sign that stated "Kansas, wind and grasshoppers ahead."

"You're leaving home behind you for sure now, Ma," Hiram said. "You still all right?"

"You just keep those mules pointed west and I'll be all right."

11

THE TEXAS FRONTIER

Mac looked at the hanged men and asked, "What do we do with them?"

"Leave them right where they are," answered Luke with grim determination. "Might be a lesson to others of their type."

Jerrod put his hand on Luke's shoulder. "No, my friend, that would make us as low down as they are. I understand your feeling, Luke, but leaving them hanging is just not the thing to do. We have no shovel so we'll heap rocks over them. I'll take this wagon and go pick up our gear. I'll pick up that other man, too. We'll bury them all together."

They were soon ready to move the herd north. They left the poorest horse for Jones and drove the others toward the herd, stopping long enough to rope the horses, nose to tail, intending to turn them loose as soon as they were sure they'd stay with the herd.

After looking over the raiders' Texas saddles, the three men decided they were more suitable for cattle work than the McClellan saddles they had inherited from their cavalry days.

Mac swung the new saddle onto his black. "The saddle horn alone makes them more usable. Having a rope makes some sense, too, with something to tie it to."

Luke chuckled at Mac. "I longed for a good many things in the cavalry, Mac, but a rope was never one of them."

Jerrod was all for dropping the unneeded saddles on the ground but Mac's frugal nature rose again.

"Might could be we can sell off or trade those saddles. We ain't so rich yet that we can afford to throw away good saddles."

They cinched the McClellans' onto the spare horses and rode out. They had looked over the wagon but decided that they couldn't spare a man to drive it so they took what provisions they could use and left the rest.

THEY MOVED the cattle out with no words spoken. Each man was quiet thinking his own thoughts or perhaps not thinking about anything at all. The violence of the morning had been unwelcome but not totally unexpected. Mac had been unprepared for the action that Luke took in actually hanging the two raiders. It was grim work. Although one had still been unconscious from the whap on the skull, the other was awake and terrified.

Mac knew he would have come to the same decision as Luke, given time, but he was shaken nonetheless.

They moved the cattle nearly twelve miles that day, switching saddles to fresh horses as needed.

Sitting around the supper fire that evening, Mac looked over at his partner. "Luke, I ain't judging you and I've decided that you probably done the only thing possible but I wasn't quite ready when you dropped those men from their horses' backs. I seen a sight of men die in that war and more than my share of blood and misery but I never seen men hung before. You ever decide to do that again, you give some notice so that I can find some other place to be."

After a few moments, Mac continued, "The other thing, Luke, is that you called this the McTavish herd. It ain't no such thing. I suppose we ought to call it something, have a brand or some such, but it ain't my herd and I'll not have you calling it such. We agreed before that there's no leader here, that we are all equal partners. You think up a name and a brand and we'll call it that but I don't want to hear it called after my name again. I ain't the leader here."

Jerrod looked at Mac and chuckled. "My friend, you're saddled with leadership for the rest of your life and you can't even see it. You've been the leader of this group from the first morning. I was a captain and Luke was a sergeant in an army with a lot of officers and non-coms in it. But you have more natural leadership ability than most of the officers I served with and you don't even know it. No, sir. You're doomed, my friend. This is the McTavish herd and this is the McTavish outfit and everywhere you go you're just going to have to face it. Folks are going to look to you whether you like it or not. Oh, we'll think up a brand for our outfit but it's you the buyers will want to see and it's you the crew will work for. You might just as well get used to it. Luke and I have known it for weeks. You might just as well know it, too, since you could say it affects you somewhat."

Jerrod chuckled again. "Just the way of the world, soldier, just the way of the world."

Mac grumbled something under his breath and stomped away from the supper fire. "There's work to do. I might just as well get at it."

"See," Jerrod said and laughed. "Just a natural leader, can't be stopped."

The drive went well for the next week, averaging between twelve and fifteen miles each day. They had one dry camp where both men and animals suffered through a hot, waterless night. But by noon the next day they arrived at a slow-running creek. They spread the cattle along the creek and Luke built a coffee fire. Two hours of rest left them refreshed enough to move out again.

"We can't be too far from the Red," hollered Jerrod over the noise of the walking cattle.

"Never been there," answered Mac. "This is all new to me but it seems that we've come a far ways."

"Luke and I crossed the Red riding south and while I don't recognize any of this country, the distance feels about right. Although Texas is an almighty big place so I could be wrong."

Three more days of brutally hard labor later and another fifty dusty miles north, the three riders - yipping and yelling like seasoned drovers - settled the cattle in along the edge of a shallow lake.

Most of the cattle had settled into following the two lead animals and the trouble with bunch quitters had lessoned considerably from the first few days of the drive. But one crooked-horned brute had finally gotten to the end of Luke's patience. He rode up beside the steer with his campaign knife in his hand but the wily old cow would have none of it, not allowing the rider closer than a few feet. Luke finally drove her far enough away from the herd to where he felt the sound of a shot wouldn't bother the other cattle and he shot the brute. He gutted her out where she lay and dragged the carcass up to the campsite, his horse skittish from the unexpected burden as well as the smell of blood.

This was the first of their own animals they'd butchered having relied on side meat purchased at the general store or venison they had managed to bring down along the way.

Mac studied the western sky for several minutes before turning to Luke. "I'm thinking we might get wet tonight. What say we get some supper under our belts before the rain starts?"

Luke lifted his eyes to where Mac was looking. Miles off, the western sky was beginning to collect considerable cloud cover. The clouds were roiling and tossing in the high-up winds. Ominous black clouds were piled high over the leading edge of the storm, rolling through the sky like a giant wheel. They seemed to be supported by a mass of lighter gray beneath them. A lower band of even lighter gray was moving in the opposite direction to the upper black mass. The setting sun was lighting it all from behind, casting sunrays in all directions beyond the edges of the storm.

Luke turned to Mac. "I expect an artist would say that was a pretty sight but the artist wouldn't have a field full of restless beef to worry about. I think our best hope is that some artist miles to the north of us gets to admire it. I wouldn't feel slighted for the loss. But you're right about supper. I'll get on it while I can still find some dry wood. At least we have lots of fresh beef."

After a quick supper of fresh beef steak cooked on sticks that Luke had pushed into the ground beside the fire and the last of the few potatoes they had bought at the settlement, they sat back with one eye on the cattle and the other on the sky. The cattle had slaked their thirst at the lake and were now lying down, seemingly content. A change in the wind coming out of the south finally drove the black clouds off to the north. The three men watched until they were sure the storm crisis was over.

"Well, that's another danger passed. I can't say I'm sorry." Luke grinned as he spoke.

They pushed the cattle off the bed grounds early the next morning and headed north, covering the most of fifteen miles with Luke and Jerrod holding the two sides of the herd and Mac riding drag. Without point riders, they often didn't know what was ahead of them until they reached it.

They headed their herd, the spare horses roaming loose beside it, over a grassy knoll and down the short slope on the other side toward a line of willows that promised water. The cattle, smelling water, broke into a run.

A few seconds later, a racket to waken the dead arose from the other side of the hill as women screamed and men hollered to warn the driven cattle away from their camp. The crash of clanking and bending pots and pans and the squeal of terrified horses added to the din.

Luke, who was riding right flank, finally saw the camp and began a futile effort to work the cattle away from it.

Mac saw Luke frantically trying to push the cattle to the left and knew something was wrong.

He rode hard toward the front of the herd and was in time to see a man and a boy rushing to throw saddles onto tethered horses while the horses screamed their fear and pulled on their tether ropes. Two women were anxiously lifting three smaller children into the back of a canvas-covered wagon.

The fire and cooking utensils were a shambles of hoof-smashed metal and charcoal. The wagon shook as a few cattle dodged that way, not quite clearing the wagon in their rush to water. One big old brindle cow hooked her massive horn onto the rope stay of the sleeping tent and dragged the tent and a bundle of blankets fifty feet before it came loose.

The packhorse calculated that it had gone far enough for one day and trotted over to get acquainted with the team of wagon horses.

The herd was soon past the camp and it only took a few minutes to spread the tired cattle along the water's edge about one-quarter mile from the camp. But considerable damage had been done in their passing.

Mac rode back to the camp while Jerrod and Luke settled the cattle down.

"Sorry, folks, we didn't go to cause harm. Anyone hurt?"

"No one hurt," answered the man, now on horseback. "But the camp's a mess and the womenfolk are a tad frightened. I'll say you gave us a mite of a start coming over that hill with no warning." He sounded a little shaken but Mac detected no anger in the response.

He did, however, detect considerable anger in the next voice he heard.

"You are not likely to receive an invitation to supper this night, sir." The voice was a cross between anger and aston-ishment.

Mac turned to see a girl walking up from the wagon.

She pointed around the wrecked camp. "You have smashed our camp and most of our dishes. Do you always charge about the countryside not looking where you are going or is this a first for you? It is certainly a first for us."

Mac looked at the girl and felt something freeze up inside him. She was probably eighteen years old, taller than most girls, filling out her simple dress in a most attractive fashion and the late afternoon sunlight reflecting off her red hair. He was pretty sure that when she smiled she would be very easy to look at. But she wasn't smiling right at that moment.

He quickly doffed his hat and ran his fingers through his unruly and overgrown hair. "Ma'am, I surely am sorry about the damage and about frightening y'all. We ain't seen a living soul in over two weeks. The last thing we expected was your camp. This is the emptiest country I ever did see excepting for parts of Kansas. At the first smell of that water, the cattle took off running. There's not much that can stop a running herd until they get where they're going. I'll be glad to purchase new dishes for you, ma'am, and pay for any other damage done."

Mac took a quick look at the man on horseback who had first spoken, as if pleading for help, and then back at the girl.

Not in the least mollified by Mac's offer, the girl said, "And I suppose you are just going to run down to the local store to do that, are you? It might make supper a bit late but we'll just have to wait for you to get back. Or maybe you carry extras somewhere. I don't see much for supplies on that packhorse of yours and I don't see a wagon coming. So just what is your plan, sir?"

"That's enough, Margo." The mounted horseman was obviously the father. "These men didn't do this on purpose. It is just a thing that happened. A sharp tongue will fix nothing."

"Reminds me an awful lot of my father," thought Mac, looking at the speaker. "Always the peacemaker. Be wrong to judge him lightly though. I expect he'll stand when a storm comes. Can't but notice the strong, work-hardened hands, his wide, sloped shoulders and that he's rail thin. Looks like they've all been on tight rations for some time."

Turning to Mac, the horseman said, "It does leave us in a bit of a fix though. We're going to miss those pots and dishes. And that kettle held the last of a small buck I shot a couple of days ago. If you just had to drive that herd through our camp, it would have suited us better if you had waited until after we had eaten and stowed our wares back in the wagon. I guess you had no way to know but it does leave us in a bit of a fix."

Mac looked from the horseman to the girl and then over to an older woman who was now helping the younger children out of the wagon. "Don't guess I can get to a store and back before nightfall but we might have enough fixings to get a meal put together. I'll pull that lazy packhorse off down to the river and see what I can dig out. One thing that is on that packhorse under that tarpaulin is a hindquarter of beef and the most of a second. Fresh yesterday so none of us need go hungry. If you can gather that fire back together, I'll be back shortly." He directed a halfhearted nod toward the girl, placed his hat back on his head and turned his horse to go.

Jerrod and Luke herded the cattle while Mac unloaded the packhorse. Slung over his saddle, he carried the few utensils they had as well as the quarter of beef and a small sack of coffee beans up to the campsite.

"Sorry, again, ma'am," Mac said to the still angry young girl. "Could be these will help. You can at least have coffee and this beef should keep you for a few days. You're welcome to whatever else we have, ma'am. We'll leave you this beef and if you see anything else you want, why, you just sing out."

"I guess I should thank you for the loan of the pots and for the coffee beans but..."

"They aren't a loan, ma'am," answered Mac coolly before the girl could finish what she was saying. "Y'all are welcome to them. Least we can do."

"And I suppose you three will just hunch over a fire cooking beef on the end of a stick until you get to wherever you are going? Driving cattle over peoples' camps and eating off the end of a stick, is that your plan?"

Wanting no more confrontation, Mac turned and was about to walk to his horse when the older woman came over from the wagon. "I apologize for my daughter, young man. She lacks a little in life experiences. She still thinks life should be fair and having cattle driven through our camp is clearly not fair.

"I am Amelia Adkins; this is my daughter Margo. Thank you for the pots and dishes. And the beef. We have enough flour and such in the wagon to keep us in biscuits for a while. Will you join us for supper? Since we will be eating your beef on your plates, it is only right that you let Margo and I do the cooking."

Mac took a closer look at this tall, thin woman. Might be taller than her husband, thought Mac, and older than her years, just like Ma. There's just nothing at all that's easy about small-farm life.

"Thank you, ma'am," answered Mac. "One of us will have to stay with the herd but we'll take turns at supper. Folks call me Mac and my partners are Jerrod and Luke. Jerrod is the tall, officer-looking one. Luke is the one you can see down there trying to pull that dumb brute out of the mud hole. Few things in this world dumber than a cow. I expect I had better go help. If you will excuse me, ma'am?"

Mac turned to Margo. "Sorry again, Miss."

Mac saw the mother smile for the first time as he turned to glance at Margo.

Margo stared ice at him as he started to back toward his horse. He tripped over a pile of firewood that had somehow missed the onslaught of cattle, caught himself, and turned toward his horse. Mac was sure he saw Luke grin even though the other man was nowhere near.

A SHORT WHILE LATER, two men - obvious from their looks father and son - rode down to the gathered cattle which the drovers had settled in about one-quarter mile from the camp. Mac, Luke and Jerrod were sitting their horses together, keeping a watch on the cattle while they discussed their next moves and wondering how to proceed after giving away their kitchen camp.

The three drovers stepped off their horses to greet their visitors.

"I'm Ad Adkins, men, and this is my son Bill. I'm sorry our first meeting wasn't more to our liking but I think the women-folk are settling down a bit and the little ones are over their fright."

Jerrod spoke up for the first time since the cattle had run

over the camp, "Entirely our fault, Ad. And again, we apologize for the fright and the damage. My name is Jerrod and these are my friends, Luke and Mac. I hope your family will forgive us for the way we imposed ourselves on you."

The men shook hands all around.

Bill seemed to have nothing to say although he gave the cattle camp a close inspection, his eyes stopping on the piled-up bedrolls at the base of a small live oak.

Jerrod noticed the young man's inspection and said with a small smile, "Don't amount to much for comfort does it, Bill?"

Bill gave Jerrod a close study and then said, "Well, I expect it's the end result that matters more than how it's done. The Lord said we would earn our bread with the sweat of our brows and except for bankers, politicians and jack-leg lawyers, I expect that's the way it will always be."

Jerrod didn't answer but Luke spoke up, "Wisely said, young man. Wisely said."

Ad turned his horse to go. "Supper will be ready directly. If you want to come up to the fire, we'll see how that beef of yours tastes."

AROUND THE SUPPER FIRE, the other introductions were made by Ad. "Properly, my name is Hezekiah but no one except my mother ever called me that. Just call me Ad and my son here is William although Bill seems to suit him better. The little ones are Janie, Carie and Hamilton. The young ones are twelve, ten and eight years old. Bill is seventeen and Margo is eighteen."

"Pa," exploded Margo, "that's private. These men are leaving in the morning and nothing else matters."

"There's nothing to be so touchy about, little girl," Ad said with a chuckle. "I'm just introducing the family and trying to reassure the men that you're old enough to be trusted with the biscuits."

Margo wasn't mollified but she kept her peace. If she noticed that Mac was studying her under the brim of his hat, trying not to be obvious about it, she didn't let on.

Glancing sideways, Mac saw that Luke as well as Margo's parents had noticed. In his embarrassment, he was tempted to saddle up and insist on a night drive to get away from the camp and his shame.

Turning back to his plate of food, Mac was quiet and a little sullen. He felt it was his carelessness that had allowed the herd to hit the Adkins' camp. And then his first glance at Margo had not at all squared with the hostile tone of voice she had dealt to him. He picked at his supper and counted the hours until morning when they could head the herd out.

He wiped his hands on the grass, said, "Thanks for the meal," and headed back to the herd. Luke grinned his wicked grin again and watched him walk away.

"You seem tickled about something, Mr. Luke," Margo said. "Since this hasn't been the best day we ever had, perhaps you could explain." Cooking supper over a hot fire had done nothing to melt the ice in her tone.

"Well, now, missy," answered Luke, not at all concerned about the coolness of the question. "It is just that I finally see our fearless leader confronted with a problem he can't solve. Does my heart good, it does. I was starting to worry that that boy was too perfect for an old soldier like me to be riding with. Yes, sir. Old Mac, he's up a stump and I just can't wait to see what he'll do next." Luke turned his grin on Margo. She looked about ready to explode.

"What is this problem you are referring to, sir? He's moved his cattle and replaced some of our pots and brought meat to the fire. Seems to me that he's about done with problems for one day." Clearly Margo was determined to hold onto her unfriendly exterior.

Luke glanced over at Ad and then at Mrs. Adkins. Mrs. Adkins was trying desperately to keep a straight face but Ad and Luke couldn't hold it in. Ad was looking down at his plate with his shoulders shaking with mirth while Luke chuckled right out loud.

"Well, I guess it must be a private joke," Margo said, still icy, "But I have no time for it. I have work to do. How y'all can find time for foolishness when we are surrounded with troubles is beyond me."

Ad smiled at her. "Oh, we have troubles enough, daughter, but a light heart lifts many a burden. I expect we can face our troubles in the morning but this evening we have folks at our fire. Won't hurt us at all to enjoy the time."

12

JERROD WALKED UP JUST IN TIME TO HEAR AD MENTION TROUBLES. He took the plate offered by Mrs. Adkins and found a place to sit. "Good looking meal, ladies; thank you for your work. I expect someone found time to give thanks?"

Mrs. Adkins answered, "William gave thanks, Mr. Jerrod, and he particularly mentioned you out guarding the herd so I expect you can go right ahead and eat."

Jerrod took a bite of biscuit, swallowed, and then said, "Now, sir, I heard mention of troubles. What kind of troubles? Anything we can help with?"

"Our troubles are our own," snapped Margo, still not welcoming the cowboys to the camp. "I expect we can handle them."

"Margo," Ad said quietly, "I hope this is the last time I have to apologize for you. You keep this up and I am going to have a hard time making folks believe that you are really a sweet-dispositioned young lady."

Turning to Jerrod, Ad explained, "Our troubles have to do with plans that didn't work out. We came west to take over a family property only to find out that others were there before us. Others who had a family claim at least as strong as ours. So we're searching just the same as thousands of others are, trying to find a place after the great unpleasantness of the past few years. When you look at that wagon, you're looking at our home, temporary as it might be. We don't know the country so we settled down here two days ago to kind of think things over."

"That's when you came and ran us over," Margo said.

"I think you should go for a walk, Margo," advised her mother. "Take the little ones with you. Watch out for snakes."

Bill spoke for the first time, "I would say that the snakes would have to look out for themselves."

Everyone chose to ignore the comment.

"What's your background, Ad?" asked Jerrod.

"Farming is what I know best although I can turn my hand to a little blacksmithing and I've trained a few horses to saddle."

Jerrod thought for a few moments and then nodded at the other men. "Luke, Ad, Bill, let's go for a short walk. Might could be I have an idea."

The four men walked over to the herd and waited until Mac rode around to where they sat on the grass. "Take a minute, boss. We need to talk."

Mac rode up close enough to hear but stayed on his horse, his eyes never leaving the herd.

"Ad, Bill," started Jerrod, "I haven't talked with Luke or Mac yet and we only met a few hours ago. But you seem to be our kind of folks although it might be difficult to sell that idea to Margo right now. So let me lay out a thought. Nothing final, just a thought. We're desperately short-handed as you can easily see. But we're pretty much broke as far as cash money goes so we didn't hire any riders or buy any spare horses. I would also have to admit that some of the meals we put together are a little less than a feast.

"Now, we don't any of us know each other but you and your family are at loose ends and we have these brutes to drive. I reckon that we are about halfway to where we originally set out for. If you were to take a risk and work with us, we could at least pay you wages. Always assuming that we get the herd north and find a paying market. There's some risk. We already had the herd stolen once and were fortunate enough to get it back. If we lose the herd, we don't make any money and you don't get paid. But you would see some country. If you and Bill rode herd on these brutes along with us and the women could drive the wagon and put together some meals as good as that one this evening, we might all benefit."

The men all took a long study of each other.

Luke spoke first, "I don't see a problem for us in that offer as long as Ad and Bill understand the risk of not getting paid."

Jerrod glanced up at Mac and said, "Mac, we need your say."

Mac took a long look up at the camp where the women were cleaning up supper dishes. "Well, we could use the help and the meal was good but I wouldn't want to impose where we're not welcome."

Luke looked up at him and grinned.

Ad looked over at Bill and it was as if they could communicate without speaking. Again Mac thought about his own father; always knew what he was thinking.

Ad turned away from his son and glanced quickly at the three drovers. "You already told us what greenhorns you were when you started driving cattle. If you thought you could put up with two that are even greener than you were and thought perhaps you could teach us some things, I expect we might go along with you. We thought to head north anyway. We might just as well be chasing cattle as we go."

Luke said, "It would be good to have the help and, if we could drive cattle as little as we knew, I expect anyone can learn."

Ad nodded his agreement. "Before we shake on it, we need to talk about one other thing. I like what I see in you three and I always figured to be a pretty good judge of men. But I have a wife and five young ones with me so you won't mind if we talk a little here just to ease my mind. It's a far road you're asking us to join you on and a lot of trust you're asking me to place on you and you on me. It will mean living awful close to each other for weeks on end. Things can happen and, well, I would just feel better if I came right out and said it.

"I'm a man of faith and we're a family of faith. We take the things of the Lord seriously and we just wouldn't get along for any time at all if there was any question about honesty or integrity. Like I said, I judge you three to be honest men but we need to have it laid out clear. We can't start out on a venture this big without we clear the air. Now Jerrod, coming to supper you asked about saying grace. Is that just a habit or is it an indication of belief?"

Jerrod was quick to answer, "Ad, I was raised in a believing family and came to faith early in life myself. I'm a long ways from perfect and haven't always made myself proud with my actions. But I believe in the Lord and it's my intention to live honest. And maybe Mac won't mind if I put in a word for him. He is probably more devout than the average person although he is a bit sparing of words. Seems to get tongue-tied from time to time." Jerrod smiled as he spoke and glanced back up at the camp.

Ad took his meaning and smiled a bit himself.

Luke quietly stood up and walked from the fire. Ad watched him go and turned to Jerrod with a question unasked.

"Don't you worry about Luke, Ad. He's been running from the Lord as long as I have known him but I've never seen him run from anything else. Luke will be there when there's work to be done or a fight to be fought. And a more honest man never lived."

When the deal was made and hands shaken all around, Bill spoke up, "It's all and well for we-uns to decide but Ma and Margo might have something to say. I think I'll stay here, Pa, while you go tell them the plan."

Jerrod laughed and said, "Bill, you might go far in the military if you were of a mind to. Do your job and keep your nose clean. That's the military way. But I agree. It's your father's job."

The job wasn't so tough and the women agreed although Margo had considerable to say about the roughness of cowboys and their careless ways.

Mac had some doubts about the arrangement but eventually accepted the wisdom of having two more riders plus two cooks and the wagon to carry supplies. But he was a mite sullen just the same. He stayed with the herd and had nothing much to say. He came to the breakfast fire the next morning, took his plate with a mumbled "thanks," and walked several yards away to eat.

Luke looked at him and grinned. "Morning, boss."

Mac just nodded around a mouthful of biscuit.

Jerrod turned to Ad. "I would judge this to be the Red River you're camped on. Luke and I crossed east of here on our way south but it has the same look."

"We only have a hand-drawn map, really more of a sketch," answered Ad. "But I do believe you're correct. At least I don't know of anything else this big anywhere around here."

They crossed the Red with no problems and headed north. After discussing the various jobs to be done, they had Bill ride ahead to scout a path. The wagon would follow Bill in the lead but well off to the side to avoid the dust and any potential stampede. Margo was driving.

"Bill, you watch out for folks camping."

Bill ignored her.

They passed a settlement two days later and sent the wagon in for supplies, restocking on beans, flour and such along with a few more metal plates and a couple of cooking pots. Mac figured they could do that only once more before they were completely broke although trading off the three cavalry saddles eased the financial burden somewhat. They kept the extra captured Texas saddles against future need.

THE DRIVE WENT WELL for a week with even Mac showing signs of satisfaction. He spoke to Margo once and she huffed and answered sharply. Ad saw and shook his head. Later, when Margo tried to talk to Mac, he acted like he didn't hear and went back to work. Luke looked at them and grinned.

The drovers had been five days on the trail since the last settlement. They had bedded the cattle on a good patch of grass adjacent to an almost dry creek. The cattle drank what little water was available and finally lay down for the night. The women had prepared a late supper and the men had chanced leaving the herd while they came in for an after-dark meal. Bill was still out, hoping to bring in a deer.

Sitting by the fire, Ad cocked his head and listened into the night. "Hear those coyotes?" he asked. "They're far away and there's probably not more than two of them. With coyotes, two can sound like twenty. Pretty sound, but lonesome. Don't know of a lonesomer sound than a coyote. Glad they're far away though. Close up they could spook this herd and I am just too plumb tired to chase cows this night.

Suddenly there was coyote sound right close by the herd. "Yip, yip, yiieeeee, yip, yip, yiieee." And then an answering call from farther away.

The men leaped to their feet, spilling their suppers. "What the...," Mac started. Some of the cattle had risen to their feet and were searching for a reason to run.

"It's Bill," hollered Margo. "Bill, you shut up that noise. Don't you have any sense at all?"

Mac turned toward Margo. "Bill? Bill? What do you mean it's Bill? If that's Bill making that noise, I'll take a willow switch to him. Of all the dang fool foolishness."

Luke and Ad had raced for their horses but the cattle were settling down. Bill rode into the light of the campfire and asked, "What you all hollering about? I'm just talking to the coyotes. Hear them answer? They often answer if you talk to them."

"I'll talk to you with a switch if you ever pull a fool stunt like that again," answered Mac. "One more yell out of you and we would have had cattle spread from here to yesterday. Don't you ever...," Mac clenched his fists and walked in the direction of the herd. Ad walked along with him.

Saddling a horse beside Mac, Ad spoke, "Sorry, Mac. Don't know where that boy gets his wild from. I swear, sometimes I think he's a throwback to another time, him and Margo both. He's done some fool things but I don't think he'll call the coyotes again, not around the cattle anyway."

It was a full week before Mac would trust Bill out of his sight.

13

Two weeks of slow drives were behind them when they came to a river that was high with run-off from an upstream storm. They'd crossed several smaller streams without difficulty but this one stopped them. Sitting their horses along the south bank they studied the foaming, tossing flood.

Mac looked grim. "It's just too dangerous. We're going to have to wait. Perhaps one day will do. These flatland rivers rise and fall quickly. Won't hurt us to rest up a little anyway."

Ad studied the paper in his hand. "According to my map, this should be the Canadian but I wouldn't want to take a bet on that. I don't know if that fellow who sketched this map knew what he was about or not.

They spread the herd along the river to drink the muddy water and then bedded them down on good grass.

The next morning, Mac took his breakfast plate and walked over to the river's edge. The river was down considerably and they decided to try a crossing. When Mac rode his big Army horse across and back, the water didn't quite reach the horse's belly.

Margo drove the wagon across first. The men strung ropes from either side of the wagon to their saddle horns, keeping the wagon true to course. The cattle followed and all went well until just about all of the beasts were across.

Luke was bringing up the drag. He was busy pushing the last few reluctant head along and he didn't see the drift log floating downstream. The log took the feet out from under two or three head of cattle before turning in a circle and sweeping toward Luke. His horse went down. Luke went under and didn't come up. The horse kicked and thrashed while the current carried it downstream where the water was deeper. Luke bobbed to the surface once two hundred yards downstream and then disappeared again.

Bill shouted a warning from the north bank. Jerrod was well ahead with the herd but Ad and Mac came running at Bill's call. They saw the horse just getting its footing and knew immediately that there was trouble.

Bill hollered, "Luke's gone. He just went under and he's gone." He was nearly hysterical.

Mac crashed back across the river and rode full gallop downstream. Ad rode as fast as his short-legged horse would take him on the north bank. They rode and shouted for half a mile and then for another half mile. Mac raced back to the crossing with the big Army horse exhausted and trembling.

He shouted to Bill, "Get me another horse." Bill was back in record time and Mac threw his saddle on a black gelding that had proved its staying power during the drive.

Ad was changing horses on the north bank.

Jerrod raced up, followed shortly by Margo who was astride a bay mare, riding bareback.

They rode both banks for miles, searching every clump of bush and wore out another change of horses.

A half-mile downstream, Ad hollered over at Mac, "Here's his hat. I found Luke's hat."

But there was no other sign. Luke was gone.

Sunset came upon a scattered herd and an uneaten supper prepared by Mrs. Adkins. She waited for the crew where the wagon had been stopped about one mile north of the river. The drovers who had never left the river bank were quiet in their loss.

Mac said, "Ad, I would sure appreciate it if you and Bill would gather the herd onto a bed ground. Use your own best judgment. Jerrod and I will want to take one last look down the river.

"Margo, perhaps you should see if your mother needs help." He hesitated, then looked directly at Margo. She had come to help in such a rush that she hadn't bothered to saddle her horse. "You done fine. I don't know how you stuck to that horse bareback but no one could have done more. There's really nothing any of us can do tonight but Jerrod and I will want to stay anyway."

Margo returned a strained smile.

Mac and Jerrod rode the riverbank all night.

Sunrise found them sitting on the south bank a mile downstream. Jerrod gripped Mac's shoulder. "We have a herd to drive. Best we get at it."

They made a sad twenty miles over the next two days. Hardly a word was spoken among them.

The third morning after the tragedy, Bill was bringing up the horses in the last dark of early morning. The women were working on breakfast by the light of a single kerosene lantern suspended on a pole at the back of the wagon. The men were sitting on bedrolls or attending to morning duties, waiting for coffee, when a shouted voice came from the dark.

"I lost a poor-quality horse and a pretty good saddle. Lost my hat, too. Any of you seen such as that around here?"

The camp was dead silent for a few seconds before Margo screamed and Mrs. Adkins said, "Luke? Where y'all been? We were frantic with worry and finally gave you up to the Lord. We were sure you were gone. What do you mean by scaring us so?" Her tone of voice gave away the worry behind the words.

Jerrod jumped to his feet and gave his old partner a bear hug that might have crushed a tree trunk. "By Jove, boy, you're a sight for sore eyes. We really did think you were gone. You had you a swim and a walk. We must have moved twenty miles."

"I don't need a bath for a day or two, that's for sure," Luke agreed. "And these boots ain't made for walking as I've told you before. Seems like I'm doing an awful lot of walking on this cattle drive. Hadn't been for that lantern over the wagon, I might never have found you. You still got my share of the cattle or did you sell them to some passing stranger?"

Mac walked up and shook Luke's hand. The men had agreed not to talk about the war but Mac forgot for just a moment. "I purely don't know how y'all won that there war, what with cavalry sergeants that can't sit a horse without they fall off at the first opportunity."

Ad said, "Luke, we looked for hours."

"Grabbed that tree that took out my horse's legs. Hung on for dear life and had quite a ride. Must have gone five, six miles before I finally felt ground under my feet again. I was so exhausted that I just crawled up on the bank and lay there all day and the most of the night. Started walking the next morning. Lost my hat," he said again.

"We have your hat. Now, if you'll put it on, have some breakfast and climb aboard a horse, we have cattle to drive. Unless you figure you need another day off." Mac spoke gruffly but he didn't fool anyone.

They saddled up and moved the herd north.

14

On the western trail

HIRAM LED his family into Kansas, heading west. He considered teaming up with a group of wagons but decided against it. "I expect we'll want to turn south in not too many miles. We'd be leaving the others anyway so we might just as well set out ourselves."

A few days into Kansas, a small group of four soldiers who had apparently decided not to recognize the surrender rode up and confronted the caravan.

"Hold up there," demanded a bearded soldier. His filthy uniform hung rumpled under a gray overcoat showing three collar bars that said it had once belonged to a Confederate captain. Whether it was his own coat or not, the man called himself "Captain."

He had a rifle aimed at Hiram. "I'm Captain Moses Hawkins. We're authorized to commandeer supplies for the 'cause'. Everyone out of the wagons."

The women had been taking their turn at driving and on Hiram's signal they pulled the teams to a halt.

"Now get out of the wagons, all of you," shouted the captain.

"Why sure, just as you say," answered Jonathon who had been riding in the back of the wagon. He jumped down off the open tailgate, turned toward the raiders and leveled his carbine on the shouting man.

Bobby and Jeremiah followed Jonathon's lead and had their carbines out, aimed at two of the other soldiers. Jessie stepped out of the lead wagon holding a pistol at the ready.

The young raiders, not much more than boys, looked at each other, unable to hide their fear. One asked, "Captain? What do you want us to do?"

By that time, Hiram was reaching for his saddle gun but the captain raised his weapon. "Touch it and you die right here."

A female voice said, "I don't think so. Not today, not my man, and not by scum such as you."

This statement was punctuated by the blast of a shotgun. The captain's weapon fell to the ground while he slid from his blood-splattered saddle. He lay in a lifeless heap on the prairie grass.

"Don't!" shouted Jonathon at the remaining three soldiers who were raising their weapons. "You can die as quickly as your captain did."

The oldest of the three licked his lips and glanced at his two riding companions. Finally, making a lifesaving decision, he slid his carbine back into his saddle scabbard and raised his hands. His two friends did the same.

Jonathon stepped a little closer to the riders, still holding his carbine steady. "Now that's sensible. The war is over. You boys are following a trail to a lost dream with a fool for a leader. Well, that leader is gone and the dream is ended. Go home. Get rid of those gray uniforms and go home. If we see you again, you'll die just like that old fool did. Now git."

The three young men turned east and started to ride away.

"Wait," hollered Nancy.

The three riders stopped and turned around, ready for more trouble.

"How long since you boys have eaten anything?"

There was no answer coming but the look on their faces told the story.

"We have some cold leftovers from lunch. One of you ride carefully over here."

The three looked at each other and finally the oldest stepped his horse toward the wagon.

Nancy disappeared under the canvas cover and was back in a few moments with a lump wrapped in an old newspaper. "It's not Christmas dinner but it might do for today."

"We take that kindly, Missus. Much obliged."

Watching the boys ride away, Jonathon said, "I wouldn't have thought to do that, Nancy. But you're right. They are hungry. Good for you."

Hiram rode up to the front of his wagon and carefully took the shotgun from his wife's trembling hands, lifting it to safety. "Mother, that was a foolish, brave thing you did and you probably saved our lives. Ain't like you though. It surely ain't like you."

"You all right, Ma?" asked Jessie.

For an answer, Ma McTavish picked up the reins and slapped the mules into action.

Jonathon grabbed the shovel that was tied to the side of the wagon and waved Nancy forward. "I'll catch up in a few minutes."

Nancy's two brothers stayed with Jonathon to help with the digging. Burying the dead captain was the work of just a few minutes. Jonathon took the captain's weapons but nothing else.

"Should we check his pockets?" asked Bobby.

"He's got nothing I want," answered Jonathon. "Fill it in and let's ride."

"What about his horse?"

"No telling who might recognize that brand. Leave him be. Drop the saddle and bridle on the ground and leave the horse."

"I was sure surprised when those men rode up," Bobby said as they rode to catch up to the wagons. "They scared me half to death."

"You're right to be scared, Bobby. I was, too. What really scares me though, now that I think on it, is that these were just boys led by a fool. There's every chance that there are other groups just like them that won't be so easy to deal with. It will pay us to keep our eyes peeled."

Hiram had called the wagons to a halt just a mile from the shooting and had taken his wife for a short walk.

Nancy had a coffee fire going when Jonathon and the boys rode up. Even from a distance, it was clear to Jonathon that his mother-in-law was crying. "Ma needs some time alone with Pa," Nancy told Jonathon. "She isn't going to easily get over that shooting."

"Boys," said Jonathon, "let's unhitch those mules and let them graze a little. Turn that cow loose, too. We can take as much time as your ma needs."

Although there was no water, a situation that was fairly common on the Kansas prairie, the travelers camped there for the night. The next morning, they had another family talk. As always, they looked to Hiram for a decision.

"I figure that we should travel west until we find some kind of a settlement. Perhaps someone there will know where the Texas trail is. Although this is bigger country than I can rightly get my mind around, the known trail has to follow water. Walker and his herd should be somewhere on that trail."

The family agreed and headed west again. It took several days but they finally arrived at a stick and canvas settlement. The oldest building could have been less than six months old.

Hiram looked the small group of buildings over. "It ain't much but someone here might know something."

Hiram and Jonathon walked into a small saloon tent, stood until their eyes adjusted to the dimness, and approached the barman.

"What'll it be, gents?"

"Well, rightly I'm not much of a drinking man but I'll pay for a beer each if it comes with a little information," answered Hiram.

"It's precious little I know, friend, but I'll give you honest answers if I can." He drew the two beers and set them in front of Hiram and Jonathon.

Jonathon ignored the mug of beer. "We're looking to meet

some folks coming up the trail from Texas with a herd. What we don't know is just where the trail's end might be. They're hoping for a railway but there surely are no tracks anywhere around here that we've seen. Can you give us some idea of where the most likely trail might be?"

"Well, the good news is that where you want to be is probably right about here. Even when the rails get built into the west, you have to figure that the herds will stay as far to the east as they can without they get into trouble by crossing into Arkansas. That means they will just naturally end up around the Arkansas River and that will lead them to Fort Gibson. And if they keep coming north they will end up right about here. So my guess would be that you could wait here or turn south to the river and see what you can see.

"There's been no herds come this way yet except one that the Chisholm people brought through a while back. Your son must be one of the first to take on that task."

Hiram turned to leave. "Much obliged, we'll be moving on. Hope to meet up with you again someday."

The saloon man held up a hand to stop Hiram. "You don't want to move on just yet. If those are Texas longhorns your people are driving, could be they don't know. Kansas has a law against bringing them into the territory. Kansas and Missouri both. Right closed-minded about it, too. They bring them this far, the vigilantes are just liable to impound them and your friends will come up short a herd. Of course, the vigilantes will sell them their own selves, divvy up the money and call it a good day's work and a public service. But none of that will help your friends any. Best they stop before they reach the Kansas border."

"I didn't know that and I'd be willing to believe that they don't either," said a worried Hiram. "Friend, your information is worth another beer. This time for yourself." He laid a dime on the counter. "Thanks again."

"Good luck to you. If it turns out that I'm wrong and you can't find them, why, you come back and I'll give you your dime back."

Jonathon laughed and tipped his hat at the man as he left.

15

AFTER THE SEARCH FOR LUKE, MARGO WAS ALMOST FRIENDLY toward Mac a time or two. Anyone watching would know she was having a hard time trying to remain aloof.

Mac was having a difficult time hiding his own feelings, too, but he handled the crisis like he handled most things: with long hours of hard work.

The drive couldn't have gone better. Except for Luke going down the river and the raid by Mr. Jones' gang of thieves, it was almost without incident. Mac knew they'd been fortunate. He knew about stampedes and Indians and outlaws and that another drive might face all of those things plus lightning storms, hail and just about any other kind of weather a man could think of. But this trip they'd run in good fortune.

They'd managed to hold the herd together during the thunderstorm and the herd had even stood fairly firm with lightning dancing on their horns. They knew none of their success was because of their knowledge of cattle. They figured that if this herd got through with as little knowledge of cattle as they had, another time just had to be at least as easy especially if they managed to hire a few men.

That night, gathered for the evening meal, Jerrod called everyone together except Luke who was with the herd. "Folks, we're in the habit of giving thanks for our meals but this evening I'd like if we could take a few extra moments to give thanks for our safety and the success so far. I know we all feel it but the Lord might like to hear us say it."

Margo spoke, "That sounds like a right good idea, Jerrod, but you just wait a few moments. Mac, can I borrow your horse?"

Without waiting for an answer from Mac, Margo swung up on the big black and headed out to the herd.

In a couple of minutes, Luke rode up. "Margo said you wanted to see me."

Jerrod smiled and said, "Swing down, Luke. Join us for a bit."

Jerrod then prayed, giving thanks for the care of the Lord in the drive and especially for the rescue of Luke from the river. Then he prayed for their new friends and finally for the food. He no sooner said 'amen' when Bill started to pray.

Mac had never heard anyone pray with the fervency of the young man. He glanced over at Bill and was startled to see Bill standing with arms raised above his head and talking to God as if he was his personal friend.

Pa would like that, thought Mac.

When Bill's prayer was finished, Luke mounted and turned his horse toward the herd without saying a word.

Margo was soon riding back on Mac's black and they all dished up their meals. Several times during the meal, Mac took questioning looks at Bill. The past few minutes seemed to be in stark contrast to the coyote incident and he wasn't sure what to think.

After the meal was finished, Mac walked over to where Margo was clearing away the dishes. "That was a right good idea you had to spell Luke off. Thanks."

Margo gave him a small smile. "I didn't think much before doing it. I hope Luke wasn't offended."

"No, you did fine," Mac said before walking off.

As the first hint of dawn was showing the next morning, they rousted the longhorns off the bed grounds and started them north.

Mac was anxious to complete the drive. Except for the fact

that they were in an area of more than usual brush, the drive was going well. Yet he couldn't help but worry about all that might still happen to spoil their plans.

The next day, Ad and Bill were with the herd while Mac had ridden back to the wagon with Luke and Jerrod for a mid-day meal.

"We get us some money from the sale of these beasts," Luke said, "we're going to do this again. Maybe several times. I'm going to watch the river crossings pretty carefully though."

Jerrod nodded his agreement at Luke and then looked at Mac. "Well, boss, you've done real well. Considering what little any of us knew when we started, you've done real well. Like I said before, you're just a natural leader." Both Jerrod and Luke chuckled at the private joke.

"I ain't rightly no leader," answered Mac more seriously than the occasion called for. "Don't want to be the leader. This cattle driving is a lonely business, not seeing any other human folks for days and weeks, and taking on leadership just works to make it lonelier. I'd be happier just driving cattle."

Surprising everyone, Margo spoke, "It might not be so lonely if you had someone by your side." Realizing what she had said, she blushed and turned away.

Mac looked startled. He craned his head around as if to check that his horse was still there tied to the wagon tongue in case of need and then slowly picked at his food.

Luke looked at Mac and held back a laugh. Jerrod couldn't hold back a smile and neither could Margo's mother.

Margo made the situation worse by saying, "What I meant to say was...,"

She was interrupted by outright laughter. Luke started it followed closely by Jerrod and Mrs. Adkins. Mac set his plate down and, climbing into the saddle, rode over to relieve Bill.

Mrs. Adkins rescued Margo. "Margo, I believe your little sister could use some help over at the wagon."

Ad had ridden in for lunch and arrived at the fire in time to hear just the last part of the conversation.

"Dumbest smart man I ever rode with," laughed Luke,

watching Mac ride away. "He'd eat a porcupine with the quills still on. Don't know how he got this far in life. Why, that man could lead an army across an uncharted wilderness but he's too dumb to see ten feet in front of him. Dumb, that's what he is. Don't know as there's any help for it." His laughter was in danger of startling the herd.

When Jerrod stopped laughing he suggested, "Ad, I think our leader needs an older man to talk with him. Kind of help him along into adulthood. Now, I figure you might just be the one."

Ad's answer was, "No you don't. I just work here. I saw through you and your scheme right from the start. Don't you get me involved in that scheme especially since you've given the lead role to my own daughter. You might say I have a vested interest. No, sir. You leave me be."

Luke was grinning from ear to ear.

The next day after a brief nooning, the crew continued pushing the herd north. They were forced to follow an established trail that wound its crooked way through a considerable growth of bush and rock. There was a scattering of larger trees here and there but mostly it was bush.

Over noon coffee they discussed their situation.

Mac said, "I truly didn't know what to expect. I had always thought of Indian Territory as plains country with maybe a river or two. I'm somewhat taken back by the mountains we've seen and the rough travel. I expect we should have angled more to the west but since none of us knew, we'll just have to carry on. But the next herd will have to be shown an easier trail."

"We'll manage," commented Margo.

Luke looked from Margo to Mac and nodded.

Jerrod scouted ahead while the others were taking their nooning. He rode back and spoke to Ad and Bill who were riding left and right point. "Narrow the herd down and stay to the trail. Once they start down the trail you'll have to sit back and let them go. The trail is too narrow for riders. There's about one-half mile of heavy bush ahead with a considerable hillside of rock and if these critters get in there we'll be all summer getting them out. Push them hard so they won't get the idea to stray."

They had been through three days of rough going with a lot of broken terrain and a lot of brush so they didn't figure the cattle would be spooked by the narrow trail and they moved right along. Still, it made the drovers long for the open prairie grass of Texas.

Jerrod rode ahead again to give the lead animals something to follow.

Riding back into the brush-strewn trail, Jerrod was startled when his horse's ears suddenly went forward and its head came up sharply. Just as he pulled his mount to a stop, two shots rang out, the two sounding almost like one. It was his abrupt stop that saved Jerrod's life. One bullet passed harmlessly a few inches ahead of him but the second shot took his horse in the side of the head. A foot more travel would have cost Jerrod his life. As his horse was falling, Jerrod left the saddle faster than he ever had before and scrambled into the bush, alternately rolling and crawling but taking his carbine with him.

He dove forward onto his belly desperately trying to make it to a cluster of small boulders when two more shots hurried him along. One shot created a small explosion of dirt, grass and debris right in front of his face. He ducked his head instinctively but kept moving. The other shot rattled off a boulder behind him. He huddled behind his small shelter curled into the smallest ball he could manage. More shots ricocheted off the surrounding rocks. He wriggled toward a small opening between the rocks and slid his carbine forward, looking for a target.

The lead cattle were close enough to be panicked by the noise. The two lead bulls suddenly turned back into the closely bunched cattle causing confusion that soon turned into a ragtag stampede back the way they had come.

Ad and Bill rode hard trying to stop the panicked cattle until they heard Mac hollering, "Let them go! They have Jerrod pinned down in there."

"Who is it?" Ad asked.

"There's no way of telling who it is but it doesn't matter. Bullets are bullets no matter who pulls the trigger."

The women had held the wagon to the side where they had found a widening in the trail. Luke cautioned them to stay there.

"Take cover, stay back," he shouted as he rode past, dodging the stampede.

The four men pulled up at the edge of the bush, sizing up the situation.

Ad said, "Bill, I want you to get back and protect your mother."

Bill was all set to object until Mac said, "That's an order, Bill."

Ad gave Mac a quick look of thanks while he swatted Bill's horse with his hat. "Git, your mother needs you."

Luke offered his opinion, "No telling how many there are in there or who they are but this looks like footwork to me. Not much we can do in this bush sittin' a-saddle."

Mac turned to Ad. "How do you see it?"

"I'd say Luke has the right of it. How about you two take the far side, going boulder to boulder? I'll take this side, all the time trying not to get ourselves killed."

Mac overruled him. "You go with Luke, Ad, down the right side. I'll see what I can find over here and try to join up with Jerrod."

"Men," he cautioned, "this ground isn't as level as it looks. There will be rises and small coulees through those trees. And there is no telling what's in amongst those boulders. You watch every step you take. I have no intention for any of us to die for a few head of cattle."

Luke and Ad nodded agreement; they all looked grim and determined.

On Mac's signal, the farmer and the two ex-soldiers ran their horses to the nearest heavy brush, dropped out of their saddles and ran for cover behind the trees and boulders. Several shots sent lead whining past, alarmingly close.

Luke dropped behind a sizable fallen tree and grinned at Ad who was hunkered down behind a rock. "I do believe these boys are serious about wanting our cattle. But I've become quite fond of these brutes and if we lose them, we lose our summer wages. Don't hardly seem like a thing to look forward to. So we'd better dig these thieves out. But this ain't anywhere near farming, friend. You keep your head down. All right, here we go."

Luke moved with an eager agility that was surprising for such a strong-built man. Three quick steps and he was flat on his belly behind a large boulder. Almost immediately Ad landed full weight on top of him, knocking out most of his wind.

Luke gasped, "You're going to have to decide whose side you're on, Ad. About one more belly flop like that and I'll be tying a white cloth to the end of my rifle barrel." Ad wasn't sure if Luke was grinning or not.

"I ain't never done anything before where there was a distinct possibility of getting killed."

"You could get killed shoeing a horse. Just happens there's no glory in getting killed that way."

"I guess I just never really considered the glory. Don't know how I could have overlooked that." Ad sounded less than sincere.

Mac's feelings toward battle had often been a bother to him. He knew the usual feelings of fear and dread that infest anybody going into battle and, in a way, he hated every minute of the human waste and carnage. In another way, he had always become exhilarated once the battle had actually begun. With death so close, he always found it a puzzle that he could feel so alive in battle, the goal clear, his every thought and action working toward that goal. He had that feeling now; the feeling that he had been put upon and threatened by thieves and he intended to put a stop to it.

Mac's only thought was to move forward to overcome this enemy the way he had overcome so many times in battle. He'd found a trail of sorts that rose upwards and through a clump of nearly impenetrable brush. Starting up it, he hoped to flush the raiders out of hiding and into the sights of Luke and Ad. He'd gone several feet with Ad watching him from over the top of the downed tree that he had crawled behind when a shot rang out and Mac dropped as if he had been hit, twisting as he fell and losing his carbine.

Ad saw the shooter above and to the left of Mac. He stood looking where Mac had fallen. He had his carbine resting on the top of a rock, ready for a second shot. Ad lined up his sights on the man's chest and pulled the trigger. Ad watched mesmerized as the man threw his arms in the air, his carbine flying upward and then flipping into the trees behind him. As the man crumpled out of sight, Ad said, "I believed I might have killed that man."

"You ever kill a man before?" Luke asked after a moment.

Ad looked over at Luke with a stricken look on his face. His silence was answer enough.

"Well, don't let it get to you. These boys chose their own way through life. They knew the consequences. Anyway, when it's a question of him or me to line up for a plate of beans this evening, I would much rather that it be me."

"They got Mac," Ad said in a trembling voice.

"I saw that. But there's nothing we can do right now. We set out to clean out this nest and we still have most of it to do."

"Judging from those shots, I would say that there are six at the most and maybe not even that. They're all bunched just over there." Ad pointed toward a group of mostly hidden boulders not far from where Mac fell.

Luke was silent for a few moments, looking the situation over. "Mac had the right idea. You stay here. I'm going around to the right. Get higher up. Keep watch but keep your head down."

"Which do you want me to do? Keep watch or keep my head down. I doubt as how anyone could do both."

Luke grinned at him. "Just try not to get yourself shot and if you see anyone thinking about taking a shot at me, why you just go right ahead and return the favor."

Luke moved from tree to tree exposing himself just once but still drawing a shot that barely missed, ricocheting with a terrible whine and spraying poplar bark fragments.

After a few more moments of waiting, Ad heard Luke chuckle.

"Well now, boys," Luke shouted. "I can see all of you clearly and it wouldn't be any problem at all to pick you off one at a time. It's a little difficult to see under that floppy hat but I do believe that's Mr. Jones hiding behind that rock like the coward he is. You should have let me hang you last month, Mr. Jones. It would have saved you a long ride and a lot of trouble to say nothing of wear and tear on your horse. As it is, I would say you have just about run my patience dry. I'd say you have no need of making any long-term plans."

Jones and the others dove behind larger rocks and out of sight.

"Mr. Jones ain't no smarter than you need to be in this life and he was just bound to end up badly." The voice came from across the trail.

"Mac? That you Mac?" shouted Luke. "We saw you fall. You hurt bad?"

"Just some bark fragments in my eye. But it's clearing up now and won't affect my shooting none. You figure we should root these characters out and hang them or just go ahead and shoot them?"

Jones spoke up, his voice sounding hoarser than ever. "You'll play hob getting at us boys. We're pretty well dug in here and I figure we can last as long as you. You can't no way see us and if you try to sneak up, we'll drill you one by one. And in the meantime, your cattle are scattered. But when we're done with you, we'll go and gather them for you. We'll sell them and collect the money for you, too. That I'm really looking forward to."

A new voice came from just past the hidden outlaws. "I can see you just fine, men, and you're well within the range of this twelve-gauge I'm holding. I suggest you just give it up. You can't no way win."

Mac was startled to hear a voice he knew but hadn't heard since before the war. "Pa? Is that you, Pa?"

"That's me, Walker; me and a few others. Come to find you. Heard the shooting and thought we would take us a look."

"Who all's there, Pa, and how in the world do you come to be way over here? Who's minding the farm? And where's Ma and the kids?"

"Ma is down by the wagon making supper and the kids aren't really kids anymore. You been gone a while, son. Your two brothers are here with their rifles held on these no-goods down here. Your brother-in-law is here, too."

"Brother-in-law? I didn't know I had a brother-in-law."

Jerrod spoke for the first time, "This is shaping up like a real good family reunion but this isn't hardly the time. Stand up, Mr. Jones, and throw your guns out. It's all over. Do it now before we all lose patience with you."

First one and then two more carbines were tossed out, followed by three belt guns.

"All right, don't shoot, we're coming out."

A younger voice that Mac took to be his brother said, "Well, it ain't that you really have much choice."

The outlaws made their slow way through the brush until they were all standing on the trail with their hands raised. They were as disreputable a bunch as Mac had ever seen.

One by one, Mac and his friends emerged from the brush. When they were all there and had made certain that the outlaws were unarmed, Mac hollered, "Pa, come on down. It's safe enough now."

Ad and Luke pulled the neckerchiefs off the raiders and used them to tie their hands. The thieves were soon sitting on the ground with their hands tied behind their backs.

Mac's father, two brothers and one brother-in-law were soon walking toward the group.

Mac shook his father's hand and then his brothers'. He then turned to the man he didn't know and said, "You must be Nancy's husband. I'm Walker although all these others know me as Mac. Y'all are a sight for sore eyes and as soon as you say hello to my friends, I want to hear how you come to be here."

Mac's brother-in-law introduced himself as Jonathon. Mac's first impression was that Nancy had chosen her husband well.

He peered past his father and asked, "Who's that sneaking up behind you, Pa? Looks somewhat like a girl-child." There was a hint of humor in his voice.

Hiram didn't even turn around to look. "That will be Jessie, your sister. Never was such a girl to get involved in men's business. She was carrying a rifle and following us up here before I turned her back. She's a caution, she is. I've just about given up on her ever becoming a lady. Jessie, come say hello to your brother."

"Hello, brother. Don't you let all that talk influence you. I can be a lady when it's a lady that's needed. But when it's another rifle that's needed, why I expect that mine would be just as good as anyone's. As good as these two brothers anyway. We all saw Bobby miss a shot at a perfectly eatable goose a few days ago. Never saw the like."

"The goose was flying pretty high at the time," objected Bobby.

The gathered group chuckled at Bobby's defensive answer and Mac put his arm over his brother's shoulder and said, "I've missed a few that weren't in the air. Don't you let her rag on you. Girls will do that if you give them half a chance."

Luke spoke up with a grin, "Bobby, if you were to take in everything your big brother knows about girls, you still wouldn't know anything. You want to find out girl information, you need someone else to trust."

Trying to ignore the grins and laughter around him, Mac started making introductions.

By the time all the introductions were done, Bill was carefully approaching the pass. He said, "We didn't hear any more shooting and Ma wasn't content to wait any longer. Sis is a bit anxious, too, but I'm not sure who she is most anxious about."

Mac told his father, "We'll get your story later. Right now, we have a herd to gather up. If you'll take these three pieces of trash and tie them to something so they can't run off, we'll go see if we can find some cattle."

"You take your brothers with you. You'll find them a help with the cattle. Jonathon and I can handle these troublemakers. We'll take them back to camp just as soon as they bury their partner."

Bill said, "Ma saddled up. She and Margo and I have most of the cattle grouped down by the wagon."

The cattle that were still loose had run only about one-half mile before settling down. They were enjoying their first hours of freedom in many weeks. Most allowed themselves to be caught without too much trouble but a few were making a fair show of heading back to Texas. It took considerable time and horse sweat to turn them back. It was nearly totally dark by the time the cattle were all driven through the short pass and bunched on reasonable grass on the other side.

Margo pulled their wagon up beside Hiram's on the side of a pleasant little stream. There was water all through the hills so it was a good camp considering the rough terrain.

Mac introduced the women and then moved off to help with the cattle.

Jessie and Margo both started gathering more wood for the supper fire. Before long, they were making a contest of this simple task although neither one would have admitted it. It started to appear that one small camp may not have room in it for two beautiful and headstrong teen-age girls.

16

THAT EVENING, HAVING A LAST CUP OF COFFEE, MAC ASKED HIS father again, "Pa, you surely took me by surprise today with your showing up. I'm awful glad to see y'all but now I need the story. There's nothing small about this country and that you found us is close to a miracle."

"Perhaps not quite a miracle. We had some help. Talked to a bartender in a little stick and canvas settlement up in Kansas. He pointed out the trail to the Arkansas River and we came right along hoping that was your route since it's the best water anywhere around. And then when we seemed to have come a far ways, we asked some folks traveling north and they told us about the military having a fort just up the road a piece."

Jonathon took up the story. "We went into the fort and asked around. No one had seen you or any other cattle herd. We decided to come a ways from the fort, set up camp, and watch for you or maybe see your dust if you were east or west of us. We set up camp here four days ago. When we saw dust in the south, we decided it was still best to just wait. Then we heard those shots and came running."

"We're all glad you did," Jerrod told them. "You were right where you were needed at just the right time. We could as easily have chosen to travel west of here and missed you by fifty miles.

So it may not be altogether a miracle that we met up but it's something pretty close."

Mac was still waiting for more explanation. "That's all well and good but none of that explains what you're doing here in the first place."

Mac's father looked at him and said, "I've thought a good bit about the west and about our farm since you left, and I finally got around to talking to your ma about looking at new pastures. Hoping for greener grass, you might say. She tried to talk to me about that farm twenty years ago and we chose not to agree so we just let 'er lay for all this time. But now we found ourselves thinking the same. So we sold off the farm to Collie. You'll recall that he farms the piece next to ours. When I made the offer to sell, he was right excited but he had no way to raise all of the price without he went to the bank. He refused to do that, having the good sense to not trust bankers. So we took what cash he had and trusted him for the rest.

"That gave us enough to buy those wagons you see over there and get us outfitted for the road. Bought all new weapons, too. Good guns and a far cry better than loading shot and powder. We took us a family vote and every danged one decided to come. I was a mite surprised at Nancy and Jonathon. Thought they might just stay. Jonathon was working steady at the sawmill and they were doing all right."

Mac's mother spoke up, "Actually, it was your letter that started it all. The one where you told about the cattle and that you were hoping to find the rails in about two months. But maybe we were ready for a change anyway. I would have to admit that having the war fought through our barnyard changed our thinking on a lot of things."

Hiram continued, "You told as how there was just the three of you to drive eight-hundred head of cattle and that didn't seem very likely. So we made up to see if we could track you down, maybe give you a hand. It's an awful big country out here but we figured you'd be pointing at the rails so we come right along with that in mind. Turns out there's no rails in Kansas yet. None to speak of anyway.

"It took considerable asking around to find out where the rails were. We figured you would have to wind up there soon or late. Then we come to find out that the rails are nowhere near where you need them to be. And if that isn't problem enough, we found out that Kansas has the same law against these longhorn cattle as Missouri. Your cattle are just not welcome at all anywhere north of here, or east either for that matter."

The drovers all looked surprised at the news about the longhorns.

"We knew about Missouri but not about Kansas," said Jerrod. "That doesn't leave us a whole lot of places to go. This drive is sounding more and more like a lot of work with no good result."

"Tell them, Jonathon," said Hiram with a smile.

Jonathon looked over at Mac and his friends. "There is a market. And it's only about twenty miles from here. Place called Fort Gibson. It's not a big fort but it's manned by the US Army and they're responsible for a settlement of Indians. We went to see them on our way down here and mentioned you and your cattle. The clerk we were talking to went right away to tell his commanding officer about the cattle and he came out of his office with a smile on his face and his hand out ready for shaking. Turns out that these Indians need cattle for food and that officer is responsible for supplying them. So all you have to do is go there and make your deal."

Bobby said, "I didn't see noth'n but Northerners there. I'd say you had better watch out for sharpers."

Luke grinned at Bobby.

Nancy confirmed what her father had said before. "When we read in your letter about just the three of you driving all those cattle, we thought to find you and offer our help."

Mac's mother spoke up, "Of course, we didn't know you had partnered up with Ad and his family. Margo told me how y'all met. I thought I had taught you better than to drive your cattle through someone else's camp, Walker, especially folk such as these and a nice girl like Margo. I think you should spend more time with Margo, Walker. She might teach you gentler ways." Ma flashed a small smile at her son. "Seems you might have become a bit rough around the edges over the past few years."

Margo looked down at her coffee cup but not before she took a quick sideways glance at Mac.

Mac noticed the glance but chose not to respond.

Jessie looked over at Margo with a look that said you've impressed Ma and you might think you're the queen bee of this gathering right now but we will see about that by-and-by.

Jerrod addressed himself to Hiram, "That's good news about the fort. Do you happen to remember the commanding officer's name?"

"True. It was Lieutenant Colonel Lewis C. True, if I remember rightly. Seemed like a likable enough fellow although I will admit that I still don't take any comfort from those blue uniforms."

"I know him," Jerrod said with some excitement. "He's with the 62nd Illinois Volunteers. We were stationed together a couple of years ago. Mac, with all these folks here, you and I are not really needed to drive this herd. How about we ride on ahead in the morning and see if we can sell these beasts. I'd like to get reacquainted with Lewis, too."

They saddled up early the next morning and headed for Fort Gibson taking Mr. Jones and the other prisoners along with them. At the fort, they turned the renegades over to the staff sergeant who promised to deliver them to the civil authorities in Fort Smith along with letters of complaint from Mac and his friends. Mac wasn't sure that the court would act on the strength of a letter but he had no intention of traveling to Fort Smith to appear in person.

By noon, Mac and Jerrod were sitting in the officers' mess with Lieutenant Colonel Lewis True. "It's good to know you made it through the difficulties, Jerrod. You too, Mac. How are the family, Jerrod, and that young lady you used to talk about?

"Most of the family wasn't there when I went home, Lewis. The difficulties as you call them took an awful toll in our area."

"Took an awful toll everywhere. And the young lady?"

"I'm not real sure if it was mostly her or mostly me that had changed but when we met up, it somehow just didn't feel the same. We decided to give it some time."

They were all silent for a while, each struggling with their own memories.

"Let's talk cattle," suggested Lewis. "How many do you have, what shape are they in and how much do you expect to be paid for them?"

Mac answered, "We started out with eight hundred and three. We haven't tried to do an accurate count lately but, what with river losses and a couple butchered for food, I'd guess that we have around seven-hundred seventy-five. They've been putting weight on. There's good grass along the trail and as slow as we've been driving them, they've stayed in good shape. As to price, I'd reckon that we need to talk a bit about that."

"I'm authorized to make the purchase," said the officer. "But they've changed commanders so often in this post that no one really has much of an idea of just what the expectations are. I've only been here a couple of weeks myself.

"I do know that the price in Chicago would be around thirty dollars the head for good stock. But you can't expect that here. I'm thinking the government might not sink out of sight with debt if you were to accept twenty dollars."

Mac looked over at Jerrod but he couldn't read his thoughts. They both knew that this offer was in excess of their original expectations but Mac had no intention of accepting the first offer.

"The cattle will be here tomorrow. If you could take immediate delivery and pay in gold, I expect the partnership would be happy with twenty-two dollars."

The post commander smiled at him. "Well, at least you came back with an asking that can be divided in half without me having to get pencil and paper to do the ciphering. Let's agree on twenty-one and we'll count them together."

Again, Mac looked at Jerrod. "Done," Mac answered and reached to shake the commander's hand.

"Now, for a second matter," said the commander. "How soon can you get me another herd? If you could deliver another this fall and another next spring, that would relieve me of some worry."

"Our drive started in far south Texas, Lewis," Jerrod answered. "We left arrangements with a friend down there to have cattle waiting for us when we get back. If he's been success-ful, we could be back here in about ten weeks. That's pushing the season considerably but we might take the chance for a sure sale."

"You have a sure sale and I'll give you written directions to that end and leave instructions just in case I get transferred out of here. Would that set your minds at ease?"

"I think that should do it but we have others we would have to confirm it with. We can do that right away and let you know."

"Good. Now I don't usually drink in the middle of the day but if you men will follow me back to my office, we just might find a small tonic to share."

17

THE CATTLE WERE SOLD AND PAID FOR AND WERE NOW UNDER THE care of the military. They would hold them until the riders from the tribe arrived. These had been warriors just a few years before, more familiar with battle or the buffalo hunt. They had been known to treat cattle like buffalo, running them and then bringing one down with a well-placed arrow.

The crew was relaxing around the fire. There was no work to be done for the first time in many weeks. They'd discussed the idea of bringing another herd that fall and all had agreed. They wouldn't all be required for the drive but that would be decided after they saw how things lay back at Ty's ranch.

Jerrod had gone to inform his friend Lewis and had come back with the signed agreement.

They had cut out the two lead bulls and were taking them back to Texas with them.

Hiram sold his milk cow for fear she would slow down the return trip. He also took the old retired mare to the settlement to find it a new home. He saw a young boy playing out behind the sutler's store.

"Howdy," Hiram said. "I see you playing with that stick horse. How would you like to have a real horse?"

The boy stared as if he was afraid to speak.

"It's all right, son. You got a father or mother nearby?

The boy nodded and pointed at the store.

Hiram walked into the store and addressed the sutler, "That your boy out there, sir?"

"Is he causing trouble?"

"No trouble from him. My trouble is with an old mare that we brought along. She's just not able to keep up and I offered her to your boy. Probably should have spoken to you first. I apologize for that oversight. But if you would let me, it would please me to give the mare to your boy."

The sutler looked out the doorway at the horse. "If you're sure, I see no harm in it as long as you say the mare is gentle. The boy's young yet and he couldn't handle a troublesome ride."

"This mare will give him nothing but gentle enjoyment. I'm pleased to let him have her."

Hiram and the sutler walked to the rear of the store building. The boy was holding the lead rope and stroking the nose of the mare. "Can I keep her, Pa?"

"You promise to look after her and say thank you to the man and she's yours."

THE TWO LEAD bulls had a long walk to make getting back home and Mac was attempting to check their feet. They weren't real happy about it but with some help he got it done. He had developed a fondness for the animals.

Looking at the group gathered around watching, Mac said, "First sizable settlement we come to we'll see if we can find a couple of bells. A neck bell for each animal. Kind of make these bulls feel special and we'll always know where each one is."

Hiram had kept the two red hounds tied close to the wagon out of fear that they would stampede the cattle. All the hounds knew from the Missouri farm was the placid milk cows and the equally placid small herd of beef critters Hiram had kept. The red hounds might make cattle dogs eventually but while making a drive through rough country would have been a poor place to test it out.

After the herd was delivered, he turned the dogs loose and they immediately approached the two lead bulls. After much sniffing and howling and prodding of hoofs, the animals decided to accept each other.

Mac had never seen his mother look so well-fed and relaxed. Clearly a few weeks on the trail without the never-ending farm chores had done her good. Mac thought she was even gaining back some of her youthful beauty. And there was no doubt that her two daughters were close copies of her. Even a brother could recognize that.

Hiram had lifted his wife's rocking chair out of the wagon and she was enjoying another cup of coffee, rocking the evening away, when she reached in her pocket and dragged out her old pipe. She packed it with tobacco brought from home and lit it with a small brand from the fire.

She inhaled deeply and blew a puff of smoke into the night sky, then returned to the subject she had brought up the previous day.

"Walker, it seems that you and your friends have a good thing going here for you along with the Adkins family. Adding in all of us, that makes quite a bunch. Is it too many, Walker? Perhaps your Pa and I should keep on west."

Jessie looked like she was about to say something but Mac ignored her. "We three set out working as partners, Ma, with Ad and his family working for wages for the last half of the trip. We promised them the option to be partners for the next drive and they haven't turned that offer down yet so I expect that's how it will be. But there's no reason we can't all work together. Just takes some planning is all."

A rumble of voices confirmed that they all agreed.

Margo looked over at Mac and said, "You're not broke any more. The job can only become easier with a bit of money."

"It's been good to be able to pay y'all, too. There was some risk that this venture would come to nothing. I wonder if you folks will really still want to throw in with us. Do this all again. It's a hard life."

Hands on her hips, Margo blurted out, "You can't get rid of

us that easily, Mr. McTavish. We already talked about it; my folks, Bill and myself. We'll stay and we'll do it all over again. And we'll do it as often as you will. Anyway, it's not all that bad and it will be easier when we can buy the things we need."

Mac cringed at the harshness of the words. "Didn't have any intention of getting rid of any of you."

Mrs. Adkins walked over to Margo and led her away toward the wagon. "Young lady, you still have some things to learn. One is that you can catch more flies with honey than with vinegar. That's a nice young man. I think I know why you treat him so rough but you might want to think it over."

"He's very aggravating with all his rightness and duty and all, Ma. He does aggravate me so."

"Yes, honey," her mother agreed. "Menfolk are often aggravating. They most certainly are. But it's all we have. There's just men and women. So we have a choice. We can live with them or we can live alone. There is just no other choice. The best you can hope for is to find you a good one. That won't stop the aggravation but it might make it a little easier to tolerate.

"You might also want to consider that it's largely because of his hard work and the attention to duty that this drive was successful."

By noon the next day, the group was making preparations for the long ride south. They had divvied up the money and they had all made simple purchases at the sutler's store. The group took turns at the tent bathhouse in town; the children first, then the women and then the men. They all purchased new clothing and made a ritual out of burning their old clothing, what was left of each piece, over the campfire that evening.

Luke dropped his torn and faded blue shirt on the fire. "That's the last of my uniform. I can't say as how I'll miss it or ever want another. Somebody else starts a war, I think I'll head for Canada." There was general assent among the group.

They spent some time deciding how to work a partnership with so many people and finally came to an agreement. Mostly it involved about half the group staying in Texas to round up cattle while the other half drove them north. Over Mac's strong objections, they decided on the Bar-M as a brand; a large M with a flat bar under it.

Supplies were purchased, plans were made and the entire group headed south again. Ad had put a new canvas cover on his wagon and the two mothers laid in enough food to feed them until Fort Worth. A second wagon and team was bought for hauling the provisions the women planned to purchase once they got to Fort Worth. It would double as a sleeping wagon for rainy nights.

Margo drove one team while her mother drove the other with the children taking turns.

Jessie preferred riding horseback. "You never know when one of these men might take a wrong turn and have to be guided back. I'd best stay close by."

As they were pulling away from their campgrounds, the boy rode out on the old mare and waved them off, grinning from ear to ear.

"Ride careful, cowboy," hollered Hiram.

THE LONG RIDE SOUTH WAS WITHOUT INCIDENT. MAC FIGURED
that they were a large enough caravan to discourage any but the
most determined outlaws. After delivering Mr. Jones and his
partners to the care of the military at Fort Gibson and receiving
their guarantee that they would see to their delivery to the
Marshall's office in Fort Smith, Mac was sure he would be quite
content to never again see an outlaw.

"I expect there's a goodly number of folks along this way that
wouldn't be altogether comfortable singing in the choir," Mac
said to his father. "But I would just as soon not get to know any
of them."

They all carried a small amount of pocket money but the
bulk of the gold they hid between false walls on the wagons,
under floorboards in cavities that they built for that use, or
stowed in steamer trunks.

Hiram had dug up Mac's tin can full of hard-saved money
that had been hidden under the rock stoop back on the farm. He
showed Mac where he had hidden it in the wagon. "Your old can
was all rusted out when I dug it up. But this new one should see
you to wherever you're going before it, too, rusts out."

They rode into Fort Worth and checked into a hotel, taking
up all of the second-floor rooms. The men had haircuts and

again they all lined up for baths. The women couldn't resist the shopping. Mac grumbled that the wagons were going to be loaded down to the breaking point but his complaints had no effect at all on the ladies.

It took almost two weeks to ride from Fort Worth to the ranch. They reached it late one afternoon and were amazed at the amount of activity taking place. There was a new corral full of horses, perhaps a dozen men busy at various activities, and hundreds of cattle spread out on the grass surrounding the ranch headquarters.

A shout arose from one of the men at the ranch and all activity stopped while the crew watched the wagon caravan wind its slow way down the light grade and into the ranch yard. Ty ran out to meet them. Luke, Jerrod and Mac were riding the lead. Ty grabbed Mac's stirrup, trotting along beside him.

Mac reached down and shook his hand. "How goes it, partner? Looks like you're in the cattle business for serious judging by that gather in the pasture."

"Wait until you see all we've done, my friends and I. You can't see but a small part of the cattle from here. Anyway, how was your trip? We've sure all been wondering."

"Let's get this bunch settled, Ty, and then we'll tell you all about it."

They pulled the wagons up beside the ranch house and everyone stepped down. The work had stopped and the ranch men started to gather around. They were all Mexican.

"Mama," hollered Ty, *"Ven!"*

A slim, wiry Mexican woman stepped from the house followed by three younger women, all Mexican. Mac figured the younger women were maybe twenty years old at most while Mama might be thirty or she might be fifty. He would have been afraid to guess. They were wiping their hands on their aprons and trying to shape their hair some.

Ty turned to Mac. 'Of course, she's not my Mama. Actually, she's Manuel's mama but everyone calls her Mama and she seems to like it. You'll meet Manuel later. When he saw you coming, he rode out. He's not much on folks that aren't Mexican.

He's not much on most Mexicans either for that matter. Spends most of his time alone. But if trouble comes, you'll want Manuel nearby."

There were a lot of introductions to make and it took a while.

They decided that the happenings of the past couple of months could wait until after supper.

Ty noticed that the women had the sheet-iron stove out of the wagon and were starting to load it with wood. "What are they doing?" he asked Mac.

"I expect they plan to prepare some food for the evening."

"They mustn't," responded Ty urgently. "Mama would never forgive them. She is very proud of her role here as cook and she and the young wives do all the cooking."

Jerrod overheard this and commented, "This is an awful big group for Mama to cook for. Wouldn't it be better if our ladies helped?"

"She'd never hear of it," Ty answered. "Mama would be very insulted and might never get over it. You tell your ladies to back off and wait and see what Mama can do. If they want, they can go to the house and offer to help. Mama will shoo them away but they could at least offer. In a few days, Mama may let them help a little."

Mac carried the news to the ladies. He figured that was all he could do so he headed toward the corral to look over the horses. He looked back once to see the two mothers heading toward the house. All he could do was hope for the best.

Ty was as excited as a kid at Christmas but that didn't stop him from noticing Jessie. He'd been introduced to her, of course, but he noticed her now as an individual, not as a part of a group. And he liked what he saw. He saw a girl a little younger than himself, about five and one-half feet tall and proportioned in a way that could not be ignored. He thought he saw a hint of freckles although he'd have to be much closer to know for sure. He looked forward to having that opportunity. Her long blond hair was twisted into two braids that hung halfway down her back.

Trying not to be too obvious, he glanced at Jessie as he followed Mac toward the corral and then glanced again. The glances were brief but Jessie saw. She smiled a little and then looked to where Margo was caring for her younger sister. "Looked at me, not you," she said to herself and then felt foolish for the immature thought.

Ty joined Mac at the corral. "Looks to me like you've done real well, Ty. You're looking good, too. You must have put on twenty pounds since we left out of here."

"Beef and beans and Mama's biscuits," he smiled and said. "Not much for variety but always a plenty."

"You didn't feed this bunch on that little bit of groceries we left you."

Ty laughed. "The gardens these folks grow down along the river would amaze you and, of course, there's beef to hand when we need it. We make out. But until I got organized, your supplies were sure welcome."

Mac waved his arm toward the horizon. "You're not quite as alone as you were either. We saw signs of some of the old ranches taking on new life as we came along."

"A few old friends and neighbors have found their way back but I'm afraid we'll never again see most of those that left. Lots of new folks trying their hand but between the big ranchers claiming everything in sight and the Mexican raiders, they might find it not quite as easy as they hoped. The Mexican raiders have left us alone so far but we're a big group to tackle. So I expect they've gone after easier targets."

"I'm glad this has worked out for you, Ty. Seems the arrangement might be good for everyone; you, our group and the *vaqueros*. But there's still lots of mouths to feed so we bought supplies along the way. We must have a thousand pounds of foodstuff in the back of those wagons. Should provide a bit of variety anyway. We'll have to let the women work out what to do with it all."

Mama indeed did do wonders on the cast-iron kitchen range. Quantities of food such as Mac had never seen before were prepared. There weren't enough pots and dishes for the large group so Nancy gathered up what they needed from the wagons and carried it into the small house.

Ty went into the house to check on the preparations. In a few moments, he came out and clanged a metal bar on the big iron triangle that hung from the front roof overhang. He looked over at Luke who was resting there in the shade and said, "I know I could holler out. No need really for the triangle but I just enjoy doing that. Maybe it's knowing there's food to be had, or maybe it's just the noise."

He and Luke grinned at each other.

Soon everyone was gathered around the tables that had been set up in the yard. Mama and three of the younger Mexican wives were ready to serve. They appeared to not need or want any help.

Ty clanged the triangle again to get everyone's attention. He hollered over the noise in the yard, "Mac, do you want to return thanks?"

"Well, I will another time. But right now, I think I'd ask my father, who's the oldest here, to do that."

Hiram took off his hat and stepped forward a bit. Most of the men responded by taking off their hats or sombreros but a few didn't.

"I don't speak any Mexican, folks, but I expect the Lord does just fine at it so we will have to leave that part with Him."

He continued, "Lord, we are very thankful to be here among these good people and for safety for all of us as we traveled and as our new friends gathered these cattle. And right now we are especially thankful for Mama and her ladies who have prepared this good food and for Your hand that has provided. Thank you in our Lord's name. Amen."

"Amen," repeated many of the Mexican folks, crossing themselves.

One of the young women spoke English. She translated for Mama and the other two women.

Everyone stood back waiting for others to move forward. Mama gestured at Mac and said, "Ven, ven."

Ty looked over and tipped his head toward the gathered

Mexicans and said, "They aren't going to move until you do so you might just as well step up."

Mac took his mother by the elbow and led her toward the food-laden table. He then stepped back as the other women came forward. In just a few minutes, the plates were full and everyone was finding a place in the yard to sit.

Luke took his first bite of the beans, placed his plate on the ground and made a strangling noise.

"Suffering saints," he blurted when he had caught his breath. "I sure never tasted anything like that. Like to have burned off the roof of my mouth."

Ty laughed. "I should have warned you. Mexican food is heavy in spice, mostly chili. It grows on you after a bit."

Several of the women had tears running down their cheeks while they held their hands over their mouths. They were all reaching for cups of water, trying desperately not to make a scene.

Mac had yet to take his first bite. He glanced over at a *vaquero* sitting on the grass and watched as the man bit a red chili in half and chewed it. Mac shuddered.

Jerrod noticed a few Mexicans watching and smiling to themselves. *"Que buen chile,"* (good chili) one hollered over with a laugh, waving a small red chili in front of him. Jerrod smiled back and nodded.

Most of them finished up their meal with some taking longer than others. Mac's mother called Ty, "You come translate for me, Ty. I want to talk with Mama."

They walked over together. Ty motioned to a young woman. "This is Maria; she speaks good English. She'll translate for you."

"Mama," said Mrs. McTavish, "that was delicious. Thank you very much. It will take us a while to get used to the chili but I bet we can do it. Maybe you can teach me how to cook like that. Perhaps we can talk about it tomorrow."

Maria translated: *"Mama, estaba delicioso. Muchas gracias. Nos tomara tiempo para acostumbrarnos al; chile pero te apuesto a que lo podemos hacer. Quisas me puedes ensenar a cocinar asi. Quisas podemos platicar manana."*

Mrs. McTavish continued with a smile, "Now it's our turn. You take your supper and your ease. We'll clean up and put things away. Is that all right with you?"

Maria translated: *"Ahora es nuestro turno. Usted tome su cena y su descanso. Nosotros limpiaremos y pondremos todas las cosas en su lugar. Le parece bien?"*

Mama nodded her understanding. She and her helpers went to fill their own plates. The visiting women started the cleanup with the smallest children collecting the used plates and carrying them to the wash pan.

Mac was looking at what the women were doing but his mind was on cattle. He called Ty over to where the men were sitting with their coffee.

"How many critters do you figure you have collected now, Ty?"

"We're well over one thousand mixed cows and young bulls. Some calves at foot. We turned back the old bulls as possibly being too much trouble."

Mac explained, "We have an immediate sale for a herd. Same fort as we sold that last bunch to. They have a more or less settled reserve of Indians up there that need to be fed. They want another herd this fall and one as early as possible in the spring. I'm thinking we could make better time with just young stuff. Cows with calves or ready to drop a calf would slow us down too much."

Ty looked over at the gathered cattle. "I'm guessing that if you were to want a herd of young stuff we would be around six hundred, maybe seven-fifty. We could probably get it up past eight hundred if we sorted out the older dry cows."

"Could your crew start on that right away? We need to be back on the trail in two or three days."

Ty nodded confirmation. "We have several men who stay here to care for the gather. The others just arrived the day before you. They spend most of their time urging these critters out of the breaks and coulees. They were going to head back south tomorrow but I'll talk with them, get them going on sorting. We can have the herd ready but are you sure you want to turn right around and head out without you getting some rest?"

"We can rest when we're old."

Luke grinned at Ty and Ty just hunched his shoulders and went to talk to the crew.

After supper, the *vaqueros* started sorting out the cattle. Mac called again to Ty, "I take it that is Manuel down at the barn. I would like to meet him. Will you come with me?"

The two men walked toward the barn. Manuel was sitting on an upturned nail keg weaving a halter from green cowhide. Although his face was sheltered by his sombrero, Mac knew that he saw them coming.

"Manuel," said Ty, "this is my friend Mac. He wants to talk with you."

There was no translation so Mac assumed that Manuel spoke English.

"We're leaving again soon, Manuel, but a lot of our folks and most of our women and the kids are staying here. I'd like to hire you to stay here and look after them. Our men are good men but they don't know this country or its people. They'll need some help."

Manuel was silent for so long that Mac started to wonder what to say next.

Finally, Manuel lifted his head and looked at Mac. "I will go north with you and with Mama and my wife."

Ty took over the conversation. "What do you mean by that, Manuel? Are Mama and Imelda planning on going with the herd? When was that decided? And how did any of you know about it? We have just now been talking about it."

Manuel showed just the hint of a grin. "Who knows when women decide? Or what they decide, eh. Or where they hear things. But Mama and Imelda have decided to go to look after me and they can't do that if I am not there. So better I be there, no?" In Manuel's mind, it was all settled.

Ty and Mac walked over to where Mama and Imelda were making tortillas and stacking them in a neat pile.

Clearly, Imelda could also speak English. How she and Manuel had learned was a mystery but Mac let it go.

"Imelda," asked Ty. "You and Mama plan to go with the cattle? Why do you want to do that?"

"We have to go to make good food for Manuel."

"But Manuel says he is going just to look after you two."

"So? Is good, no?" Imelda smiled at the two men.

Ty and Mac walked off toward the wagons. "Did you understand any of that Ty?" asked Mac.

"All I really understand is that you have a cook and a guard for your trip north. I don't suppose there is really anyone who could explain how that came to be but there it is. But Manuel will make sure you're safe and Mama will make sure you're well fed so might could be it will all work out."

Still wondering about Manuel and Mama, Mac called a gathering of his entire group.

"We're moving north in two days. We have a lot of work to do. We need to repair the wagons and check all the horses for shoes or injuries and we have to pack our foodstuff into the trail wagon. We have to decide on who's going and who's staying. Manuel has just told me that he's going to look after Mama and Imelda, and Imelda has just informed me that they are going to make sure Manuel is well fed. If you can get your head around that circle, you are doing better than me."

"Do we get any say in that?" asked Margo.

"It seemed pretty much decided."

The gathering was quiet for a few moments while they let that soak in.

"We leave day after tomorrow. So we have to decide now who goes and who stays. This is going to be a fast drive if the cattle cooperate and a fast ride home. It's going to be real late in the year before we're done. We could see some cold nights. I'd like to see eight riders besides a horse wrangler and the cooks.

"As for those staying here, this ranch is pretty much on the frontier and there's some cause for concern in a lawless land. I asked Manuel to hire on as a guard for you all here at the ranch but he's determined to go with the herd."

Mac turned to Luke. "Luke, how would you feel about staying here and making security your full-time task?"

Jerrod smiled over at Luke. "No rivers to cross here."

"I ain't ever going to live that down, am I? But I'll stay here as long as I don't have to tackle that brush again, chasing cattle that prefer not to be chased. I had about enough of that."

Mac turned to Ty. "Do you think you could get a few *vaqueros* to make the trip with us, plus a horse wrangler? We could sure use their knowledge of cattle."

"Several have said they would go if Manuel was going. And it's no good asking me how they knew Manuel was going. We're friends but that don't mean they tell me everything."

Margo spoke up, "I'm going."

Mac nodded at her. "You'll be a help and welcome. Who else wants to ride?"

When the talk was finished, it was agreed that Mac, Jerrod, Ad and Bill would go as drovers along with four *vaqueros* and a teen-age Mexican boy as horse wrangler. They would take one wagon only with Margo doing most of the driving. Jonathon had offered to go but Nancy wouldn't hear of it.

Mac asked Jessie, "Do you want to come along and help with the camp work?"

Jessie glanced over at Ty. "I might do more good right here."

Ty agreed on six dollars a head for his cattle and the gold was paid out. He paid the *vaqueros* and still had a considerable amount of money left. He kept some out for supplies and hid the rest in the root cellar.

Those staying behind were determined to set up winter quarters no matter how temporary and Nancy had agreed to take on the task of school-teaching for the younger Adkins' kids.

Before full dawn on the second day, the *vaqueros* pushed the sorted beef off the bed grounds. Ad gave his wife a goodbye kiss and hugged the smaller children. Margo looked over at Mac and caught him just turning his head away from her.

She put the wagon well out to the front to avoid the dust and smiled over at Mama. "I'll teach you to drive the wagon if you'll teach me how to make corn-flour tortillas."

Imelda translated and Mama nodded with a small smile.

Margo continued, "Maybe you could teach me some Spanish, too."

Imelda said, "I think so. We will have lots of time sitting on the wagon. We teach."

They bought provisions in Fort Worth and moved north. The driving heat of the summer was over and the days were pleasant. Even the odd rainy day didn't bother the travelers.

Just short of the Red River, a hard-case bunch of riders approached. Mac was still wondering what their intentions might be when Manuel appeared with his saddle gun leveled at the lead rider. Mac had no idea where Manuel had come from. He just seemed to appear.

"It is a poor time for a visit, hombre." Manuel's vicious smile and the pointed carbine left no doubt as to the words' meaning. "You are too late for coffee and we have no time for stopping. Best you move on, eh?"

The riders took a hard look at Manuel. Their leader spoke, "I ain't exactly used to taking back talk from no Mex. Best you keep still while real men talk."

Manuel directed his wicked grin at the man. "Hombre, this is one Mex that will gladly cut your tongue out and skin you for the leather. Now you move on."

The hard case took another look at Manuel and a quick note of the other drovers who were making their way around the herd. "Perhaps another time."

"Maybe best not. Best you visit someone else, eh?"

The leader nodded and turned his horse with the others following. Manuel followed along for perhaps a mile before disappearing into some scrub brush.

It would have been good to have him back at the ranch, thought Mac, but it's good to have him here, too.

Mama showed real fear at the prospect of crossing the Red in the wagon. She spoke quickly to Imelda and Imelda hollered and waved at the young man driving the remuda. "Bring a good horse," she hollered. "For Mama."

The horse arrived and Mama swung on bareback as easily as

any of the *vaqueros*. She headed for the river and was soon across, standing on the north bank wringing out her soaked dress.

Imelda said to Margo, "Mama rides pretty good; not so good on the wagon."

Margo smiled in wonder and put the wagon into the river. The men were there with their lariats to guide her across.

In just over five weeks, the herd was bedded down on good grass within sight of Fort Gibson. Mac and Jerrod rode in. "We're here to see Lieutenant Colonel Lewis True," Jerrod said and gave his name and Mac's.

Within minutes, they were sitting in the commander's office. After the formalities, Lewis True asked, "How many head?"

Jerrod answered, "About the same as last time, just over eight hundred. We heard some talk in Fort Worth. The talk was that prices were up some. What have you heard here?"

"If I remember correctly, you received twenty-one dollars in government gold for the last batch. I was expecting you so I sent a courier to Fort Smith with a wire to army headquarters. He got back just a couple of days ago. I can offer you twenty-six dollars this time with no bargaining. That's the price. Take it and be happy."

Mac answered by saying, "Where will we drive the cattle to?"

"Leave them where they are. Just herd them for another day or two and I'll have some riders from the tribe here to take them off your hands. They'll drive the whole bunch to the reserve and butcher them as they need them."

As before, the commander reached into his desk and found a bottle to share.

As they visited, a thought occurred to Mac. "Colonel, when we started out on this cattle venture, we sure didn't know anything. The fact is the first while we made mostly mistakes. All we knew was that the market was north of Texas some-where. So we made up our minds to drive to the rails wherever they were. Then we found out that Kansas had closed its border to Texas live beef. That set us right back on our heels until we found out about this fort and the Indians needing food. You and your Indians were a godsend to us. Now the news is that the rails are moving west into Kansas but not fast enough to suit us. So I got to wondering if there are other forts in Indian Territory that may have the same needs as you."

Jerrod looked at Mac as if he was asking himself why he hadn't thought of that same thing.

The colonel answered, "There's several forts with Indian responsibility and a couple of old forts that the Indians have taken over for themselves. Our communications are not real good between forts so I don't know their situations. But I can give you a list of the forts and their approximate locations. The rest is up to you."

"We couldn't ask for more. We owe you our thanks again."

Two days later when the Indian riders arrived, it wasn't just a few men. It appeared to be the entire village; men, women, children, dogs and all. It was no time at all before hide teepees were pitched and cooking fires were letting smoke into the air.

The cattle were soon in the care of the Indian riders. Bill took the opportunity to mingle with some of the men in the village. He walked through the large and colorful group, talking and nodding and gesturing with his hands although it was doubtful if anything he said was understood.

At one point, Mac saw Manuel talking with a small group of Indian men. He wondered what language they were using.

Margo asked her brother on his return, "What did you see over there?"

"Just folks; like us, only different. We're all God's children."

The group headed the wagon and horses south that afternoon, led again by the two bell animals.

To visit the other forts was a considerable distance out of the way and the travelers were pushing the weather. Mac suggested that they could split up with the larger group heading straight home while he and a couple of *vaqueros* visited the forts. The group led by Margo would hear nothing of that plan so Mac gave in and they made the side trips together.

On the way south, they visited Forts Towson, Washita,

Arbuckle, and Cobb. They found a welcome from the commanding officers at Cobb and Arbuckle.

Fort Towson was no longer in use but the local Choctaw Nation, led by their Principal Chief Allen Wright and the Indian Agent Mr. Colman, met with the group.

"We need cattle only because so many of ours were stolen and driven off during the war," reported Allen Wright. If we buy your animals for food, we can keep our heifers and cows for future herd growth. None of that seems to be how it should be but there we have it. Most of our cattle are gone and that is a fact. You drive some here next spring and we'll deal with you."

Mac and his group rode away with mixed feelings. They were happy for the sale but embarrassed that their fellow countrymen had stooped so low as to steal cattle from the peaceful Choctaw Nation.

"There's always someone prepared to take a shortcut to wealth," Ad observed.

There was considerable urgency about the return trip. There had been no snow but there was frost on their blankets some mornings and a couple of times Imelda had to break ice on the creek as she was dipping water for the morning coffee. The cook fires were made larger than usual to try to encourage a little heat into the riders as they ate.

Saddle blankets and bridle bits were warmed over the fire before the horses were rigged out for the day's work.

Their clothing was inadequate for the chill fall winds. Bill cut a hole in the center of one of his blankets and pulled it over his head, wearing it like a coat. Others followed that good idea.

After crossing the Red back into Texas, they stopped and built several fires even though it was just mid-day. A blanket was hung on the off side of the wagon to give the women some privacy as they warmed up and changed into dry clothing around their own fire.

Mac said, "I'm guessing that the worst is behind us now. It will get warmer from here on south and we should be home at the ranch within three weeks or so." They made it in eighteen days.

Again, they bought supplies in Fort Worth, this time to see them through the winter. The sleeping beds were removed from the back of the wagon as it was prepared to receive the load of purchases. When the women were done with their buying, the vehicle fairly groaned with the weight.

Everyone slept on the ground; the women under the wagon and the men wherever they found a piece of ground to their liking.

Mac found an old open wagon that the liveryman was willing to sell. He purchased it for just a few dollars along with a team of mules that cost considerably more. They loaded as many sacks of oats on the old wagon as they felt the wheels would carry.

Mac said, "I don't know if our animals will remember oats but they might come through the winter a little better for the extra feeding."

When they arrived back at the ranch, it was obvious even from a distance that there was trouble in the yard.

Mac called Jerrod and Ad over and pointed at a group of rough-dressed men. One of them was holding a gun on Luke while the others huddled around. "What do you suppose that's all about?"

"Hold those wagons here until we find out what this is all about," Jerrod yelled at Margo and Imelda who was driving the second wagon.

Mac, Jerrod, Ad and Bill spurred down the light grade toward the ranch yard. Again Manuel had disappeared but Mac no longer worried about him.

They rode up behind the group of visiting riders with saddle guns pointed. "Explain yourselves and be quick about it," demanded Jerrod in as fine an officer's voice as Mac had ever heard. "Lower that weapon and point it away from my friend. Do it now."

The weapon wavered but did not drop. Instead, the holder of the gun turned halfway around and said, "This man is under arrest. I'm the sheriff in this county and I'm taking this man into custody."

Jerrod gave him a hard look. "Mister, you are going to be the deadest sheriff in all of Texas if you don't drop that weapon. I will not tell you again."

"And I'm telling you again that I'm the law."

Mac wasn't sure where Manuel had come from but suddenly he was standing beside him. Manuel had a habit of just appearing. The others were still on their horses.

Manuel stepped forward and before anyone knew what he was doing, the sheriff had a knife pressed firmly under his jaw, the point drawing just a pinprick of blood. "I think maybe you do as my friend say. Now would be a good time to not be holding the gun." His smile was deadly.

The sheriff stretched his neck to get away from the point of the knife but Manuel held it firmly against his skin.

The sheriff dropped his weapon and said to his companions, "Do as they say, boys. We'll have them all facing the judge by-and-by."

"Maybe you die first, eh?" Manuel responded with a smile. "I think I would like to see that happen."

Manuel pulled his knife away and the sheriff and his crew stood in mute obedience.

Mac could see that this had become Manuel's show and he wondered what might happen next.

What came next for the sheriff was Luke. His work-hardened fist exploding against the sheriff's mouth and nose. His head snapped back. His lips were ruined and blood poured freely from his smashed nose. He sagged to the ground without making a sound. He lay there still awake but showing no sign of wanting to get up and challenge Luke.

"Mister," Luke said in a voice trembling with rage, "you ever pull a gun on me again you had better pull the trigger. You won't get any second chances like here today. It's only that there are witnesses here that's keeping you alive right now."

Jerrod stepped over to Luke and pulled him away before he could do more damage. "Easy, friend. We'll get to the bottom of this now."

Ad picked up the weapons dropped by the sheriff and his

friends. After checking the men carefully for more weapons, he said, "Prop up that sorry excuse for a sheriff and sit down there beside him. And keep your mouths closed until you're asked something."

When they were all sitting, Jerrod turned to Hiram and asked, "What's this all about, Hiram? And how did this fool manage to get the drop on Luke?"

"Well, he got the drop on Luke because none of us saw harm in any of them. We saw that badge and welcomed them. They came looking for Ty and Luke was just explaining that Ty wasn't here when next thing we know this here sheriff pulls his pistol and points it at Luke. He called Luke a liar and said as how he expected that Luke was really Ty and was lying about it. None of us expected anything such as that."

Jonathon added, "Luke was getting set to make him eat that pistol and I was afraid he was going to try. That's when you all rode over that rise and made yourselves known."

The sheriff was still spitting blood and broken teeth and was in no condition to answer questions.

Jerrod turned to one of the other men and said, "I told you earlier to explain yourselves. You still got that to do. You have just no time at all to get with it."

"This ranch is being taken because of unpaid back taxes. And the owner, a Tyrell somebody, is being arrested for cattle theft. The judge sent us out here to arrest him and to clear off anyone else that was here. He appointed Tiny here as sheriff and me and these others as deputies. Gave us this here job to do."

"Where is this judge?" Mac asked.

"He's a circuit judge, travels around a lot. Right now he's holed up in a flyspeck of a town over east of here about twenty miles. Name of Wayward and well-named if you ask me."

Jerrod asked, "Have you done dirty work for this judge before?"

"Not us. We was just passing through. Stopped for a drink and to pick up some more beans and such when someone hailed us down and said the judge wanted to see us. We found the judge sitting at one of the back tables in the saloon. Sitting there with a fat man wearing expensive clothes and a look on his face that I didn't really take to. That judge, he offered us this job and twenty dollars. It looked good because we're nearly broke with no job prospects that we could see."

"Have you been paid?"

"Tiny, he wouldn't take the job lessen we was paid first. Said he didn't trust that judge. Told him right to his face, too."

Jerrod looked over at Mac and Luke who was still in a fit of anger.

The three men didn't often make a decision without a full discussion but Jerrod made one now.

"You unpin that sheriff badge and give it to me. Then you lift your friend onto his horse and get out of here. We ride around a lot so I would say that you need to be a long ways gone by night-fall to keep us from seeing you again. Believe me, you do not want us seeing you again.

"Do we get our guns?"

"You get your guns. If you should happen to be careless where you point them, it will be the last thing you ever do. Now git."

The four men mounted and rode out of the yard. The sheriff sat slouched over, holding onto the saddle horn with both hands.

Jonathon watched them ride away and then turned to Luke. "Luke, I don't believe I have ever seen a man hit harder than that. You changed his looks and his life with that one punch. I heard bones break. Don't take that as criticism though. I kind of wanted to hit him myself although I admit I couldn't have done the job as well as you did."

Luke, watching the men ride away, didn't acknowledge hearing the comment.

Mac asked, "Where's Ty?"

Jessie answered, "He's down with the *vaqueros* gathering cattle. We're not expecting him back for a few days yet."

Mac turned to Manuel. "Do you think you could find them? Send Ty back here? It would be a big help to us."

Silently Manuel swung onto his horse. He rode over to say a

few words to his mother and Imelda, then swung his horse to the south and rode out of the yard. As if by some unseen signal, the other *vaqueros* spurred their mounts to catch up. Mac had paid them all in Fort Worth so there was nothing keeping them at the ranch. There were homes and wives and sweethearts and cattle calling them back south. Mac idly wondered about the order of importance of those things.

When Manuel and the *vaqueros* cleared the ranch yard, Hiram walked over to Mac and shook his hand. "Good to see you all back here, son. Come, have a coffee and tell us about it."

Mac gave his mother a hug, nodded to his two sisters, then asked his father, "Where's Bobby and Jeremiah?"

"They insisted on learning the *vaquero* trade. Ty promised to look after them but I must say we've worried some. They came home just the once a couple of weeks ago covered with scrapes and scratches and torn clothing, chewing on red chili peppers and smiling from ear to ear. I guess they're all right or else they've taken full leave of their senses, one or the other."

Jerrod walked over to where Mac was talking with his father. "You've done some work here. I never saw a house built from brush and sticks before but you've sure done it. If that brush roof holds out the rain, it might just make a winter shelter."

Hiram answered, "The Mexicans showed us how to do that and stayed long enough to get us started. They call them jacals. I don't know what that means in Mexican. In English, it might mean poor excuse for a house. They sure wouldn't keep out a Missouri winter but they might do in this desert. As soon as we finish the three you see, we intend to start another. They're not difficult to build so if we need more we can do that, too. It would be a mite crowded if all of us bedded down in just the one.

"As much as these women have purchased, a body can't hardly get into the main house for bags and sacks and boxes. So we decided to use the house just for cooking and food storage and to move the beds into the jacals. I don't imagine shacks like these will last more than a year or two but the winters are short in south Texas and we don't plan on staying here so we'll make do all right."

Mac's thoughts always went in the same direction. "How about the cattle? How is the gather going?"

Hiram pointed toward the chosen pasture. "The boys have about five hundred on grass here now. The gather is a bit slower than it was before, according to Ty. There's others trying for the same cattle so it will take some time. And a couple of the big ranches are making noises about owning all the cattle. That's bound to cause trouble soon or late but Ty is sure we can have a good big herd by spring."

The men discussed the cattle and the trip for a few minutes. By that time, Margo had the wagon pulled up before the house and Bill had the team unhitched and was walking them toward the corral.

Imelda had stopped her wagon in front of the barn where the oats would be stored against the needs of winter.

"Come on, Luke," said Jerrod. "We'll unload those oats. Take our minds off sheriffs and traveling judges."

Hiram and Mac walked over toward the house where the women were standing behind the wagon wondering where to store all the provisions.

Mac's mother looked at the wagon load in wonder. "Land sakes, I never saw such a heap of truck. We take all of that into the house, we'll have trouble moving around."

Hiram smiled at his wife, remembering the many years of counting pennies on their small farm. "It is a goodly amount, I must admit. But it's a comfort to me and I welcome it. You decide what you want to do with this lot, you give me a call. I expect I can still tote a bit if pushed into it."

"The first thing you can do is figure out some way to build some shelves. That would be a big help."

Mac wandered over to where Margo was standing by herself. "That was a long, fast trip with a lot of work and not much sleep. You did real good. You did good at teaching Imelda and Mama how to drive that wagon, too. How's your Spanish coming?"

"I can say a few words."

"Good for you. I picked up a bit working with a Mex on the freight wagons but I don't seem to have much of an ear for it. Even the parts I should know I miss because they talk so danged fast.

"Anyway, it's good to be back. We won't leave again until spring so we have considerable time to rest up. Wouldn't hurt you to take a few days to yourself either after all your work on the trail."

Margo stood speechless as she watched Mac walk toward the barn. She saw Mac's mother out of the corner of her eye. She turned to her and said, "In all these months, that's the most words he's ever directed my way. What am I to make of that?"

Mac's mother had heard most of his talk. She smiled at Margo. "Be patient, he's just like his father. Work has always come first and easy. Words come harder."

Margo nodded at the other woman and continued to watch Mac make his way toward more work unloading the oats.

When the wagon was empty, Mac drove it over to the house. Mama and Imelda showed him which provisions they had purchased for themselves in Fort Worth and he loaded these for them. The two women then headed the wagon south to join up with their men with Mama driving the team like a practiced professional. They promised the return of the wagon and team at their first opportunity. Two *vaqueros* had stayed on at the ranch, waiting for the ladies. They rode out, one on each side of the wagon, watching for trouble.

Three days later, Ty rode into the yard with Bobby and Jeremiah. Jessie watched them ride in although she only had eyes for Ty.

Ty hollered, "What's this I hear about a sheriff visiting?"

Mac and the others explained and asked about the taxes.

"Never missed a single year. Got the receipts right there in the house."

"You get yourself cleaned up and try for a night's rest and we'll ride into this Wayward in the morning. We'll show those receipts to that judge and convince him to forget the whole thing."

Luke said, "I never seen a judge hung. That might be a thing to do." He hadn't grinned much since the sheriff's visit.

Jerrod suggested, "Let's put that out of our minds."

Mac looked at his two brothers. "Wouldn't hurt you two to head down to the creek with a bar of soap and a change of clothes."

The boys laughed and slapped each other on the back.

Bobby said, "That creek water gets any colder the cattle might just refuse to drink it, and you want us to go and have an all over bath in it. Cruel is what you are, big brother. It's hard to believe you come from the same loving family. But I expect we have it to do, else we'll never hear the end of it. Come on, Ty. We'll go together. Sort of protect you and keep an eye on you at the same time." They looked over at Jessie and laughed some more.

"Protect me from what?" Ty asked.

Bobby laughed. "You and Mac, neither one of you is any smarter than the horses you ride. But never mind, we'll watch out for you. Go get your change of clothes."

The following morning, Mac, Jerrod, Ty and Jonathon headed out to see the judge. Ty had dug out the tax receipts and buttoned them safely into a shirt pocket. The ride took just over two hours. They found the judge sitting at a back table in the saloon just as if he had never left since appointing the sheriff. With him was a man that fit the description the deputy had laid out.

The four men walked into the saloon and spotted the two at the back table immediately; all four wore side arms. They walked shoulder to shoulder through the small saloon, all grimness and purpose.

The bartender watched them walk past. He turned to the customer leaning on the bar with a beer in his hand and said quietly, "Wouldn't surprise me none if there were to be thunder and lightning right here inside this saloon. Those men appear to me like they've been over the hill and through the crick. I think I would rather have them as friends than enemies. I wonder what the judge and old Hodgson have tried to pull now."

The men stood in a semicircle facing the judge and the second man. Mac took the lead. "I assume you to be the judge."

"Judge July Bradshaw, sir. What can I do for you?"

Mac jutted his jaw toward the second man. "Who's this?"

"Why this is Mr. Hodgson, a rancher around these parts. And who are all of you?" asked the judge.

Hodgson spoke, pointing at Ty, "I'll tell you who this one is. He's the cattle thief I was telling you about. The one you sent the sheriff out to arrest."

The judge tried his best to make his words sound impressive. "Ah, I see. And just where is the sheriff and his deputies?"

Jerrod flipped the sheriff badge onto the bar table. "I doubt as how any of us will ever see him again around here. We explained to him how short and unpleasant life can be in this climate. Now I will explain just exactly the same thing to you. And to your friend Hodgson who just called my friend a thief. Hodgson, I know all about you and your kind."

That was a stretch of the exact truth but Jerrod said it in that officer voice that had so impressed Mac. It clearly impressed the judge and Hodgson, too. Hodgson adjusted his considerable girth in his chair and looked around uncomfortably.

Jerrod returned Hodgson's look. "But I'll get back to you in a moment."

Returning his attention to the judge, Jerrod said, "Judge, that poor excuse for a sheriff that you hired tells us that you intend to take my friend's ranch from him."

"Even in Texas you have to pay your taxes."

Jerrod turned to Ty. "Show him, Ty. And you, bartender, and you three over there at that table, I would appreciate if you would all come over here. Just for a minute or two to witness these papers."

The three strangers and the bartender made their way over to the judge's table.

Ty laid out the tax receipts and stood back.

"I want each of you to take a look at these tax receipts. They're signed by a Millicent Stony and it says that she's the clerk of the county office. There are four receipts, one for each of the last four years. Would you all agree with that?" Jerrod looked at each man in turn.

"That looks right to me," answered the bartender.

One of the men from the other table looked at the receipts. "That's old Millicent's handwriting; would know it anywhere. And the receipts are exactly like my own,"

Another man took a look and said, "Tyke here, and myself, we can't read writing, not either of us. Can make out newspaper printing a little, given time and good light."

The bartender spoke up again looking over at Ty, "Don't know who you are, son, but you must be one of the few ranchers in the whole territory that has his taxes paid. Going to be tough for you to get this feller's ranch, Hodgson. I imagine that's what this is all about. You've gobbled up a few. All better men than you, too. But you're not going to get this one, looks like."

Hodgson looked at the bartender with venom in his eye. "Shut your mouth, saloon man. I'll tear this shack down around your ears and you with it."

The bartender gave him a scornful look. "You scare me just none at all. You come for me, you better bring help. You're too fat to do it yourself and you fight me you, have to fight the whole town. The townsmen, we already have a plan in place for the likes of you. Be showing wisdom if you was to just walk softly while in town."

Jerrod thanked the men and turned to the judge. "All right, that's settled. Now, let's talk about cattle theft."

The judge was clearly shaken and was now uncertain of his position. "Mr. Hodgson has asked that charges be laid. He claims that this man and his friends are stealing his cattle, driving them out of the country."

Jerrod said, "And you believed him with no evidence of any sort. I know that because there is no evidence. Just what kind of a judge are you? Of course, you're not really a judge. I think it's time you laid your commission on the table for us to examine. My guess is that you and Hodgson worked out this judge thing between you. Lay out your papers." It came out as an order.

Mac figured that Jerrod would have had no problem getting men to follow him during the recent Northern aggression.

The judge sputtered, "Why, you have no right. I, I mean, I'll, I'll..."

Jerrod scooped up the tax receipts and passed them to Ty. "Just as I figured. Now I'll tell you what you two are going to do. Hodgson, you're going to get on your horse and show us your back. You be out of town within five minutes or we'll help you along. You wouldn't enjoy that at all. And don't you ever come near Ty or his ranch or his cattle, you or your men either. And you, Mr. Bradshaw, you're leaving town, too. We're going over to the cafe for lunch. When we finish, I don't want to be able to find you. This ploy of yours is finished. Are you both perfectly clear on this?"

Neither man spoke but both got up from the table and left the saloon.

As Jerrod and his friends were walking out, the bartender said, "You men made yourselves some friends here today but you made a couple of enemies, too. Don't you take those two lightly. They're just as apt to lay up somewhere and back shoot you. You be on your guard."

"Thanks for the advice, friend. We'll be careful."

Jerrod led them from the small saloon and across the sun-blistered street.

Seated around a table in the cafe, Ty turned to Jerrod. "I'm not sure I fully understand what happened in there."

Jerrod answered, "The plaintiff decided to drop the charges and the judge decided to return to his former occupation, whatever that was."

Ty still looked mystified. "Well, I'm sure that's a good explanation but it would probably be better if I knew what a plaintiff is."

They all laughed and Jerrod said, "That's the one making the complaint."

Jonathon thought the situation over for a few moments and then asked, "Just exactly what was your occupation before the war, Jerrod?"

"I farmed part of the time."

Jonathon couldn't hold back a grin. "And what did you do the remainder of the time?"

Jerrod seemed reluctant to answer but finally did. "I did some lawyer work when there was a call for it. Our small town couldn't keep a lawyer busy all the time."

Mac looked as if he had found a fly in his soup. "You're a lawyer? You been to school and all that?"

"I'm afraid so," Jerrod answered with a nonchalant smile on his face.

Mac shook his head in wonder. "We rode all those miles together through scorching heat, downpours of rain, through swollen rivers, slept on the same lumpy ground, fought outlaws and halfway starved together and you never thought to tell me that you were a lawyer? It ain't as bad as if you were a banker, but still, a lawyer? Seems like you might have given a hint or something. You know, kind of prepare me for that news."

Ty laughed and looked at Mac. "You want me to shoot him for you, Mac?"

"That might be excessive but we'll see what happens in the future. Might have to resort to that eventually."

Jonathon, Ty and Jerrod were all laughing and Mac was having trouble keeping a serious face.

Jonathon said, "Mac, there's folks that think becoming a lawyer is a badge of honor, showing hard work and achievement."

"I never met such as that."

Ty had the last word on the subject. "Well, that was good lawyer work in the saloon today. Better than some dumb cow nurse could have done. Left to myself, I would have probably settled it with my gun and I'm not sure if that would work out too well or not. I owe you my thanks, Jerrod."

The ride home took them until early evening. They rode warily but saw no sign of Hodgson or Bradshaw.

19

THE GATHERED CATTLE HAD TO BE HELD FURTHER AND FURTHER from the ranch headquarters as the grass was eaten down. With everyone home from the fall drive, there were enough men to work on both the cattle gather and to guard the herd. There were the normal problems of bunch quitters and the constant fear of stampede but the large crew had no real difficulties. And the two bell animals were acting more and more like herd leaders, seeming to enjoy the task.

Hiram had been working with his red dogs. He didn't trust them near the herd so he had isolated just a few cattle in a makeshift corral out past the small barn. The first time he turned the dogs into the corral they worked the cattle into a frenzy that resulted in a broken corral fence and a wild chase across the prairie, the dogs baying and howling and the cattle terrified.

"That worked well," Jessie said with a grin.

"Young lady," answered her father, "you go find some dishes to wash or something."

Jessie laughed. "I think I might learn more right here."

With patience and a few more failures, the dogs had started to figure out what their master wanted. Hiram hoped that by spring the dogs might be an asset on the next drive north and perhaps even in the brush during the gather.

When the dogs seemed to have the hang of it, Hiram called Bobby and Jeremiah over to the corral. "Now pay attention; this is serious business. If you boys can pick up on this dog thing, we just might have something going here. I want you to watch me for a bit and then try it yourselves, one by one."

The boys sat on the top rail of the corral and watched as Hiram put the dogs through their paces. Hiram had set up a small "bush" in the center of the corral. He tied the dogs outside the corral while he worked the steers into this bit of brush made of cut-off tree stems and branches buried butt down in the corral dirt. He then brought the dogs in one by one and told them to ease the cattle out. With a soothing voice and gentle hand commands, Hiram got what he wanted from the dogs.

Instead of the dogs charging in and running the cows, they slowly entered the bush and, with barks and small nips on hind legs, drove the cattle out and into the corner of the corral.

After an hour of this, Hiram turned the cattle into another corral and put the dogs out. He then brought in a few more cows and a couple of young bulls that he had kept back for later use.

"Your turn, Bobby. See if you can get the same work out of the dogs. You have to remember that we don't want to terrify or run the cattle. We only want to get them out of the bush to where the *vaqueros* can herd them. Now come and try."

The boys and the dogs were old friends and the boys had no trouble at all doing what their father had done.

After two hours of working the steers, Hiram said, "Well done, boys. Now you go and get Walker and a couple of others and we'll take these dogs down to that brush just west of here. I know there's a few head hiding in there because I rode down there yesterday and I seen them. That will be a good test for all this work."

Most of the men were with the herd so Mac joined his father and brought Margo and Jessie with him. "You girls have seen it done often enough although you haven't been involved your-selves. You ride to the far side of that brush and I'll stay here.

Dad and the boys will take the dogs around the other end and we'll see what happens. You girls watch yourselves. Some of these brutes were born with a troublesome attitude. You look after yourselves and your horses first. We can always get more cattle."

Margo said to Jessie as they rode away, "These brutes aren't the only thing with a troublesome attitude."

"I wouldn't say too much about that, were I you."

"Well, at least he invited us along. That's something."

"I'm probably not the one to give advice, Margo, but I'd ease up a bit if I were you. That is, if I rightly understand your goal and I think I do."

Margo took a slow look at Jessie, gave a slight nod, and said no more.

Hiram was too far away to let Mac know the dogs were turned loose but the howling told him what he needed to know. It took perhaps ten minutes before the first steer emerged from the bush. Jessie went to ride forward.

Mac hollered, "Wait! There's more."

Jessie stopped and rode back to Margo. In a matter of minutes, eight more wild brutes ran from the bush looking for something to fight or to blame for being disturbed. Mac and the two girls rode slowly in behind the cattle and kept them moving away from the brush.

Bobby and Jeremiah came charging around the outside of the bush laughing and cheering.

Hiram dismounted and called the dogs. He slipped a short piece of rope through each of their collar rings to keep them from following the cattle and, down on one knee, rubbed each dog behind the ear and told them what good dogs they were. "Let's go home."

The two boys caught up with Mac and the girls, pushing the cattle toward the home corral. There they would be branded before being turned into the gathered herd.

That evening, Hiram said to his two younger sons, "Boys, I would like it if tomorrow morning you would put a team on that small wagon and drive these dogs down to where the *vaqueros* and

Ty are working. Won't do much good if the dogs are footsore before they get there so you ride them down in the wagon. You handle them yourselves and make sure that no one else gets them riled up. If they do good, you keep them there. If it doesn't work so well, you load them back up and bring them home. Make sure you keep them well fed and watered and whatever you do, don't let them run any cattle. One run could undo all this hard training."

When the boys weren't back in a week with the dogs, he figured the idea must be working.

On their return from Wayward, the men had discussed the potential risk from rancher Hodgson and others like him. The big ranches had suffered, too, during the recent conflict but some of them had the resources to recover quickly. Resources of authority, if not actually of gold coin.

Mac figured that the worst of human nature was to be found in the wealthy as well as the poor and struggling and perhaps even more so in those that used to be wealthy but were so no longer.

Mac said to the men, "Pay to keep our eyes peeled for trouble. This gathered herd might become a serious temptation to someone who has allowed his Christian upbringing to become faded from memory."

Mac talked with Bill. "I would appreciate if you would do something. If you thought you could handle those dogs, I'd like if you would ride south and find Ty and the *vaqueros*. Have the boys work with you a bit with the dogs and see how it goes. If things work out all right, you stay there and send Ty and the two boys back up here. I have something else for them to do. How would you feel about that?"

When Bill was saddled up, ready to go, Jessie teased, "You watch out for those young *senoritas*, Bill."

Bill pretended he hadn't heard and rode off.

Ty and the boys returned with glowing reports of the work the dogs were doing and how quickly the herd was growing.

Mac sent Ty and a *vaquero* named Ernesto off on a scout to buy horses. With a larger crew for the next drive, there would be more need of horseflesh. Bobby and Jeremiah went along to help drive the horse herd. They had wanted to see the countryside and get away from their herding duties anyway so the task pleased them.

A couple of evenings later, Margo approached Mac and Jonathon who were whittling on sticks while they drank their after-supper coffee, enjoying the evening and helping the sun go down.

"I don't suppose you two would have noticed but there are too many women here for one kitchen. I'm going to take my turn with the herd. There is just no sense in me sitting around here all winter doing nothing. Mac, you pick me out a good horse and saddle and I'll take my turn in the morning."

No such a thought had ever crossed Mac's mind and he wasn't ready for it now. "You'll do no such a thing. Why, I never heard of such a thought. I'll hear no more about it now. I'm not going to be responsible for someone getting hurt who shouldn't be there in the first place." He stood up as if to leave.

Margo, hands on hips, fired back with, "I wasn't really asking for your permission, Mr. McTavish. If I recall correctly, you started me thinking this way when you called me out to help when there were no men available. I enjoyed it and I don't see as I gave you any room for complaint. And anyway, we're partners and we all have some say. And I say I'm going to ride herd. I'll be here in the morning. There had better be a horse and saddle waiting for me. And you don't have to take on any responsibility that doesn't suit you."

Mac looked ready to burst but Jonathon spoke up, saving Mac from saying something he might come to regret.

"Now wait a minute here, Mac," Jonathon said and laughed. "Why can't she take a part? It's a long drive in the spring and some experience here this winter might make it possible for her to be a really big help on the drive. Anyway, what can it hurt? And as far as that goes, Nancy and Jessie might want to give it a try, too. The two mothers have laid claim to the kitchen and I doubt as how anything will change their minds. So the young women aren't needed there. Come on, brother-in-law, loosen up a bit. I'll bet they can do a fine job."

Margo gave Jonathon a strange look. "Jessie's already riding herd. It was her idea first. She's out there now with my father and the *vaqueros*. Dad says she's doing well, too. If she can do it, there's just no reason at all that I can't. And I'll bet my singing voice is a lot better than the most of you. I'm going to do it, starting in the morning. But not Nancy."

Jonathon returned Margo's strange look. "Why not Nancy? She's a good rider. I'll bet she'll want to do it."

As Margo turned to walk away, she said, "I wonder if all men are dumb or just the ones I know."

The men watched her.

"Now what in the world was that all about?" asked Jonathon.

"I have no idea at all," answered Mac. "I find there's a lot of things I have no understanding of. I might just as well go pick out a horse, else I'll never hear the end of it."

Jonathon waited for a short space of time and then wandered over to where Nancy was sitting in the setting sun peeling potatoes. He squatted down beside her.

"Had a talk with Margo. She and Jessie are taking a turn riding herd but when I mentioned that you might join them, Margo said you wouldn't be doing that. Actually called me dumb. Can you believe that? Everyone knows you're a good rider and you're not really needed in the kitchen so I suspect your secret is out."

There was silence for a full minute while Nancy peeled another potato.

"I've been meaning to talk to you about that. I know it was my idea to not say anything but I've seen the other girls looking at me with some suspicion. So you're probably right. Our secret is out. We might just as well tell folks and then you won't have to act dumb anymore." She smiled at him. "I wouldn't want to be responsible for ruining your reputation."

Jonathon reached over and took her hand, stopping the peeling. "All right, I'll leave it with you. You tell when you're of a mind to. It will bring up all kinds of possible problems in people's minds, like babies being born on the trail in a wagon and such, but at least the pressure of trying to keep it secret will be gone."

"Well, probably everyone on the ranch is already wondering so it's really not much of a secret. Except for Walker, of course. He won't have noticed anything. I believe an eagle could land on his head and he wouldn't do more than brush it off so he could get back to work. No, Walker wouldn't notice a little thing like that my dresses don't fit anymore and that you and I are going to have a baby."

"Well," said Jonathon, "I was just going to start a job of work before this all started. Guess I'd better get to it. You still feeling all right?"

"Yes, thank you, I'm feeling just fine. And I have spuds to peel."

Within ten days, Ty and his small crew were back with nineteen horses. They came in from the south, the horses running flat out and the drovers steering them toward the yard.

Hiram saw them coming and gave a yell toward the barn. "Open that corral gate," he hollered. "Horses coming."

By that time, the thunder of hooves was overshadowing all else in the small yard. Mac and Jonathon ran to open the gate. They had barely enough time to and jump out of the way before Bobby slapped the shoulder of one of the lead horses, turning him toward the corral. Ty did the same on the other flank and the horses flooded into the corral with a swirling of dust along with the din of hooves and yelling drovers.

Mac swung the gate closed and turned to Ty and the other drovers. "I reckon you found that to be exciting, boys, and I will admit that you got everyone's attention. But just the same it wasn't smart. There's women and little kids here that those horses could have trampled and men, too, for that matter. You ever do anything like that again I'll take the double of a rope to you."

"Relax, big brother," answered Jeremiah. "We had everything under control. You really have to learn to relax. You might not live any longer that way but you'll enjoy the time more. Margo might explain that to you if you were to ask her." Jeremiah's grin angered Mac almost as much as the charging horses had.

Ad walked out to look over the horses. He entered the corral and walked among them, rubbing their shoulders and looking them over.

"What do you think, Ad," asked Mac who was leaning on the top rail of the corral. "You told us one time that you had some experience breaking horses to ride. Think anything can be done with this bunch?"

Ad walked around the horses a few more moments before replying. "I would say they've been ridden but that doesn't mean they're trained or can be trusted. I'll get a start on them in the morning. I'll set Bill to helping me. He rode in about an hour ago. He's down at the house and his mother has him sitting at the table with her trying her best to fatten him up. He said one of the *vaqueros* was doing better with the dogs than he was so he wasn't needed. Be good to give him something different to do. Might be good to brand these nags, too, in case any decide to head for home."

Most of the crew was still eating breakfast the next morning when the turmoil of stomping hooves, whinnying horses and yelling men arose from the barnyard. The men dropped their forks and rushed outside in time to see one of the new horses put its rump and hind legs in the air, fishtail completely around and dump Bill out of the saddle onto the ranch yard dirt. Bill did a neat feet-over-head flip in the air and landed with a dust-raising thud. He lay there trying to catch his breath as the men rushed over from the house.

Bobby and Jeremiah were yelling and waving their hats at the horse, trying to haze it back into a corner where the corral met the barn and where they could catch it again. They didn't see Mac bearing down on them.

Mac was so angry he was sputtering. When he finally formed his lips to get out real words, he said, "Of all the confounded foolishness; I never seen the like. You two buttons are just bound and determined to either get yourselves killed or maimed and injure a good horse in the doing of it. Don't you ever do anything so downright dumb again. I should have known when you ran those horses through the yard last night that you couldn't be trusted to act with common sense. Not you nor Bill either. Not a lick of sense in the three of you. Now catch that horse and turn him into the corral. Be gentle. Ad intends to bring these nags along gentle. You put that horse away and go ride herd. You've done enough here for one early morning."

"We ain't had breakfast yet," answered Jeremiah.

"You can have breakfast tomorrow morning. Now get out there and try to remember that all our futures depend on those cattle."

Ad had helped Bill to his feet. When he determined that nothing was broken and that Bill had no more serious hurt than smashed lips and a bleeding nose, he lit into him even more harshly than Mac had done with his brothers.

Bill and the two younger boys looked contrite but Mac wasn't at all sure that it would hold.

Margo arrived with a cloth and a pan of water and was all set to help Bill clean himself up.

Ad told her, "You take that cloth and water and leave him alone. He has work to do and it starts now." The words left no room for discussion.

Margo pointed at Bill's face. "He's bleeding,"

"I said go.

Margo returned to the house and Mac thought to himself first time I ever saw that girl do anything she was told.

Ad was giving Bill no reprieve. "Now, Mr. Horse Trainer, you get in there and slip a halter on another horse and bring him out here. Easy like."

Bill wiped his bleeding nose on his sleeve and went to catch a horse.

20

Once they got a pattern going, the horse training went well, mostly with Ad supervising and Bill doing the riding. Bobby and Jeremiah got the chance to help from time to time. They kept it gentle and the horses responded well to the treatment.

Ty had gone south and soon arrived back with the *vaqueros*, driving another four hundred longhorns. They now had well over one thousand head on grass. It was taking more riders to herd them as the grass became eaten down. They were herding most of the horses also as the supply of cut hay was very limited.

Margo and Jessie were taking regular turns herding and Mac had said no more about it. He had ridden out once in a pouring cold rain to relieve Margo but she refused to leave before her shift was up. Mac had purchased a slicker in Fort Worth but she refused the borrow of that, too. It was obvious that Jessie was not going to leave before Margo so they both stubbornly rode out the storm soaked to the skin as if it was a competition.

Later, back at the house, warming herself by the fire and wrapped in a blanket, Margo told her mother about Mac's offer which raised a quizzical look and a short response.

"Young lady, I see you pining away and then I see you being stubbornly foolish. You might live to regret some of this."

Margo pulled the blanket more tightly around herself and stared into the fire, saying no more.

The cold evenings and the skim of ice on the water pail in the morning convinced the crew that summer was truly over. Hiram called for attention at the evening meal.

"Folks," he said, "if we don't get a little more set up for winter, we just might find ourselves in an uncomfortable situation. I can tell you that, for my family, we need some warmer clothing and something to replace this worn-out footwear. Y'all might be in the same situation. I've talked with Ty and he tells me there's a fair-to-middling general store at this Wayward place. I'm going to suggest that we make up a group of us and go on in there. Most of the men will have to stay with the cattle but maybe we could make up a list of things wanted and shop for each other. Or the ones that don't go now could make another trip in a day or two." He stopped talking and looked around at the gathering.

"Sounds good to me," answered Ad. "The boys have been working hard on the horses. A day off probably won't set their work habits back too far. Could be there's a few of those nags that could benefit from a ride of that sort, too. Can you ladies be ready by morning?"

The general agreement was that everyone could be ready to go and that each man staying behind would make out a list of things wanted. Luke greased the wheels of the big wagon and got it ready. Ad caught up the wagon team and put it in the barn for the night with a gallon of oats each. The men all wrote out lists.

Margo walked over to where Mac was writing out his list. "Would you trust me with your shopping?"

After a few moments, Mac looked up from where he was sitting. "I never once thought of you doing that. I was going to ask my mother to take my list. Why would you want to do that for me?"

"I might do other things for you, too, if you weren't so almighty self-sufficient." She immediately wanted to take the words back. "I'm sorry. I didn't mean to sound like a nag. I just thought it might be good to do something for you. I am fully aware of all the things you do for the rest of us. Maybe this will just return a little bit of that."

"Well, I'd be pleased if you want to do it. I'd like a sheep-hide coat if they have one. But wait to see that everyone else gets their wants before you pick one out. I need some long handles, too. If that bothers you, just let one of the men take that part."

"I've scrubbed enough pairs of long handles. I expect I can manage to pick out some new ones without it stunting my mind too much."

Margo took Mac's list and the gold coins he offered and stored them carefully away.

Her mother had been watching from a distance. She smiled and nodded at Margo. "You're learning."

The group left for Wayward in the early morning and returned late that same day with a loaded-down wagon.

Mac saw them coming. As they neared the house, he pulled his hat off and scratched his unruly hair. "I swear, that looks almighty like a cow you're dragging along behind that wagon, Dad. We ain't exactly short of cows that you had to bring another from town."

"Well, son," Hiram responded. "Unless you plan to try to milk one of those longhorns, I expect you might find this critter useful."

"Who's going to milk it, Pa, and don't you be looking my way?"

"You needn't worry yourself, son," answered Hiram. "No one mentioned you when we saw this cow. Anyway, she's not going to freshen for a couple of weeks and we'll have it all sorted out before then."

The wagon was unloaded and the purchases distributed. Margo called Mac to come see what she had chosen for him.

Mac carefully removed the string and the paper wrapping knowing it could all be used again for some need in the future. He lifted each item and studied the pile. At the very bottom was a waterproofed canvas coat with a sheep's wool lining and a pair of warm gloves. The coat was the only item he tried on. He swung his arms, testing for fit.

"You did real well." He smiled at Margo. "Thanks."

"I'm glad you like the coat and all," answered Margo. "I've been a bit nervous that you might not. There's not a lot of choice in Wayward."

"Nothing to be nervous about. I don't know as I ever had a better."

The group made another trip just before Christmas. The supplies in the general store were limited but a few things were found that would make passable gifts for the littlest children. The adults agreed among themselves that for this Christmas they would be content to just be together. Gifts could wait for another year when the shopping held a little more promise.

Luke and Ty went hunting and came home with three turkeys. "Not exactly grain-fed fat," Luke said. "But I can guarantee that they're turkeys. Least ways that's what we would call them back home. I expect they'll do."

Ty guided some of the women to where a few pecan trees grew by a stream where they gathered a good many of the nuts. Christmas was a simple affair with good food, a few songs sung together and a few stories told. Hiram told the Christmas story from memory.

Mac insisted on riding herd during the celebration. Margo joined him although he had claimed that he would be all right by himself.

"You spend too much time alone working all the time. No need to spend Christmas alone. I'll saddle up and be right there."

21

WINTER WASN'T LONG BY THE CALENDAR BUT WITH THE CROWDED conditions and with the wind and occasionally rain sifting through the walls and roof of the hastily thrown up picket shelters, the weeks seemed to drag.

Cattle kept arriving and it was becoming more and more difficult to find good grass. It was more difficult to watch for trouble, too, as the herd was further away and more spread out.

There were other ranches within a few miles and they all had cattle looking for grass. As the herd fed closer and closer to the other ranches, a line of riders was formed to keep the herds apart. The other ranches sent out riders also. If the herds got mixed, there would be days or weeks wasted in sorting them all out.

Mac and his father spent considerable time visiting the surrounding ranches buying cows for Mac's ranch herd as well as several likely-looking young bulls.

"I need young stuff for keeping and we don't have the time to gather that many," he told the ranchers. "I want about one thousand head in total plus the bulls and I'll pay a fair price in gold coin come spring. I'll want you to keep them close to your ranch over the winter and to try to settle them down a bit. I don't want them right out of the breaks. There's enough to go wrong on a drive without we try to drive stock that doesn't want to be driven. You gather them, brand them with my iron and, come spring, you have a sure sale."

Several ranchers had been talking about a drive north, making up a herd with their neighbors. But that plan would have to wait for the rails in Kansas which were at least a year away. It also meant they had breeding cows they were more than willing to sell to Mac. Most ranchers were desperately cash poor. Mac sealed the deals and earned their undying gratitude by paying a modest amount up front, giving the ranchers cash to make necessary purchases. For some, it was the first serious cash they had seen since before the war.

TY and his crew turned back any branded stock they came across. "There's thousands of head of branded stuff down in those breaks," he told Mac. "Brands from close-by ranches and some I never saw before. Be a sight of work for the ranchers to dig them out but with the northern markets opening up and the rails being built, my bet would be that by spring most of those critters will be brought back to the home ranches. The other good news is that we've found a goodly number of Bar H stuff, too. It will be good to see my brand back on my own land."

Signs of new life in the surrounding countryside created restlessness in the crew and added a sense of urgency to the preparations for the drive. The nights were still cold and a fire needed in the stone and clay fireplaces in the houses but the harsh winds had ceased. A welcome rain felt warm and Mac convinced himself that the grass was starting to green up, maybe just a mite. A honking, V-shaped flight of geese heading north left everyone in the ranch yard staring at the sky. Even the cattle were showing more life and the riders were anxious to be under way.

Mac couldn't see any real difference in Luke over the months except that he didn't grin as much since the visit by the make-believe sheriff. But there was a change in Jerrod. He was often seen sitting his horse rereading a letter that had caught up to him in Wayward, an answer to one that he had sent north earlier. He was sometimes melancholy and spent considerable time looking toward the north. He hadn't talked about it and no one asked.

It was clearly time to be making final decisions and to get the drive pointed north.

Mac called a meeting. The herd was left in the care of the *vaqueros* they had hired. "We need to keep this short," Mac said. "I don't like having just the *vaqueros* at the herd although they're all good men. But I thought we should run over the plan again just so we all know what we hope to do. You all know that a couple of us were down to Wayward yesterday. The news there, brought in on the telegraph, is that the rail lines are moving into Kansas and that no one is fussing much anymore about bringing in longhorns. So my guess would be that drives to the rails could be done in about one year. But for now, we have a market waiting for us and no real competition for the trail grass.

"We have just over two thousand head on grass and even with the winter conditions they seem to have gained weight. The grass looks dead but the cattle are doing well on it. But there's not much feed left and we can't wait for it to grow. We need to get under way in a few days, hoping the weather is loosening winter's grip as we head north. If we manage to get a few head to each of the forts and the eight hundred head that Gibson wants this spring, we'll still have some left and we'll have had a pretty good run. There's a lot of miles, a lot of rivers and a lot of ifs between this here ranch and those forts but we have it to do. I would like to start the drive within one week."

Jerrod, always thinking ahead, asked, "What comes after this drive?"

Everyone knew this time would come and that Jerrod's question would need an answer but so far no one had faced right up to it. Now Mac had no choice.

"Luke and Jerrod will recall," Mac started, "that we agreed this partnership was not a permanent thing, that I have other plans. I agreed to stay till the job was done. Well, we get this herd delivered and I'll guess it's about done. We get this herd to market and collect our money without any of us gets killed or maimed, we can call it a good go. You all know that I have been buying breeding cows from the local ranches. Those are for my own ranch and brand."

Jerrod said, "For those that might be wondering, what Mac's saying was the original agreement between the three of us. I would say, Mac, that you have done more than we agreed to and I wish you luck on your own ranch."

Mac continued, "The reconstruction government gangs are a little slow getting to this far-flung corner of Texas but we had better believe they will get here eventually. I don't want to be here when they take over. If we can move these cattle to market before they start to trouble the likes of us, we can call the venture successful and maybe avoid a site of misery as well.

"We've made considerable more money than ever I expected to make and I've been thinking of things to spend some of it on. Y'all will have your own plans but I plan to go to ranching. I don't like this hot, dry country as much as I thought I would after spending so many cold nights during my time in uniform. I've been told about a green valley along the eastern slope of the Rockies out west in Colorado where it rains once in a while and where the grass grows tall. There's a little winter there but that don't sound as bad as it used to after all this heat. I figure to go find me that valley."

"You ever been out there, Mac?" asked Ad.

"Not all the way but close. I drove wagon on the Santa Fe Trail. We cut south before reaching the mountains but I could see enough to know it's a pretty country with high-up mountains. That whole country is high as far as that goes. Going west you don't seem to be climbing but the animals know by how hard the wagon pull is. A lot of that land is five- or six-thousand feet up and the mountains twice that or more. Hard on the animals. They tire more easily.

"But there's grass as far as the eye can see. Mostly just grass in Kansas but west into Colorado there's forests. No shortage of building materials or firewood. Good looking country."

Margo's eyes seldom left Mac but she didn't think he noticed.

He seemed to have eyes only for the cattle and the work to be done. If Margo knew how much Mac had thought about her for the past year, she would have shown some considerable surprise.

Margo didn't often enter into the discussions with the men. Now she did. "Are you going to find this valley all by yourself, the way you do most things?" She immediately could have bitten her tongue but the words were out and couldn't be brought back.

Mrs. Adkins gasped and the men all looked at their coffee cups. Ad shook his head and Luke grinned at Mac. Mac straightened up and looked uncomfortably around the group.

He seldom acted to protect himself, having mostly an accepting nature. But this challenge seemed to bother him. "No, I don't figure to go myself unless you all have had enough of me. You're my friends and family and I was hoping we could go together. I had in mind to keep enough *vaqueros* on to drive this big herd of cows. Drive them north and west until I find my valley and hold them there for breeding. I figure to buy graded bulls but I'll take along enough longhorn bulls until that can happen. I expect there might still be an Indian or two where I figure to ranch but I'll just have to deal with that as best I can. There's no reason any of you as wants to can't locate a place, too.

"If some of you wanted to make more drives, you could find cattle enough and the *vaqueros* to work with but this will be my last drive."

Mac waited for one of the partners to speak and when no one did, he continued, "Now, as to doing it all myself and since you brought it up, Margo, I guess you'd not be too much of a burden if you wanted to come along. That is, if your mother can spare you from the work and if your father would approve. Generally, a man and a woman would talk about these things privately and I had it in mind. But there's just not much privacy the way we've been living. I guess we'll just have a public proposal. Comes of living too close together for too long, I'd guess."

"Walker Samuel McTavish," sputtered Margo. "Of all the

boneheaded proposals. So you don't think I'd be too much of a burden. Well, let me tell you...,"

"Margo." Ad laughed. "Daughter, shut up and sit down. I swear, woman, sometimes you could drive a bird right off its nest. I'll allow as how some of this is a little unusual but these are unusual times. We've done mostly work for all of the past many months. It's left little time for private matters. Still, you two have gotten to know each other about as well as any two people can. If you was to say yes, no matter how the proposal was done, your mother and I would approve and be pleased to."

"That's all well and good," Margo fumed. "But a girl wants to hear the words. That big overgrown boy is not going to get away that easy. Cowboy, you have to say the words."

Mac grew red everywhere that wasn't covered by hat or shirt and said, "Margo, I'd admire if you'd agree to travel with me as my partner...,"

"Not partner," interrupted Margo. "Wife, married, you have to say the words. There's nothing happening until you say the words."

Mac knew he was as close to anger as he had been since the run-in with Mr. Jones on their first drive. By the time he was over that anger, one outlaw had lain dead in the grass and two were hanging from their saddle ropes. He had no desire to turn his marriage proposal into a bloodbath like that. His solution was to walk over to his horse, step into the saddle and ride out to the herd.

There was a stunned silence around the gathered group as Mac rode away. Even Luke had quit grinning. Jessie, who had given up her private competition with Margo shortly after seeing Ty for the first time, found herself feeling sorry for Margo. Slowly, everyone found something to do somewhere else; even Margo's mother, who left for the house directing the smaller children ahead of her.

Margo and her father were left alone, looking at the ground. "Well, girl, I don't know as I ever saw anything quite like that before."

Margo was weeping until her shoulders were shaking.

Finally, she managed to say, "Pa, what am I going to do? I'm so in love my heart hurts. I think about this man every waking moment. And then the next thing I know I've said something that I'm going to regret. Sometimes I don't even know where the words come from. I've waited and prayed that he would ask me to marry him and then when he did, I made a mess of it. What am I going to do, Pa? I love him so."

Ad reached over and gave Margo a hug. "Since you asked, I might suggest that right yonder there stands a saddled horse. Why don't you take the borrow of it and go find Mac. Tell him what you just told me. And no more harsh words. Mac's not much for words, you should know that by now and accept it. But there's more than words that are important in this life. You're never going to find a better man. Let him be the way he is. I'm pretty sure he will accept you the way you are if you'll just learn to bite your tongue."

Margo found Mac sitting his horse on the far side of the herd. She rode slowly around so as not to spook the cattle or Mac either. With a lump in her throat and an ache in her heart, she slowly rode up to face him.

Mac sat stoically, both strong hands wrapped around the saddle horn. It was impossible to read the look on his face but clearly he was in no mood for any more nonsense.

Margo hesitated, finally saying, "Mac, I would admire to talk to you. Try again, kind of." She hurried on before anything could break her train of thought. "I've said too many harsh things to you over the past year but I didn't really mean any of them. It was mostly my way of protecting myself. I fell in love with you the minute I saw you riding into our cattle-wrecked camp with you all full of apologies and offers of help. My feelings right that minute scared me half to death. You were nothing at all like the boys I knew from home, all strong and sure of yourself. I didn't know what to do so I tried to drive you away with harsh words. Those harsh words became a habit mostly because I couldn't see you noticing anything but cattle. You never seemed to pay the slightest attention to me but I was watching you every minute. And every minute I was going deeper in love until it hurt just to be near you. Mac, I love you with all my heart and I would very much wish to be your wife. I apologize for my foolishness this morning. Can you forgive me? Can we start again?"

The two were silent for an uncomfortable length of time. Finally, Mac spoke, "Rightly, I'm not much with words. Mostly what I know is work. And war although I hope to never see another. You may think that I haven't seen you but you would be wrong. I nearly fell out of my saddle when I saw you for the first time, climbing down from that wagon after the cattle were cleared from your camp. All my growing years I had a shadow of an idea of the woman God had set aside for me. I kept that idea before me all through the war. That and the idea of trying to stay alive.

"Many a cold, scared night I huddled in my blanket listening to the cannons pound out their death and thought about finding just the right woman. I knew that right woman was you the minute I saw you. But you weren't at all welcoming so I tried to put the thought out of my mind and concentrate on the work to be done."

"I'm sorry I wasn't more welcoming," Margo said with a shy smile.

"Well, I have most certainly seen you. Seen you working after others had gone to their bedrolls. Seen you looking after the little kids. Seen you cooking and serving food in difficult circumstances, fighting dust and flies. Seen you stubbornly riding in the rain when you didn't have to. Seen you sacrificing your own comfort to help the others. Seen you mature into a beautiful, desirable woman. Oh, yes, I have most certainly seen you.

"But I remembered getting my hand torn on a thorn bush when I wasn't but maybe six years old. I didn't enjoy that at all. And as much as my heart said that you were the one for me, my head was telling me to be watchful of the thorns."

Margo smiled perhaps the first genuine smile that Mac felt was just for him. "I'm sorry about the thorns. If I promise no more thorns, will you take another look and reconsider the question you were trying to ask me back yonder?"

"You have to understand something, Margo. Poverty and war didn't leave much room for lightness or gentleness. Or happiness either for that matter. The war is over and so is the poverty unless we meet up with circumstances that take it from us. And maybe in time I can learn gentleness. If you can live with that, I would sure like to have you spend that learning time with me."

"I have some problems of my own to work on," answered Margo. "Perhaps we could work on them together."

"If you would agree to be my wife, Margo, that would be a long step toward fixing some things anyway."

"I would love to be your wife. I've wanted to be your wife for all of the past year. Yes. If you want a really short answer, yes. Wife. I like the sound of that. And Mrs. Walker Samuel McTavish sounds great, too."

"Then it's settled and we'll forget all about thorn bushes and poverty. But I am real anxious to know who told you my middle name. I've been wondering a little about that."

Margo laughed and said, "I'd better get back. I'm sure everyone in camp has only one thought this afternoon. Are we going to have a wedding or a burying?"

"You go tell them. I have cattle to mind."

"Mac, you've never even held my hand, never mind kissed me."

"I don't have any real experience in that area but perhaps that's something we can learn together, too." Mac put his hand gently behind Margo's head and pulled her toward him.

22

LUKE AND JERROD RODE OUT TO SEE MAC LATER THAT DAY. LUKE had his grin back. "Thought you'd never get around to it."

Jerrod reached to shake Mac's hand. "We're all real happy for both you and Margo although some of us had about given up." he said with a smile.

Mac figured it was best to say nothing.

Jerrod continued, "We had another meeting. This will be our last drive. Everyone wants to have it that way. I don't know as everyone will go to find that green valley but no one wants to stay here. Jessie might be the one exception."

"Jessie?" asked Mac with considerable surprise. "Why would she want to stay here?"

Luke answered, "Friend, sometimes I don't know how you get your shirt buttoned straight of a morning as poor as you see. Jessie was pretty determined to stay here the minute she laid eyes on Ty. I just don't know how you miss things like that." He was grinning again.

"I just plain didn't see it. Busy I guess. But that's between those two. I have troubles enough for one man."

Luke changed the subject. "We've been considering. We have a lot of cattle here and a sizable investment. And I'm not too sure we've seen the last of that phony sheriff and his friends or that land-stealing rancher that tried to push Ty aside either. Were they to let their greed get in the way of their common sense, we might expect a visit. And I'm afraid that carpetbag judge is just a warning for what's still to come."

The three men were silent for a few moments while Mac thought this over.

"I was expecting trouble right after the foolishness with that make-believe judge but I had pretty much put it out of my mind lately. But I do believe your thoughts need some attention paid to them. What do you two suggest?"

Jerrod responded, "Our suggestion is that we hire all the *vaqueros* we can get our hands on. There's some expense to that but losing the herd would be pretty expensive, too. We are expecting a drive of more cattle within a few days. There will be maybe ten or twelve men making that drive. Let's see if they will delay their return south for a few days. Just as insurance. We had been planning on hiring some of them for the drive north anyway."

That's good thinking," Mac said. "But let's take it even further. What would you think if we had Ty ride south right away? These are his friends. He could tell them what we're concerned with. I'm of the opinion that some of the *vaqueros* would rather fight than do almost anything else."

Luke turned his horse. "I'll see to it right away."

Ty listened to the plan as Luke explained it. He saddled up immediately, inviting Bill to ride with him. He was back in two days leading a group of tough-looking, well-armed *vaqueros*.

The *vaqueros* headed out to the herd after Mac thanked them for coming with Ty translating although Mac had picked up a bit of Mex lingo.

"I didn't see Manuel," Mac said to Ty.

"He'll be along in a few days. He and a couple of others are escorting Mama and Imelda in the wagon. He has the dogs riding the wagon, too. The *vaqueros* love those dogs. You might have a problem claiming ownership again. There's still a handful of *vaqueros* coming along also, driving the last of the cattle."

"I wasn't expecting the women," Mac said. "That surprises me a bit. Do they know this is a one-way drive, that we won't be coming back?"

Ty smiled at Mac and shook his head a little. "As soon as I told the plan, Mama started to gather things they need for the trip north. She plans on making sure the men are well fed and you'd be wasting your time trying to talk her out of going. Or Imelda either for that matter."

"Luke and Jerrod are sorting all of that out. I'm happy to be out of it."

Ty spoke up again, "There's another thing. Remember I told you I had a sister who ran off in a wagon with a neighbor boy when the war started? Todd, his name is. They're back, riding the same old wagon but now with a boy riding a horse as big as his dad's, stuck there like a burr in a blanket, and a little girl sitting beside her ma as she drives the wagon. They spent all this time in Old Mexico. They all look good so I expect the years have been kind to them. They're coming along with Manuel and the other wagon."

"Interesting that they should show up just now."

"It didn't just happen. Seems the Mex's knew all along just where they were. A couple of them rode over and suggested it was time to come home. I guess it was time all right and I wish them well. There might still be a couple of old war dogs around here who won't forget that refusal to wear the gray but we'll have to see what happens.

23

THE CAMP WAS A TURMOIL OF ACTIVITY WHEN THE WAGONS AND the additional cattle from the south arrived. The cattle had been branded Bar-H as they were driven from the breaks so they drove the new bunch right up to where the larger group was gathered.

The women stepped down from the wagons and Hiram and Ad immediately led the teams over to the barn where they were rubbed down and given a good feed. They cleaned up the wagons, greased the wheels and re-nailed any loose boards. They then drove the wagons down to the creek to soak the wheels that had dried out over the winter.

Ad set Bill, Bobby and Jeremiah to currying horses, checking saddles and gear, and making what repairs were necessary. Ad himself checked each horse for shoes and packed up the extra shoes as well as the anvil and what blacksmithing tools were available.

Mac, Luke and several *vaqueros* set out to pick up the breeding stock from the surrounding ranches. Mac had talked with Manuel about hiring all of the *vaqueros* and the deal had been struck. They would drive two herds, keeping them separated by at least a couple of miles. One bell animal would go with each herd.

The ranchers had the cattle ready in anticipation of seeing more of Mac's gold coin. Ad had put together several Bar-M irons which the ranchers used to brand Mac's gather. The Bar-M would become Mac's brand after the larger drive was completed. Each rancher thanked Mac with a firm handshake and one rancher's wife wept openly at the sight of the gold. Each rancher either came himself or sent along a rider or two to help with the drive. A few cows with calves they had dropped in the past few weeks were cut out and left with the ranchers. Cows with older calves were kept, with the hope that the calves would stand the drive.

Three days later, they arrived back at Ty's ranch with over one thousand young cows and fifty young bulls. They gathered the bunch a mile east of the ranch, well away from the other herd, and left them with the *vaqueros*.

Arriving back at the ranch yard, they were met with gloomy faces. Jerrod saw them coming and came out to greet them.

"We had some trouble."

"What is it, someone hurt?" Mac asked.

"It happened just after you left. That land-robbing rancher we had the trouble with snuck up on the herd with several of his men. He had somehow joined up with the make-believe sheriff, too. It appeared to me like they were real surprised to see the *vaqueros*. Seems they had not been expecting so much resistance. When they saw they couldn't get the herd, they took a few shots and left out running. Before our boys got the situation under control, Ty and one *vaquero* were down."

Mac and Luke both stepped off their horses. "How bad hurt are they?" Luke asked.

"The *vaquero* is not too bad. He has a bullet hole in his shoulder but the bullet went right through. Barring infection, he will be all right in a couple of weeks. Ty took two shots. One went through his side just above the beltline. The other is still lodged in his leg. That bullet has to come out and we have no real help anywhere close by. Ty is pretty sick with fever."

Mac looked at the activity around the wagons. "Is there

anything stopping you from getting a wagon under way right this afternoon?"

Jerrod looked grim. "Nothing at all. We were just waiting for you and using the time to get the wagons ready, and hoping that Ty's fever would come down. The wagons are now packed and ready. We made pallets for the boys in the big wagon. We were going to leave this afternoon whether you got back or not."

"I'm ready," Mac said. "But I think the cattle need to settle down overnight before we start the drive. But that doesn't stop y'all from heading out with the wagons."

"The drive won't be able to keep up with the wagon anyway. We will have to meet up down the road a piece."

"Did the herd run?" Mac asked.

"It did and it might have been a real problem except for all the men we have here, especially the *vaqueros*. The herd ran maybe a mile but the boys got it back under control. The few that strayed off were picked up the next morning. No losses as far as I can figure."

"You didn't tell what happened to the raiders," Luke said.

"The rancher and two of his men are dead and buried. The sheriff got away, heading east and nursing a wounded arm. The rest ran as hard as they could. I don't expect to see them again."

"I'll catch up to you," Luke said grimly. "I've got unfinished business to take care of."

Luke rode over to speak to Manuel and in a matter of minutes they rode off together heading east. Manuel had shown no intention of becoming any more friendly than he was before but he had developed a friendship of sorts with Mac and Luke. Luke and Manuel had found in each other a mutual love of combat. It probably was not a real friendship; more of a trust in battle. Still, a lot of men have walked together for years with little more than that in common.

Mac went to see the two wounded men. He went first to the *vaquero*. "Thank you for all you have done. You are a good man." Ty, who was awake but clearly hurting, translated, *"Gracias por todo lo que has hecho. Eres un buen hombre."*

The wounded man smiled. *"Gracias, senor."*

Mac turned to Ty. "How is it, cowboy?"

"Well, I've had better days but I expect I'll be all right by-and-by."

"You ready to get under way?"

"Until this happened, I had no intention to leave Texas or the ranch. But with my sister arriving back home with a family, I expect I can leave the ranch in good hands and front them enough money to see them well on their way to prosperity and a small herd to get them started. And then Jessie has convinced me that there might be some real advantages in going along with the group. So, yes, I'm ready to go."

"We've avoided San Antonio on our drives, Ty, but my father and the others are leaving right now to get you to San Antonio just as fast as they can. That's the closest big center. We'll follow along with the herd. You hang on and don't worry about a thing. We'll look after everything. All you have to do is get well again."

They shook with the Mexican abrazo, each man's hands gripping the lower arms of the other.

Ty and the wounded *vaquero* were both loaded into the wagon. The *vaquero* was able to walk on his own but Ty had to be carried. He gritted his teeth at the pain and broke out in a sweat but he didn't cry out. Ty said his good-byes to his sister and her family and they pulled out, heading north and a bit east with Hiram and Ma McTavish. Bobby and Jeremiah and two *vaqueros* were riding guard. Jessie had her horse tied on the back of the wagon while she rode inside, paying special attention to Ty's needs.

Before they left, Ty confided to Jessie where his gold was hidden down in the root cellar. She dug it out and hid it again in the wagon.

Mac came over to see them off. "You make the best time you can to San Antonio. We'll meet you there in a few days."

The drovers let the cattle rest for the remainder of that day. At daybreak the next morning, they moved them out. They put one bell animal with each herd. He immediately moved to the front of the drive and the rest of the cattle fell into place after some jostling and crashing of horns. They had enjoyed success with slow, easy drives before and intended to follow that pattern. As there were no other herds moving, they had the choice of grazing and bedding areas. They knew that might change after Austin as other herds started to converge on the drive north. Mac figured that as soon as the rails reached into the vastness of the west, there would be a great movement of Texas cattle to a hungry eastern market. Still, he wanted no more part of it. This herd raising dust ahead of him would be his last.

It took the herds twelve days to reach a bedding ground a few miles from San Antonio. The wagons were driven in for supplies. Jerrod went along to see to the condition of Ty and the injured *vaquero*. Mac stayed with the herd along with most of the other drovers. Luke and Manuel found him there.

"Get your business all straightened up?" Mac asked.

"All done," was the reply from a grim-looking Luke.

Manuel was looking equally grim.

Mac figured it was best neither he nor the others knew what Luke and Manuel had been up to so he didn't ask.

Jerrod returned with the news that the doctor was able to remove the bullet from Ty's leg and that most of the fever was gone. He was advised to rest for at least another week but Mac doubted that the young cowboy would be content to be left behind.

Mac and Margo rode in to see Ty after the rest of the crew returned. When they came back, they were riding beside a young man and woman in a top buggy.

Arriving at camp, Mac introduced the crew to the Reverend and Mrs. Isaiah Brockton.

Another buggy followed along behind. This one was driven by the livery owner with Ty and Jessie sitting up on the seat beside him. Ty looked weary but determined. Jessie also looked weary from lost sleep from looking after Ty but equally determined.

Margo stepped up beside Mac. "You had better explain before these folks burst with questions."

"I don't much see what the questions would be. Seems like everyone here but me had this figured out a long time ago."

"Tell us, Mac." Jerrod laughed. "Make it official."

"What's official, if that's what you want, is that Margo and I are getting married. This afternoon. Right here. We can't all leave the herds so we thought to bring the minister out here. And here he is. So the soonest we get this done and over with, the soonest the Reverend Brockton can get back to town. I expect we could get under way just about any time at all."

Nancy spoke up laughing, "Whoa, hold on there, cowboy. The lady might want a bit of time to fix herself up a mite and practice looking shy or whatever she feels needs doing. I suggest you go find a cup of coffee and sit for a spell. We'll tell you when you're needed."

After two hours, Mac had drunk all the coffee he could hold and listened to all the advice this group of bachelors could give him about married life. Mac figured that, except for his father and Ad, the total sum of the knowledge of the rest wouldn't make a decent sentence if a man set out to turn it into a speech.

Luke and Jerrod had ushered him down to the creek and passed him a bar of homemade lye soap. He bathed and shaved and got into the new set of clothing that Margo had purchased for him.

"I wonder what else she's gone and done," thought Mac. "These new clothes are a clear extravagance. Might have to keep a close eye on expenditures in the future."

The Reverend Brockton broke into his thinking. "If you would like to come with me now, sir, I do believe your bride is ready."

Mac knew that Margo had spent considerable time in San Antonio going to several stores but all he had seen at the end of the time was wrapped packages. He had no idea what was under the brown paper wrapping.

When he walked over beside the wagons and the gathered group, he wasn't quite prepared for the change in Margo. Mostly he'd seen her in simple dresses and lately in men's pants that allowed for easier riding and more comfort. But this Margo was all set out in a dress that was unlike anything Mac had seen since the summer he had worked on the riverboats. There he had seen wealthy ladies all decked out in finery that was unimaginably costly in the eyes of a simple deck hand. He never expected to see the like again but here it was right in front of him and waiting to marry up with him. It stopped him in his tracks and took away the most of his breath.

The ladies had managed to set Margo's long blond hair in a series of curls that fell one over the other across her shoulders and down her back. Mac wondered how they had managed that.

He stood rooted to the ground until the reverend gently took his arm and said, "Come, your bride is waiting."

The wedding was short and Mac had a bit of trouble understanding that such a long change in his life could happen in so short a time.

When the minister said, "You may now kiss the bride," Mac was tempted to look for a saddled horse again but he finally got it done amidst much cheering and encouragement.

Mama and her helpers had been busy preparing a small feast with even more chili than normal if that was possible.

They ate and celebrated and laughed and joked.

Finally, Margo gave both of her parents a hug, Mac kissed his mother and shook hands with his father and Ad, and the newly-weds climbed into the back seat of the Reverend Brockton's buggy with their saddle horses tied on behind.

Mac lifted a hand in farewell. "We'll catch up in about a week unless we decide we've seen enough of San Antonio before that time."

"I don't think San Antonio has much to do with it," hollered Luke.

The married couple rode off to much laughter and cheering.

They arrived in town well after dark, having found it difficult to get away from the celebrating friends and families.

Mac fussed with the horses in the livery barn until Margo finally burst out laughing.

"Mac, if you don't quit your fussing over those horses and come along, folks are going to think you're just putting in time, not wanting to face being alone with me. Why, there's some might even think you're afraid, maybe even a coward."

With a bit of a grin, Mac stepped back from the horse he was brushing. "I guess I am. I used to wonder if I was a coward when those cannons started to roar. That was a new experience, too, but somehow I made it through."

Margo slipped her arm under Mac's and said, "Come on. Pick up that carpetbag. We'll go face the cannons together."

It was a two-block walk to the hotel. On their earlier trip to town, Mac had booked the best room the hotel had to offer.

The grinning desk clerk looked as if he was tempted to make a comment. Maybe say something about newlyweds and such.

Mac gave him a look that could have frozen a boiling pot, suggesting that the young man might have a happier future if he said nothing. He passed them a key and said simply, "Welcome."

It was a good decision.

Mac and Margo started up the stairs arm in arm. Margo may have been tugging just a little bit.

24

The newlyweds spent five days exploring San Antonio and eating in restaurants, an activity that neither of them had any experience at before. They became comfortable with each other but Mac still insisted on blowing out the lamp at bed time. Margo continued to tease him about being a coward. He didn't let it bother him.

On the sixth morning Mac brought their horses up from the livery stable. Margo stood in front of the hotel waiting for him, their small bit of luggage at her feet.

Mac was just finishing tying their bedrolls, small tent and the war bags behind their saddles when a voice said, "Ready to move out? It's about time. There's work to be done."

Margo looked around and started to laugh.

Mac turned. There sat Luke and two *vaqueros* saddled up and ready to ride.

Mac searched for words for a moment or two and then said, "You had better have a good explanation for being here, boys. And now would be a good time to come out with it."

Luke was grinning his exasperating grin. "We took a vote. A few thought you could look after yourselves but most figured someone had better trail along and keep the boogers off. No telling what someone in your frame of mind could step in. We figured that were you to step in something unpleasant, you might need help getting it off your shoe. I drew the short straw and these lazy Mex's with me thought to get out of a few days of real work. So here we are and ready to go just as soon as you finish tying down that bedroll."

Mac knew that the *vaqueros* were two of the hardest working of the crew and that both could speak passable English so had understood what was said. He also knew they had proved themselves to be eager, almost anxious, for a fight which might be why they were chosen. They were grinning almost as widely as Luke.

It took Mac most of the morning to accept the fact that three men had been sent to escort them. Margo saw the humor in it and started to tease Mac. His silence caused her to rethink that idea.

THEY CAUGHT up to the herd on the second evening just in time for supper. The herd had moved a bare sixty miles.

After a boisterous welcome from family and friends, Mac left Margo with the other women and rode out to the herd. He did a slow circle of the market herd and then an even slower circuit of his breeding herd. Jerrod joined him along the way. They rode in silence until finally Mac said, "They look good. Any troubles?"

"Nothing we couldn't have expected. A few bunch quitters but the riders kept them pretty tight and the dogs have really picked up on what is expected of them. Herding cow critters is a long way from treeing coons. I'm amazed at what the dogs have learned."

"How is Ty making out?"

"He hurts some but otherwise he's doing fine. Up and around some each day. He'll be back in the saddle before you know it."

They found good grass west of Fort Worth and settled the herd down for a two-day rest.

The wagons were sent in for supplies. Mama, looking like she had been handling a team all her life, drove one wagon while Jessie drove the other. All the women rode along with them. Ad and Hiram went with the women, figuring they would need help to carry and tote.

As opportunity allowed, they each found time for a trip to the barber or bathhouse.

This time they were treating the shopping as their last opportunity for the next year and it probably was unless they made a trip south to Santa Fe. They not only purchased food-stuffs in quantity but both summer and winter clothing as well. It was heading up to be a sizable load.

On his return from town, Hiram talked to Ty who was sitting on the open tailgate of the wagon, Jessie hovering not far away. "Son, you seem to be doing pretty well now. Took you a short ride yesterday. If'n you thought you could manage, we could use the wagon space."

"I was thinking that very same thing," Ty answered. "I'll clean this mess out of your wagon right now and see if I still have a horse in that remuda or if they's sold it off. I sure do thank you for your care. Don't expect I would have made it without."

They crossed the Red at low water with no trouble. Again, Mama had a horse brought up for her. Somehow the wagon and water made her more nervous than what seemed reasonable but she wasn't to be swayed so horseback it was at every crossing.

The early spring grass was greening up better than the drovers had hoped for. They brought the cattle along slowly, allowing them to graze a bit along the way. After a long winter with the dead, dry grass, the critters had some condition to regain even though they had seemed to hold their weight.

The forts and Indian agencies required side trips for the delivery of their cattle. It was decided to let the two herds rest and graze the new spring grass while the deliveries were made.

They cut out the count needed to fill each order and chose who was to go with the delivery and who was to stay with the remaining herds.

Everyone who had ordered cattle the fall before welcomed the arrival of the herd but two Indian bands reduced their orders. After the final delivery at Fort Gibson there would still be a herd of nearly seven hundred head with no sure market for them.

Mac said, "We'll keep them if we have to and sell when chance offers. Not much else we can do."

Jerrod was more optimistic. "You've never seen those big, hungry northern cities, Mac. That's the ready market and where a market exists there's always someone figuring out how to reach it. We brought these beasts this far. Along the way we'll find someone prepared to take them the rest of the way."

25

There's no telling what spooked the herd. Sometimes it almost seemed like their sole purpose during the drive was to find something to be boogered at. So the crew never knew why the cattle that had been slowly walking through the long spring grass one minute was a stampeding chaos the next.

Mac was riding right flank along with several *vaqueros*. Jerrod was at right point on a roan gelding that had proven its worth on previous rides. When the animals broke into a run, the riders immediately swept toward them, pushing them into each other in an attempt to turn them into a mill to halt the maddened rush.

Jerrod pushed his roan into a run and closed in, driving the running cattle into each other with the coil of his lariat. A wide-horned old cow hooked the roan's front leg and it went head over heels, throwing Jerrod in the process. Jerrod, unhurt, got up immediately and made a grab for the dragging reins. The panicked horse leaped away and Jerrod was left unprotected.

A fear-driven animal with down-turned horns hooked him directly through the stomach. He was dragged fifty feet and then tossed to the ground like a rag doll as the maddened animal unloaded the burden. He received a dreadful tearing wound and hit the ground unconscious.

Mac and Ad both saw what happened and came riding to his rescue. They were in time to keep the herd off Jerrod, blocking the cattle with their horses. As the herd stampeded into the distance, Mac forgot about them, thinking only of his injured friend.

Mac and Ad swung off their horses at the same time and ran to their injured partner. They could see immediately that there was nothing they or anyone else could do. The horn had driven right through leaving a terrible mass of blood and gore as it pulled loose.

Mac rolled Jerrod gently onto his back and wiped some dirt from his face. He then wiped blood and froth from his lips. He had no idea at all what to do next.

Ad rode back to get Luke, quickly telling the short story to the others. The herd was left to the *vaqueros* while the partners all gathered beside Jerrod and Mac who was sitting on the ground with Jerrod's head resting on his lap. Mac, unashamedly, had tears rolling down his cheeks. Luke knelt down on the other side and picked up Jerrod's hand, clasping his arm in the abrazo that he had been using with his Mexican friends.

Jerrod was conscious again and trying to talk. He looked up at Mac. "How bad is it partner? Feels real bad."

"It's bad enough, my friend. It's no good lying to you."

Margo knelt beside Jerrod and picked up his hand and held it.

Luke's shoulders were shaking as he cried silently, oblivious to the thoughts of others.

"We'll get you into Gibson, Captain; find a doctor there." Luke knew Jerrod was beyond needing a doctor but Mac understood that he had to say something.

"I know you mean well, Sergeant, but my ride is over. It's been a great adventure. With you two as partners, and all the others, it's truly been a great adventure. No man could ask for more. I was going to tell you at supper tonight that I was leaving for home after Gibson. I guess I'm going to a more permanent home. Didn't expect that."

Margo wiped some more bloody froth from Jerrod's lips.

One of the red hounds came and laid his head on Jerrod's arm, surprising everyone.

Jerrod's words were coming out hesitantly and slurred. "I wish you would do something for me. In my saddlebag, you will find a letter. There's a name and an address on it. It's the name of a young lady that was going to be my wife until the war came along. We both decided after the war that we needed some time but now we were going to complete that original plan. I would like someone to send her a note explaining why I can't keep my promise. Send her two-thousand dollars, too. That might make her life a bit easier, for a while at least."

Margo spoke very quietly, "You have a lot more gold than that, Jerrod. Do you have family for the rest?"

"My family is right here. I have been thinking for some time that the deal we made with Ad and Hiram was mostly to our advantage. Take what I have left and split it between them. They've earned every penny." Jerrod was having difficulty talking and was showing signs of great pain.

After a short pause, Jerrod looked at Luke. "Sergeant, would you see that I'm buried on the fort grounds?"

Luke could only nod.

Hiram bent over the wounded man and touched his neck. "He's gone. Ain't no one could live through that wound. A good man gone." He gently closed Jerrod's eyes and stood up.

It was a solemn group that drove a wagon carrying their blanket-wrapped friend on his last ride. They had been less than ten miles from the fort when the stampede happened. The men were needed with the cattle so after loading Jerrod on the tailgate of a wagon, they completed the drive and halted the herds on grass about one mile from the fort.

Luke and Mac rode in.

Luke went into the officer's quarters to get permission to bury the ex-cavalry man in the fort cemetery. There was a new commanding officer in charge of the post but, still, permission was granted immediately and an honor guard assembled. A detail was assigned to dig a grave while the fort carpenter built a casket. Within a couple of hours, the preparations were complete.

While that work was going on, all the men except Luke rode back out to the cattle.

Luke stayed with the body while it was prepared for burial. The two older women cut off Jerrod's old blood-soaked clothing, washed his body as best they could, and wrapped his stomach with wide strips of clean white cloth. They then dressed him in clean clothing and, helped by a medical orderly, laid him in the newly prepared coffin. Luke placed Jerrod's hat on his chest and together they lifted the coffin lid into place.

The crew had arrived by that time. Manuel and four *vaqueros* also arrived along with the Mexican women. They all gathered around one end of the grave while Hiram, dressed in his best suit of clothes and newly shaved, stood at the other end with his worn Bible open in his hand. That he seldom referred to that old Bible but spoke lengthy passages from memory was testament to his many hours absorbed in those precious words.

The honor guard of six cavalry soldiers dressed in their best uniforms carried the coffin from the small medical center to the gravesite. Every officer at the fort accompanied the honor guard, all in their dress uniforms. A goodly contingent of enlisted men also silently gathered around the gravesite. Luke found himself wishing that Jerrod's friend, Lewis True, had been present.

They laid the casket on two poles that spanned the newly dug grave and draped ropes under it. They then stepped back and stood at attention.

HIRAM QUOTED the Twenty-Third Psalm just as Mac had done at the grave of the unknown settler family back on the Kansas plains. He then talked quietly of what he called a good man gone.

"Friends," said Hiram, "the Scripture doesn't tell us very much about heaven. But it does assure us that such a place exists and that it is the final home for those who live in faith. Jerrod was a man of faith. Living a life of faith is not easy on the frontier where the daily experience can often be harsh and unpredictable. We have all done some things that we would not have done if we were safely settled down in the city. But this is not the city.

"In a land just being settled and that still has its rough edges showing, I expect the Lord is prepared to make some exceptions. However, I never knew Jerrod to take advantage of those exceptions."

Hiram paused and looked at the gathering. He pulled a hand-kerchief from his pocket and wiped his forehead. He then unashamedly wiped his eyes. When he started again, his voice broke but he carried on.

"In some ways, Jerrod was not cut out for this land. He had more education and refinement than most of us have. He confided to me once that he felt more at ease in a settled town than he did on the frontier.

"Jerrod was a gentleman and a gentle man. It was our great privilege to have known him. Our lives were bettered by the experience. But now he is gone and we must carry on. Jerrod completed the work that was set before him. We must do no less. We will all grieve in our own way but Jerrod would not have us stop on account of what happened to him. Jerrod is in that better place.

"We too set out to find a better place on this earth. A place where we could build our homes and you young folks could raise your families. And where we older folks could have some peace and, hopefully, bring some improvement to this old world as we go through our last days.

"And then, when our time is done and our work is completed, we too can settle forever in that land that the human eye cannot see. I know that Jerrod will be there to greet us. I look forward to that day.

"This was a good man. A good man gone. We shall miss him."

Hiram look over at Mac and said, "Son, why don't you lead us in a song?"

Mac nearly twisted the brim off his hat as he held it between his two hands but, nevertheless, he started out in a strong baritone voice, *"Nearer my God to thee, nearer to thee."*

As Mac sang, several voices joined him. Margo, arm linked in Mac's and with her head resting on his shoulder, sang until she started to cry. She stopped singing then as did most of the others.

Bill sang strongly right to the end. When Mac was unsure of a word, Bill filled it in, seemingly knowing every verse. When the song was finished, Bill started to pray. He prayed a short but heartfelt prayer, ending up on his knees with one arm raised to the heavens and with his other hand resting on the coffin.

With the completion of the short ceremony the honor guard shouldered their rifles to give the traditional gun salute.

Luke spoke up, "Thank you, men. I know the tradition and I know you mean well but my captain and my friend hated guns and war perhaps as much as any man ever hated guns and war. He is more honored by our silence. No more guns, please."

The honor guard slung their rifles over their shoulders again and picked up the rope ends. As they lowered the casket into the ground, several of the women and a couple of the men could be heard to be weeping. When the casket was resting on the bottom and the ropes removed, Hiram again stepped forward. He filtered some soil through his fingers and said, "Lord, into your hands we commit our friend and your child. Take good care of him for us. Amen."

The honor guard marched smartly off and the mourners slowly made their way back to the campgrounds. Mac and Margo and Luke stood there silently after the others filtered away. Finally, they too put on their hats and walked silently out of the little cemetery.

What had to be done was done. What had to be done tomorrow would also be done. But a bit of the shine was gone from the venture.

The camp was quiet that evening but around midnight Nancy's baby decided it was time to make its entrance into the world.

MAC AND MARGO AWOKE IN THEIR SMALL TENT TO THE SOUND OF great activity centered on the wagon that Jonathon and Nancy had taken over due to her advancing condition. Mac pulled on his pants and stepped outside.

"What's going on?" he hollered over at his mother who was fussing around at the other wagon. The light from the fire plus one lantern illuminated the campground. Mac could see another lantern inside the wagon.

"Nothing that you're needed for, Walker. Your sister is going to have her baby. You go back to sleep. Let us take care of this."

"Go back to sleep? How can anyone expect to sleep with all that racket going on? You'll have the entire fort awake if this keeps up."

Hiram spoke up, "Son, I expect you know somewhat about cow critters but your knowledge comes up a bit short on human critters. If you can't sleep, perhaps you can make some coffee. And see can you do that with a minimum of grumbling."

Margo was chuckling inside the tent. "Come back to bed, Mac. You don't need more coffee and the women surely don't need you. Could be that I need you. And anyway, you will need your sleep come morning."

The two older women were joined by Mama who had heard

the ruckus and somehow knew what was going on. She announced that she had seen several babies into this world and took charge.

Mac lay in his blankets wondering what was going on.

Margo pulled him close. "Mac, go to sleep."

He was finally back into a deep sleep when he was again awakened by the crying and squawking of a small voice. He fumbled for his clothes and left the tent all ready to tell the women that the crew needed its sleep only to see that he was the last one to the fire.

Hiram said, "Good morning, son. You disappeared on me. Had to make the coffee myself. Never known you to shirk a job of work before," he teased. "But I guess I'll share this coffee with you if you want to pull up some of that there ground and sit down."

Mac finally figured out that this would be a good time to say nothing at all.

Jonathon walked over grinning from ear to ear to shake Hiram's hand. "Well, how does it feel to be a grandpa? Grandpa to a fine looking little girl."

"About as new to get used to as you having to get used to being a dad. I expect we'll both get the hang of it by and by."

The crew gathered around to shake Jonathon's hand and slap him on the back.

Margo arrived and gave Jonathon a kiss on the cheek and started in to making breakfast, calling Jessie to come and help.

Morning was a buzz of activity. The cattle were delivered to the fort and paid for. Supplies were bought and the crew was given two days of rest although they had to alternate time off with their herding responsibilities.

When the Indians arrived, it was much like before with the hide tents soon rising and smoky fires started. The men took charge of the cattle and within one half-hour, one animal was slaughtered and was in the process of being distributed to the family groups.

Bill and Manuel rode to the village and spent the afternoon visiting.

Nancy figured she would be ready to travel if she had the two days of rest. Her mother was not so sure about that but Nancy brushed her concerns aside.

There wasn't much to see at the fort and surrounding village but the crew all took turns riding in anyway. With the sale of most of the beef herd, it was decided to amalgamate the remainder with Mac's cow herd although they all dreaded the task of sorting them out again if they found a market.

A waving, smiling boy riding the old mare rode into camp. Hiram waved back at him. "How goes it, cowboy? You gettin' any work out of that lazy old mare?"

"It's not good manners to criticize a man's horse but since it was you who gave her to me, I'll let it go. And thanks again, mister. This is a good mare."

"Well, I know she's a good mare, son. I'm just funning you a little bit. My own young'uns rode her just like you're doing. Never once threw one off. Yes, I'd say that's sure enough a good mare."

"Pa made me promise not to get in the way so I'd better be gettin' back. Thanks again, mister."

"Bye, son. You ride careful now."

Six of the *vaqueros* said their good-byes after the herd was delivered to Gibson and Mac had paid them. *"Los vamos a hechar de menos. Ustedes son hombres buenos,"* Mac told them. "We will miss you. You are good men."

The men answered in Spanish, *"Dicen que han sido muchas millas y algunas senoritas van a estar llorando por ellos. Tambien dicen que tienen suficiente dinero, gracias a ti, para comprarles regalos a las muchachas; pero de que les sirve el regalo si ellos no estan alli para recibir las gracias."*

Manuel translated, "They say it has been many miles and there are some *senoritas* that will be weeping for them. They also say they have enough money thanks to you to buy presents for those *senoritas* but what good is a present if they are not there to receive the thanks." Manuel grinned and hunched his shoulders.

The men rode south with much shouting and waving of sombreros and Mac watched them go. "I'm not totally convinced about weeping *senoritas*," he said to himself. "But we will miss these men."

A bit later, Mac walked over to where Mama had her wagon set up. Manuel and Imelda were there. "What's your plan?" he asked. "From here we head north and west. It's a long way to where we're going. You're welcome and we can use your help but it's up to you. You'll be a long way from home."

Mama had been learning some English as the weeks went by. "What is there? Where you go? What we see?"

Mac answered, "None of us have been right exactly there but I've talked with people who have returned from that area. And I've been close enough to see the mountains clearly. There's grass and rolling hills for a long way without much water although we'll follow the Arkansas River most of the way through the dry country. Past that the land rises toward the mountains with broken hills and grass-filled canyons. I'm told there's lots of water with a couple of major rivers and many flowing streams.

"To the south and west, those hills rise up and become the Sangre de Cristo Mountains. A beautiful mountain range."

At the speaking of the name of the mountain range, Mama caught her breath and crossed herself. Many of the other Mexicans did likewise.

Mac's mother asked Ty, "What does that name mean in English?"

"Blood of Christ Mountains."

"My, my, what a strange name for a mountain."

Mac continued, "To the west of the Sangre de Cristos and carrying on to the north are the Rockies. That whole country is one mountain range after another. High-up country. Higher mountains than anything in the east. Snow-topped most of the time.

"But where we'll be going is on the eastern slope of the Sangre de Christos. Not in the mountains but close enough. Forests, hills, grass and lots of water. Still some Indians and buffalo and not many people. At least that's what we've been told. Just a few settlers down along the Purgatoire River."

Mama turned to Manuel and a long discussion was held in Spanish. Mac found himself wishing he had learned more of the language. Finally, Mama looked back at Mac. "I think we would like to see these high mountains. We go."

Imelda was looking a bit worried but Manuel was grinning.

Mac looked at him and smiled. "He's spent too much time with Luke," he said quietly.

Sitting alone with their coffee cups after the evening meal on the last day at the fort, Luke spoke into the silence, "Something Jerrod never told you, Mac. He wanted you to know but just couldn't find the words. That black you're riding was his brother's horse and the saddle and weapons were his brother's, too. He recognized the horse right off but he was willing to hear your story before he said anything. He was somewhat reluctant to ride with you at first but, after meeting you, he felt that you weren't the type of man to do something that you couldn't rightly answer for. Jerrod's a pretty good judge of men.

"And then it wasn't you that fired the shot that killed his brother so it would've been unfair to blame you and Jerrod always tried to be fair."

"I wish he had said something."

"He was biding his time was all. And then you will remember that I asked you about the horse. That wasn't just entirely by accident. Your story set Jerrod's mind at ease. And he no longer had to wonder what had become of his brother. He had no further doubts about you either." Mac had no answer and no more questions as he walked away.

BEFORE FULL LIGHT the next morning as the breakfast dishes were being gathered up, Mac sought out Ad. "Ad, I'd appreciate if you would get the herd off the bed grounds and under way. I'll catch up to you shortly."

Ad agreed and called out to Bill and Mac's brothers, "Get them up and move them out, boys. We're going west."

Mac saddled up and led his horse and Margo's over to where

the women were working. "I'm sure you can be spared for a bit. We have a short ride to take."

Margo dried her hands and mounted her horse. The other women watched them ride off and then went back to their work.

Margo had been wondering if they would visit the gravesite before they left but she didn't want to pick at the wound so she had said nothing. But she understood immediately that this was exactly what Mac had in mind. They rode the short distance to the fort, tied their horses and walked into the cemetery. The morning light was just sufficient to see where they were going and to see that Luke was there before them, standing alone with his hat twisting between his hands. He didn't seem to hear them coming.

Mac and Margo walked quietly to the gravesite and stopped beside Luke. Margo slipped her free arm through Luke's and gave it a light squeeze. Luke jumped at the touch and, turning, saw his friends for the first time.

The three of them stood there in silence for perhaps five minutes which can seem like a lifetime under some circumstances. When the time seemed right, Margo gave Luke a light kiss on the cheek and said quietly, "Let's go."

Arm in arm, the three mourners went to their horses. Not a word was spoken as they mounted up and made their way back to the herd.

They soon caught up to the herd and the wagons. Margo tied her horse behind the wagon and climbed up beside Mama. Mac and Luke took their places with the drive.

They moved the herd northwest, following the Arkansas.

A few days later, Mac called Bill over at breakfast. "Bill, how would you like to ride north and see what you can see? Take a couple of *vaqueros* with you. They're building the rails west but we have no way of knowing how far they've come. You take a few days and scout out the country for us. It would be good to know how they feel about longhorns now, too. And you leave those two harebrained brothers of mine here. No telling what would happen were the three of you to go together."

They let the herd graze its slow way north waiting for Bill's return. Within the week, he arrived back full of enthusiasm.

"The Kansas border is two days north of here for a slow herd. There's a settlement another day's ride north of the border. The rails are still not this far west but there's activity in a mostly tent town up there including some cattle buyers. We talked to them. They figure to be the first on the ground when the Texas herds start to arrive. They figure to graze the herds on Kansas grass until the rails come to meet them. We were told to come along, that they would deal with any quarantine issues. The quarantine is only in the settled parts of the state anyway. No real problem west of here."

Mac expressed some frustration. "Sounds like we made a lot of work for ourselves putting those two herds together. If those buyers want the beef animals, we have to dig them all out again."

They stepped up the pace of the drive, anxious to deal with the sale herd and get on their way west. They had talked a good bit about green valleys and snow-topped mountains. It was time to get on with it.

They settled the herd on good grass a mile south of the tent town. There was no good water, just a small stream. Mac wondered why anyone would place a settlement where there was a lack of water.

Morning found Mac and Luke riding on ahead to make a deal for the cattle. He located three buyers in the tent saloon having their morning coffee. Mac thought it unusual that the men were socializing together since they were competitors. He put it down to the strangeness of Northerners.

Mac made his pitch to the three men and, after some talk, they rode out to look over the herd.

"What's your count?" asked one of the buyers.

"We won't know exactly until we sort them all out again. We sold most of our beef herd to the military and Indian forts on the way up here. My current count is just shy of seven hundred animals. A few headed for home, a few drowned crossing rivers and we ate a couple. But you can make your own count just to be sure. Anything branded Bar-H is for sale."

They rode around the herd, letting their eyes sort out the beef from the cows and heifers. Then they pulled over to the wagon for coffee.

One of the buyers, a man named Steady Carlson, said, "I'll accept your count for now. But you got to understand, it ain't rightly a prime herd although I expect it's as good as most long-horns get. You have some older animals among them. If they were all young steers in good shape, I could get you nigh onto twenty-six dollars the head. As they are, I can't go over twenty-two."

The other two buyers looked at Carlson and then at each other. One, named Johnston, threw the dregs of his coffee into the fire and said, "Well, now, Steady, you got to remember that these folks worked almighty hard and took a lot of risks to get here. That company you work for is a big, rich company. I figure they could stand a little more. Now, you take our company. We're just nowhere near as big as y'all are but I figure I wouldn't get fired if'n I was to offer an extra dollar. Twenty-three, I make it, and a good deal for both sides."

The third buyer said nothing.

Carlson poked at the fire with a stick and looked at each man in turn. Then he looked over at the herd. "Johnston, we might have all been better off if your mother had done the honorable thing and drowned you the day you were born. Might still be a good idea but there's just not much water around these parts." He was quiet for a few moments and then said, "All right, Mac. I'll match Johnston and go another two bits. That's twenty-three and a quarter. If Johnston goes higher, he can have them."

The third man still did not speak. Mac figured that maybe the three took turns buying herds.

Mac looked at Johnston who didn't seem in any way inclined to say anything. They let another full minute go by and then Mac said, "We'll have the herd in town by noon tomorrow if the sorting goes well. I'll want you to take immediate delivery and have cash payment ready."

Carlson stuck out his hand. Mac shook it and stood up. The

three buyers climbed onto their horses and Mac looked over at Luke.

"You all right with all of that?"

"Right as rain partner. Let's get 'er done and get on our way."

BEING USED to herding on their own for several months and led by their bell bull, the beef animals separated almost eagerly from the breeding stock.

They drove the small herd into the hastily-built corrals in the settlement the next day and received their pay.

Steady Carlson asked Mac, "You boys going back for another herd? We could use more cattle. We figured to be first on the ground knowing the rails were on their way. Lots of grass here for holding herds until the rails arrive. But we need more animals than this to cover our costs."

"There's another herd about two days behind us. Judging by the dust, you won't have to go in search of cattle. There's more than just a few critters running loose down in Texas and everywhere we went we heard men talking about gathering cattle. But this is our third drive and that's enough. I figure it can only get more difficult to gather cattle from now on and, knowing the nature of human men, I expect that some of the larger ranchers will claim them all for themselves. That will lead to all kinds of fighting and misery and we want no part of it. We're heading west to ranch."

FOR THE FIRST TIME, THEY WERE ABLE TO POINT THE HERD directly west. That in itself seemed like a victory. There had been so much talk about the west that it had started to take on legendary proportions. But Mac figured if only a part of the story was true it was still worth the ride.

As Mac rode beside his father's wagon, Hiram asked, "Is this the part of Kansas you drove wagon through, Walker?"

"No. The land is much the same but the Santa Fe Trail is a goodly bit north of here. I'm thinking we'll meet up with the trail somewhere along west. You'll not have to ask when we see it. The wagons have carved ruts in the prairie grass that will never fill in. They'll be there a century from now. We could follow that trail if we wished but if the freight wagons come along, we'll want to give way. Those wagoners are mostly good men but they surely think of the trail as theirs. They don't welcome having to make way for pilgrims. We'll keep the herd off to the side a bit."

The rolling hills offered abundant grass but scant water. The riders took turns riding out in search of water. When they reached the Arkansas River, they decided to follow it. The Arkansas swung a ways north, adding extra miles, but the group figured it was worth it to be near water. The river eventually led them directly to Fort Dodge.

"Not a pretty place," Margo said to Mac. "Hardly any buildings. I wonder where the soldiers' quarters are."

"If you take a look along that river bank, I think you'll see."

Margo looked where Mac was pointing and was amazed to see a good number of soldiers moving about in front of what looked like small caves carved into the riverbank. "Oh, my, do you suppose they actually live like that?"

"The army takes better care of its horses then its men."

THEY SET up camp on a grassy flat about one half-mile from the fort. The cattle were herded a bit further west where the grass wasn't overgrazed. That done, Mac, Ad, Bill, Margo and Jessie rode to the sutler's store, a soddy showing no signs of planning except to keep the weather out. It was miserable looking on the outside, dark and dank on the inside.

They waited while the sutler made a note in his account book for the purchases of two soldiers who had just left. That done, he turned to the travelers. "Afternoon, folks. You're a long ways from anywhere close. I'm Jesse Crane, sutler here in Fort Dodge. We don't see many womenfolk out here. Where y'all heading to?"

Mac didn't like to be questioned but he answered as civilly as he felt necessary, "Driving a herd west. Plan on ranching if the land is as good as we hear it is."

"Oh, there's nothing wrong with the land except what's already on it. Buffalo, both dead and alive, and enough Indians to keep you sharp."

Mac didn't want to pursue the topic. "Any chance you might have seen Jimbo around here lately?"

The sutler looked at Mac and chuckled. "You men walk over to that there saloon. You could close your eyes and just listen to the sound of talking and it'll lead you directly to old Jimbo. That is one talking man."

Mac smiled at the sutler. "That sounds like Jimbo all right. I was hoping he might of run out of stories by now."

"Oh, he has. I believe he has started back at the beginning several times and the stories get longer with each telling."

The men left the women to make the few purchases they had decided on and walked over to the saloon.

A rider dressed all in buckskins was holding forth on a couple of young soldiers he had cornered.

Ad walked over to him and said, "I hear tell you might know a thing or two about the land to the west of here or is that just an old wives' tale?"

Jimbo looked Ad over carefully and then asked, "Well, now, that just might be true but I would like to know who told you."

Ad pointed at Mac. "That man sitting over there in the corner said he heard it somewhere."

Jimbo turned around and looked through the gloom of the half-dark saloon. "Walker!" he shouted. "Well now. There's a sight for sore eyes. Been so long I thought I might never see you again."

Jimbo invited them to find chairs or half barrels and sit down at his table.

The two soldiers took the opportunity to make a welcome retreat.

Mac and Jimbo shook hands after which Mac introduced the men with him.

Jimbo took a hard look at the much-matured man he knew as Walker. "So, what brings you back west? You here to stay this time?"

"There's quite a bunch of us and we have a herd with us. We figured to go find us a place to live and ranch. Thought you might like to show me that green valley you talked about one time. That is if you still remember how to ride and if that Idaho Nez Perce tribe didn't come borrow that Appaloosa horse back."

"Ride? Why, sonny, I've ridden all over this here west. Ain't no one seen more country than ol' Jimbo. Ride. You'll have to get up awful early in the morning and stay at 'er till dark to cover the ground I leave behind and then I'd probably have to stop and make coffee while I wait for you to catch up. Why, I remember one time..."

Mac stopped him with a grin. "All right, you convinced me. Now what about showing us that valley?"

"Sure as we're sitting here. Why, I was up there just last month. Or maybe it was the month before. Took some trinkets and such up to Runs His Horses. Spent about a week in their village. They've moved a little further into the hills than they were. Trying not to be noticed by the army and the reserve do-gooders. Why, I declare, those do-gooders would have every one of us on a ball and chain if it were left up to them. Met one up there who actually tried to convince me of the happiness to be found on that desert reserve the government laid out for the tribes. Said they would all be better off under government care. What a fool. That reserve is mostly hot, useless land if you ask me and this for tribes that have known nothing but mountains, green valleys and running streams. Plus, of course, a bit of snow from time to time.

"I doubt as how that government man even knows enough about the Indians to know how they live let alone where they want to live. I was somewhat tempted to try to educate him but then I gave 'er up. He'll just have to learn the hard way. Or maybe..."

Ad interrupted the talking man, "You can probably tell us about that as we ride along. But when can you be ready to go and how long do you reckon it'll take to lead a herd to this valley?"

"I'm ready right this very minute if that's what you want. Of course, I'd have to square up with that sutler. That, or sneak out of town in the dark of night. I'm a mite tight on funds right at this very moment. But as far as travel goes, I expect you could have a herd up there in about four weeks, maybe three barring trouble."

Ad continued, "That sounds real good. But we had in mind maybe two more days for the cattle and horses to rest up a bit before we set out again. And we have some wagon repairs to complete. Would that suit you?"

"Suits me," answered Jimbo. "That also gives all you folks time to take in the bright lights and see the sights of old Fort Dodge." He slapped his knee and broke into a croaking laugh. "Wouldn't want to miss all of that."

Mac stood up. "I think you should meet the others, Jimbo. How would you like to ride out to the camp with us?"

"Got old Idaho in the corral out back. I'll just go get him and meet you on the road."

By the time they left the saloon, the women were finished packing a few things into the wagon. The men joined them about the time Jimbo rode up.

Mac said, "Jimbo, I wish you'd say hello to my sister Jessie and my wife Margo. Ladies, this is Jimbo. You will remember me telling you that I met him on my way back from Santa Fe."

"Please to meet you, Jimbo," the women said almost in unison.

"Likewise, I'm sure," answered Jimbo, remembering polite speech from a previous time.

Jimbo slapped Mac on the back and said, "Wife, now that's prime. A man should have a wife. Had one myself from time to time but that was some while ago. Wife. And a right fine-looking one, too. Makes the winters seem a bit shorter if the scenery around the shack is something to look at. Looks to me like you done just fine, Walker. And you done it without my good help and advice, too. Just goes to show. Just goes to show." He slapped Mac on the back again and Mac moved sidewise to put an end to the backslapping.

"Mount up, Jimbo. We'll go out and you can meet the rest of the group. By the way, Jimbo, I got hung with the name Mac in the army and that's what all these folks know me by."

MAC INTRODUCED Jimbo around and he surprised them all by breaking into almost flawless Spanish when he met Manuel and the *vaqueros*.

He fussed shamefully over Mama and Imelda until Mac

finally said, "Come on, Jimbo. We need to go and have a meeting."

Turning to Manuel, Mac said, "Manuel, I would like it if you would leave just a few men with the herd and the rest of you come in to the meeting. Now is the time to ask questions of Jimbo and try to get all the information we can."

Everyone was called together and coffee served.

Jimbo advised that there were still some uncertainties about Indians. "Don't let that stop you from going. It's a beautiful country you have in mind. Just you keep your eyes open for trouble. And not all the trouble comes from Indians. The late war dumped a goodly number of men footloose into the West. Some no better than they need to be."

He continued, "I've been west, boys. Greatest land God ever put grass on. A land that's just crying out for cattle. Still a few buffalo around but that won't last long the way them hides arrive by the stacked-up wagons. The boys will soon have Kansas cleared of the last buf and then they'll turn their eyes on the land to the west. A few hunters out there already leaving their carnage behind. Mighty hard on the Indians, the loss of the bufs is.

"My bet is you've heard lots of nonsense about the Indians. Well now, I'll allow as how a man has to be careful but I always got along with them. Lived with a bunch for two years. Took a wife and had a son. I often wonder what became of them. You'll have your best luck if you stay friendly. Try to at least."

Jimbo seemed to be prepared to ramble on for as long as he had an audience. "And green valleys. Your biggest problem is going to be deciding on which one pleases your eye the most although I want to show you one that will please the eye of the most road-weary traveler. There's no end of grass. It's water that you need to watch out for. Still, there's no shortage of that either in most years."

Luke spoke up for the first time, "Jimbo, this here that you see is Mac's herd. I expect that what we have to find is a valley that suits Mac and Margo. We'll probably stay and help them get settled, most of us anyway. But come next spring, we'll be wanting to spread out. Find our own places. I'm hoping that where you plan to lead us has room to do all of that."

"Nothing but room up there. The entire nation could move up there and still have distance between one another. Space. Did I ever tell you about the time…?"

Mac had been watching Jimbo carefully, trying to see any falseness in him. Finding nothing obvious, he interrupted the story, "Jimbo, we'd be prepared to let you earn a few dollars showing us some of those green valleys."

Jimbo grinned, reminding Mac of Luke. "I would need a couple of those dollars up-front to pay off that sutler. Else he might nail my coat to his back door and leave me there, rain or shine. That's a hard man yonder. Counts every dollar twice, he does. Myself, I never had many dollars nor needed many.

"Sure, I'd admire to show you a valley or two. Two days of rest I believe you said. I'll be ready to go."

Mac said, "Good, that's settled. You go say your good-byes or whatever you need to do. I'll deal with the sutler."

Jimbo looked around at the camp. "Those wagons appear well-loaded. I hope the load is for necessaries to get you through the next year and not just heavy furniture and such that you can't eat."

Ad answered him, "We bought everything we figured to need in Fort Worth. Been hauling it many a mile already. If we can add some fresh meat from time to time, we should be all right for many months. And then Mac says that it's not too terribly far down to Santa Fe so, if we have to, we can make a run down there."

THAT EVENING at the supper fire, Hiram asked his wife, "Where's Jessie? I haven't seen her all afternoon."

She smiled back at him. "Just let her be. Jessie usually knows pretty much what she's doing. I expect she does this time, too."

At the sound of a running horse, they looked up to see Jessie riding into camp.

"Where's Ty?" she asked.

Mac answered, "He's out at the herd. What do you need him for?"

Jessie ignored Mac's question and spurred her horse out to the herd. Rounding the cattle until she came up to Ty, she said, "Ty, I want to talk with you. Pull off to the side for a few minutes, please."

Ty pulled off a short distance and sat his saddle waiting for Jessie to speak.

"Ty, this is more than just a little bit unusual but we're going out to the wilderness in a couple of days and who knows when we'll see a settlement again. I don't expect that's a big concern to you or any of the other men since mostly what you think about is cattle but it concerns me a considerable amount. What concerns me is that if you and I don't go visit that army chaplain and become Mr. and Mrs. Ty Hobson before we leave, it's going to be a long winter with me longing for you and you longing for me. Don't you try to deny it. You don't talk any more than just enough to get by but I see you looking at me and you have surely seen me looking at you. And then those times we rode or ate together, or on the long trail with you sick, you can't deny that they were special.

"Ty, I don't know if you love me or not but I surely love you. And that chaplain is licensed to marry people. I just came back from talking to him. I went because I was pretty sure you wouldn't think of it. We could send someone down there right this very evening to fetch him. He said he would come if we called him. It's our last chance, Ty, for who knows how long." Jessie was silent then, looking at him.

Ty looked like he had been hit by a swinging barn door. He lifted his hat and ran his fingers through his long hair. He looked off in every direction, twisting in his saddle as if there might be help coming.

Finally he said, "Jessie, I sure do enjoy your company. I'm not exactly sure what love is, never having any experience to judge by except from my ma, and I expect that's not the same at all. But if looking for opportunities to be alone with you and looking forward to the next opportunity is love, then I guess that would be me. I avoided girls even when opportunity allowed knowing that I had nothing but a bare piece of scrub land to my name and one pair of pants with holes in them and figuring that no sensible girl would want to tie her future to someone with so little prospects. But thanks to Mac and them, I have a bit set by. I expect we could take care of ourselves all right. If you wish to do it together, why that sounds fine by me. But what about your parents? We would have to get their blessing."

"You let me worry about my folks. You just come with me and we'll make the announcement and see if one of my brothers will go for the chaplain."

Ty told the *vaqueros* that he would be gone for a while and asked them to fill in for him at the herd.

Jessie spoke up, "Might be more than just a while. He won't be back tonight."

Riding toward the camp, Ty said, "Won't be much of a honeymoon what with all of us bedded down on the open prairie like we do."

Jessie looked at him and laughed. "Silly man, why do you think I bought a tent in Fort Worth?"

"You bought a tent?"

"A girl has to plan ahead if she wants anything in this life."

Ty looked at her in wonder.

Jessie smiled back at him.

They rode together to the supper fire and stepped down from their horses. Jessie's mother was smiling from ear to ear like she was a part of a secret. And she was for Jessie had talked to her before going out to talk with the chaplain.

As the two approached the fire, they realized that talk had stopped and every eye was on them.

Ty stuttered and stammered a bit but finally said, "Folks, we have something to tell you. Jessie has agreed to be my wife. Or I have agreed to be her husband. I'm not just exactly sure how all of that came about; it's all kind of running together. But anyway, we wish to get married. The base chaplain is available for legal marriages and would come out this evening if we called him.

But we need the blessing of Hiram and Jessie's mother." He stopped there, not exactly sure how to continue.

There was a collective gasp from the gathering and then silence.

Hiram looked at the two. "This is a little sudden isn't it, Jessie? You haven't talked with us about this at all."

"Pa, I respect and love you and Ma but this is really my decision to make. What we want is your blessing."

Hiram looked over at his wife. "Well, I expect from the look on your mother's face that she is way ahead of me on this as she has always been on most things. Ty is a fine young man and has shown responsibility beyond his years. I expect you two have the makings of a strong family. That is, just as long as Ty learns early who's boss.

"You been pretty headstrong, Jessie, ever since you rolled off the porch when you were still shy of two years of age. You were determined to get up off the ground by yourself and you brushed all our help away. You did it, too. Set a pattern for your life, that did. She's a good girl, Ty, but she ain't easy. You figure you're up to it?"

"I do, sir. I admire her independence."

"Well, I hope you still admire it twenty years from now. You have my blessing and I don't even have to ask her mother. Her approval shines all over her. You go call that chaplain and God bless."

Jessie looked over at her brothers who were just finishing up their evening meal. "Bobby, Jeremiah, I wish one of you would ride down to the barracks and find that chaplain. Tell him that we would much appreciate if he could ride up this way."

Bobby got to his feet and said, "I'll go right now although what Ty sees in a bossy girl like you is beyond me."

I'll go, too," said Jeremiah with his typical enthusiasm.

Mac looked at the two and said quietly, "Heaven help us. Those two are liable to bring back the sergeant of the guard by mistake or scare the living daylights out of the chaplain."

Margo elbowed him in the ribs and said, "Hush."

The women ushered Jessie down to the river with a bar of soap and clean clothes. Luke and Bill did the same with Ty.

Mac rode out to the herd.

About an hour before full dark, the two boys arrived back with the chaplain in tow. Jeremiah spoke up getting everyone's attention. "Folks, this here is the Reverend Abercrombie. Come to do the deed."

They left the introductions right there, allowing everyone to file past and make themselves known.

The Reverend Abercrombie was a middle-aged, roundish cherub of a man who would not have been remembered if he was seen in a crowd except for the massive muttonchops proudly displayed on each sunburned cheek. The smile he displayed suggested that he had never had an unhappy day in his life although he could have told a story or two if asked.

Hiram gripped the chaplain's hand and said, "Thanks for coming, Reverend. The young folks in question are not here yet but they will be shortly. You have time for a cup of coffee before then, if you'd like."

"Why, that would be just fine, sir. I take it you are the father of the bride."

"That I am but I'm not quite used to this whole thing yet, only knowing about it myself for about an hour. Takes some getting used to."

While he was drinking his coffee, the chaplain asked Hiram, "And where do you wish to have this ceremony registered, sir? I will, of course, be sure it is written in my own records but since our chances of meeting again are not all that good, you might want a register of your own."

"I figured on exactly that. I have the family Bible right here. You can register with your signature right below our son's name. He and his bride were married a few weeks ago down in San Antonio. That name at the top is our oldest daughter. That's her over there with her husband and baby."

"My," the chaplain smiled and said, "you're giving them away one after the other."

"Well, a person has to pray that we will be gaining more than we're giving up."

Ty and Jessie arrived about that time. Jessie surprised everyone by showing up in a very attractive white dress that she had also purchased in Fort Worth without telling even her mother.

The ceremony was short. The vows were said and Ty gave Jessie his first kiss, missing her lips on the first try and nearly giving up before he actually got it done.

With the kiss done, a great cheer arose and Mama ran a bar around the iron triangle that Ty had brought along and announced that she had food ready. She and Imelda had clearly had a very busy couple of hours. She had a simple but tasty meal prepared with more than enough for everyone.

After the meal, some of the men rode out to relieve the *vaqueros* who had missed the wedding while guarding the herd. The *vaqueros* rode in to take a meal and congratulate the new couple.

There was much laughter and talking as the sun wound its way out of the evening sky. Ty and Jessie were looking more nervous and more anxious as each minute passed. Finally, at full dark, Ad blew out the extra lanterns and turned down the wick on the one that was left burning hanging from the end of the cook wagon. "Morning still comes early folks, wedding or no wedding."

The chaplain shook hands with the newly-married couple and then made his way over to Hiram. "I'll be taking my leave now, sir. It has been good to meet you all. I will pray that your journey goes well and that you locate just the right place to settle. I'll pray for the young couple, too. Thank you for calling on me. It has been a pleasure."

"You all right riding back in the dark, Reverend, or would you like a couple of us to ride along with you?"

"I'll be fine, but thanks. It's not but a mile and I can't possibly get lost. I just have to follow the smell of those dugout barracks. Terrible way for men to live but there's nothing I can do about it so I see to my job and stay out of the rest. Good night, sir."

Over the many weeks on the trail from south Texas, the sleeping locations had been well established with some preferring the open prairie, some in their wagons, and a few spreading their blankets under the wagons.

Mac went to his two brothers. Knowing that they had seldom resisted a good temptation, he told them, "You two settle down and don't you get up until morning. If either of you moves this night, I'll tie you to the back of the wagon and make you walk to Colorado. You leave your sister alone. You hear me?"

The two boys grinned at Mac but they went to their bedrolls.

Jessie very nervously pulled her tent out of the pile of bedding and passed it to Ty. Ty picked up his bedroll with the other hand. Jessie shouldered her own bedroll and they disappeared into the dark.

Hiram watched them walk off and then turned to his wife. "Makes me feel old, it does, seeing one after the other leave the nest. But I believe they've all chosen well so I'm happy to let it be."

The wagons led out on a bright midsummer Kansas morning heading west following the Arkansas River. Jimbo rode a little ways ahead of the lead wagon.

With the beef herds, they had kept the wagons behind or off to one side in case of stampede but the chance of a cow herd stampeding was very small. Many had calves at foot and others were heavy with calf. They had showed very little notion to run. And with the abundance of riders plus the two red dogs, there was no chance at all of someone's inattention causing a stampede. The herd plodded after the two bell-bulls mile after mile, seemingly content with their lot in life.

The drovers raised the herd off the bed grounds to follow one half-mile behind the wagons. The excitement of nearing their destination had taken some of the edge off their travel weariness.

Jimbo had addressed the group at breakfast. "We'll follow the Arkansas to Bent's Old Fort and then swing a bit south until we cut across the Purgatoire again. Then we follow along until we come to that valley I want you to see. That's, by guess, about one-hundred eighty miles to Bent's Fort. You must have seen most of that country driving freight, Mac."

"I've seen a good bit of it but our freight wagons always

followed the Cimarron route so I never did get out to the old fort. Heard others talk about it though. Nothing left there now, just a couple of chimneys and a lot of broken adobe. You had guessed three to four weeks for this leg of our trip, Jimbo. At one-hundred eighty miles, that sounds about right as slow as these cows walk and all the time assuming that we can avoid trouble."

"You seem to have managed to avoid the trouble that comes to some on the trail. There's no end of wayward folks a body can find on the trail if he's careless. Good you never met up with any."

"I expect we saw a few from a distance. Folks standing off and taking our measure. But we have a sizable group here. And we're well-armed. We make sure that a lot of our weapons are kept in sight so that folks such as you're talking about would see that we're not pilgrims waiting to be relieved of our goods. It would take a small army to do us any real harm."

Jimbo nodded his agreement. "Well, let's hope it all stays peaceful." He loped out to see what was over the next hill.

Mac figured that was the story of Jimbo's life; always wanting to see what was over the next hill.

He rode back to where Margo was driving their wagon. "How goes it for you? Everything all right?"

"Right as rain," answered Margo. "We're nearly home and nothing could sound better than that. Seems to me you told me one time that, when you left Missouri as a boy, you had two goals. One was to escape poverty and the other was to locate a home. The first is done with considerable success and we are within shouting distance of the other. Gives us a lot to thank the Lord for. The trip has gone well but I don't deny that it will be good to stop. The only thing I would change on the trip, if I could, is losing Jerrod. Everyone took that pretty hard."

Mac was silent for a full minute. "We'll all think about Jerrod from time to time all our lives, I suspect. He was a good man. But you're forgetting about my third goal."

"What was that," Margo asked, feigning innocence.

"You know full well what it was."

Margo looked at him with a half-hidden smile. "Well, even if I do I still like to hear you say it."

"If you promise not to burn the biscuits again, I'll say it. I was watching for a good woman to take to wife. Found one, too."

Margo had been nibbling on a biscuit since breakfast. She threw it at Mac. "I never once burnt any biscuits. I'll have you know Mr. McTavish …"

Mac laughed out loud and rode off.

Margo smiled after him.

They wound their slow way along the river until they pulled up at Bent's Fort three weeks after leaving Fort Dodge. It was just as Mac had said. There was nothing left but a couple of chimneys and some broken adobe on a considerable-sized clear area. They pulled the wagons onto the clearing and set up camp. The cattle were bedded down on the flat beside the river. Since leaving Austin behind, they had never had to worry about grass. It had seemed like the entire continent was grass. It was the same in Colorado. Looking over the country around the fort, Mac figured they could graze thousands of cattle and hardly make a dent in the feed.

Around the supper fire which long ago had become the agreed to meeting time, Ad said, "We must be getting close, Jimbo. What's next?"

"We'll rest the animals here for a couple of days and then head south. That was the Purgatoire we passed a few miles back. We'll come up to it again a few miles to the south. Beautiful country all the way. This country is too good to hide for long. You'll be combing settlers out of your hair before you know it. Of course, the old Spanish land grants cut through these parts but I always found Mex folks reasonable if approached friendly. Don't expect you'll have any trouble."

He pointed off to the west. "That there way is the Apishapa River and a little further is the Huerfano. Both smallish but dependable. Smaller creeks aplenty. A few lakes here and there, too. There's snow on the Sangre De Christos most of the time. Their runoff waters this whole country. There's green valleys, some mighty rugged canyons and miles of more or less flat grassland. I'll get you to where I think you want to go and the rest is up to you. Were any of you to decide to go further west, there's more land between the Sangre De Christos and the Rockies. You might want to explore some."

They turned the herd south two days later.

Four weeks after leaving Dodge, Jimbo called Mac up beside him. He was squatting beside his horse on the edge of a valley. The valley was miles wide with grass and small brush as far as Mac could see and buffalo scattered throughout. The upper valley headed off to the northwest, the Sangre de Christos shining in the summer sun with timber-covered hills between.

"I wish you'd look at that, Mac. Is that a sight or not?"

Mac was speechless. He stepped off his horse and squatted down beside Jimbo, staring at the land before him for several minutes. Finally, he spoke quietly, almost in awe. "If there's a better, someone else can have it. I've thought about a home place for years but never in all my imagination could I have pictured such as this."

Ad signaled a halt to the herd and the caravan. Calling the others, he walked forward holding his wife's hand.

Slowly the other travelers gathered around Mac and Jimbo.

The two older couples stood together, silently staring at the wide valley before them.

Jonathon and Nancy walked up, Jonathon holding their baby.

Ty stood with his arm around Jessie.

The younger children sat on the grass with their legs over the river bank.

Mama, Manuel and Imelda stood off to one side. Mama looked down into the valley and then up at the shining mountains and crossed herself.

Margo slid her arm under Mac's and eased her head onto his shoulder.

Bill and Mac's two young brothers were silent with awe for a few moments. Sensing that their journey was over, they put their mounts down the short river valley and splashed across the shallow river, shouting and yelling Rebel yells. Bill stood in his stirrups, dropped the reins across his horse's neck and rode out into the valley, arms spread wide as if to embrace the land, still yelling those penetrating Rebel yells.

"Are we home, Mac?" asked Margo.

Mac pointed at the three boys riding across the valley. "I guess that about says all that needs saying."

Mac turned to Ty. "Ty, I'd appreciate if you would ride out to the herd. Tell the drovers to drop the cattle into the valley and turn them loose."

After a while, Jimbo spoke, "You run your cattle down and set up camp. Tomorrow I'll go see old Runs His Horses. I'll tell him you're good folks and that you aren't buffalo hunters. Might bring him down to meet you. Might ask him where my wife and son are, too."

Mac stood and faced the group. "Welcome home," he said. "It's been a long ride and a far distance. Welcome home."

A LOOK AT MAC'S LAND

MAC'S LAND IS A STORY ABOUT A FAMILY. A FAMILY WITH PARENTS, children and grandparents. A family that loves one another. A family working hard to operate a cattle ranch in the pioneer days of the West. A family with heavy responsibilities. A family with hopes and dreams. In other words, a normal pioneer family. There were thousands of them just like the McTavish family.

Don't come here looking for heroes. Don't expect to find swaggering men with hands quicker than lightening who can shoot the eye out of a squirrel at fifty paces. Come here looking for real people, people you would like to call 'neighbor, friend'.

Mac McTavish is a rancher. In a new land where the grass seemed to be never ending, he was among the first to realize that the grazing couldn't be infinite. The grass was showing more poorly as the short years came and went. As the herds grew, the land suffered and might soon die, as indeed it did in too many parts of the West.

Mac decided that on his Bar-M he would do something about saving the land. He told his neighbors that he was cutting his herds back and was fencing the land. The open grazing era had to stop.

Not everyone liked his proposal.

AVAILABLE NOW FROM REG QUIST AND CKN CHRISTIAN PUBLISHING

ABOUT THE AUTHOR

REG QUIST'S pioneer heritage includes sod shacks, prairie fires, home births, and children's graves under the prairie sod, all working together in the lives of people creating their own space in a new land.

Out of that early generation came farmers, ranchers, business men and women, builders, military graves in faraway lands, Sunday Schools that grew to become churches, plus story tellers, musicians, and much more.

Hard work and self-reliance were the hallmark of those previous great generations, attributes that were absorbed by the following generation.

Quist's career choice took him into the construction world. From heavy industrial work, to construction camps in the remote northern bush, the author emulated his grandfathers, who were both builders, as well as pioneer farmers and ranchers.

Quist's heart was never far from the land. The family photo albums testify to how often he found himself sitting on a horse, both as a child and into later life, when he and his wife owned their own small farm, complete with kids and horses.

Respect for the pioneers, working alongside skilled, tough workmen, and learning from them, marrying his high school sweetheart and welcoming children into the world, purchasing land for the family to grow on, and riding horses with the kids, all melded together to influence Quist's life and writing. Over, and under, and wrapped around his life is Quist's Christian heritage. This too, shows itself in his writing.

Quist's writing career was late in pushing itself forward, remaining a hobby while family and career took precedence.

Only in early retirement, was there time for more serious writing.

Quist's writing interests lie in many genres including children's work, short lifestyle stories, cowboy poetry, western novels, plus Christian articles and novels.

Woven through every story is the thought that, even though he was not there himself in that pioneer time, he knew some that were. They are remembered with great respect.

Find more great titles by Reg Quist and Christian Kindle News at http://christiankindlenews.com/our-authors/reg-quist/